McDowell

Other Books by William H. Coles
Guardian of Deceit
The Surgeon's Wife
The Spirit of Want
Sister Carrie
Facing Grace with Gloria and Other Stories
The Necklace and Other Stories
Story in Literary Fiction: A Manual for Writers
Literary Fiction as an Art Form: A Text for Writers
The Short Fiction of William H. Coles 2001-2011
The Illustrated Fiction of William H. Coles 2000-2012

Short Stories by William H. Coles
*The Activist, The Amish Girl, The Bear, Big Gene,
Captain Withers's Wife, The Cart Boy, Clouds, Crossing Over,
Curse of a Lonely Heart, Dilemma, Dr. Greiner's Day in Court,
Facing Grace with Gloria, Father Ryan, Gatemouth Willie
Brown on Guitar, The Gift, The Golden Flute, Grief,
Homunculus, The Indelible Myth, Inside the Matryoshka,
Lost Papers, The Miracle of Madame Villard, The Necklace,
Nemesis, On the Road to Yazoo City, The Perennial Student,
Reddog, Sister Carrie, Speaking of the Dead, The Stonecutter,
Suchin's Escape, The Thirteen Nudes of Ernest Goings,
The War of the Flies, The Wreck of the Amtrak's Silver Service*

McDowell

by

William H. Coles

Published 22 Aug, 2015

Story in Literary Fiction
99 West South Temple #1802
Salt Lake City, Utah 84101

www.storyinliteraryfiction.com

Cover art and illustrations by Anna Sokolova

ISBN: 978-0-9961903-3-6 (softcover)
ISBN: 978-0-9961903-4-3 (hardcover)
ISBN: 978-0-9961903-5-0 (ebook)

PART ONE

Prologue

Nepal, 1981
Himalayas

The sky cleared briefly before daybreak. The sharp, bitter winds eased somewhat, but the negative forty-degree temperatures penetrated to the bone. Hiram McDowell lifted the flap of a one-man tent to look in on Erick Woolf, who turned his head, his beard tinged in frost-white from his labored breathing; Woolf lifted his goggles, his pale blue eyes opaque with fatigue.

"You ready?" Hiram asked.

Woolf shook his head "no," trying to smile but his face remained motionless.

Hiram took off his outer gloves, freed up an oxygen tank from Woolf's backpack, and placed the mask on Woolf's face. Woolf rallied after a few minutes of oxygen.

Within half an hour, with four other climbers, Hiram and Woolf started for the summit. Woolf's fatigue slowed progress and after an hour they soon fell behind the others. The wind gusts increased. Woolf sank into a sitting position a few yards from a slope of snow and ice.

Hiram steadied himself on a steep vertical. For a few seconds, the visibility improved, but he saw no one.

"Go," Woolf called to him, his voice husky dry. "I can't do it."

With only slight hesitation, Hiram waved his agreement. He had only two hours or less to summit before their oxygen supply ran low. And Woolf was too weak to go on; the rest would strengthen him. At the summit, Hiram took photos and, for a few minutes, absorbed the satisfaction of his achievement and the awe of the view from the highest point on earth.

Winds picked up, and snow and haze decreased visibility as he began his descent. He pressed on. After an hour, he stumbled onto Woolf a few feet from where he had left him.

"Get up," Hiram yelled over the howling wind.

"Help me. In the name of God," Woolf pleaded.

Hiram gripped Woolf's parka to help him stand, but Hiram was too weak to lift, and Woolf fell back.

"Rescue," Woolf moaned, drifting off into semi-consciousness. Rescue from base camp was impossible until the weather improved. And they were in the dead zone, too high for helicopters.

Hiram freed Woolf's remaining oxygen supply and attached it to his own pack.

"Don't leave me, Hiram." Woolf coughed.

Hiram backed away and started down. Climbing ropes aided him for a few hundred yards. Near a rock crevice familiar to him, he stumbled on the half-buried lifeless body of a facedown climber. A candy bar and water were in the inner jacket pocket. Near the corpse's outstretched arm, a glint of silver stopped Hiram. From hard snow and the ice-solid fabric of a frozen glove-hand, he freed a silver crucifix that he pocketed for identification and to send to family. He plodded ahead. The storm abated and he felt the muted exhilaration at knowing he would not die.

On return home after his miracle survival, Hiram dreamed of immortality. He determined to climb every peak above 8000 meters in Nepal.

Chapter 1

Hiram McDowell's second wife died in the summer of 1999 a few weeks after her 45th birthday party, debilitated and demented from breast cancer. She left three children—Ann, Sophie, and Billie—for Hiram to raise. Two years later, Hiram married the widow, Carole Mastriano, whom he had met in Denver. She had two daughters, Tasha and Candice, and he bought a house big enough for two families to live more than comfortably. Only his son Billie was at home at this time; his younger daughter Sophie was at school in the east and her stepsister Ann, from his first marriage, was in college.

1999

After two months away, Hiram returned to Denver from a board meeting in Chicago at the International College of Surgeons. He entered the kitchen of the contemporary 8,000 square-foot Pueblo Ranch designed by Eiichi Ono through the side door from the four-car garage. The view of the Rocky Mountains through the panoramic window over the sink made him pause as it always did. He would be climbing again in a few months. He was yearning for the exertion and isolation that always energized him.

His third wife Carole bent over a sweeping granite counter—complete with sink and cook top—preparing dinner. She did not turn to look at him or speak.

"Hey," Hiram said, easing his bag through the door.

"You could have called," she said.

He thought better of responding. Carole practiced clinical psychology and lived in her own caverns of self-imposed hell. He walked the hall to the north wing of the house. He unpacked his bag on his bed and threw dirty clothes in the corner of the room for the maid to take care of in the morning.

Back in the kitchen he put his arms around Carole's waist from the back. She was flabby now; she'd lost all pretense of trying to exercise. "Good week?" he asked, squeezing her slightly then letting her go.

"Do you want dinner?" Carole asked, still not looking at him.

"Sure," he said. Although with jet lag, he didn't know if he was hungry or not.

Carole emptied a package of capellini into boiling water. An electric crock-pot of meat sauce bubbled on an adjacent counter. *Always too bland*, Hiram thought. She never listened to his advice. *And her girls eat anything... a banana-topped-with-peanut-butter-and-mayonnaise diet mentality.*

"Something wrong?" he asked. She busied herself, searching for the strainer to drain the pasta.

"Call the children," she said coolly.

Where was an ounce of kindness? He called into the rec room and the back bedrooms that dinner was ready. Billie, now almost seventeen, came out. "Dad," he said. He gave his father an enthusiastic, masculine embrace.

"I thought you'd be at school," Hiram said.

"Career stuff." Billie grinned sheepishly. That meant he was goofing off somewhere. He was in chronic academic trouble. "Good trip?" Billie asked.

"Nepal, great. Chicago, not good," Hiram said.

Carole's girls came out of a back room together—Tasha and Candice, short and not-so-short, blond and dusky brunette. Billie had a quizzical smile looking at the girls. They all went to the dining room.

"What do you want to drink?" Carole asked everyone. She retreated to the kitchen to fill glasses as everyone took seats. Hiram was pissed that Carole's girls rarely greeted him... or looked at him. *I'll goad them into response.*

"How's school?" he said. Carole entered with the drinks on a tray.

"Tasha made cheerleading squad backup," Billie volunteered.

Impossible to imagine, Hiram thought. Tasha teetered on the cusp of overweight with legs shaped like ice cream cones. *How could she bounce and jump? She'd splat any cheerleader she landed on and she wasn't in shape enough to support a pyramid.* Well, he was exaggerating a little. But still, she was a tragedy with a pretty face and a ballooning body.

"You could say 'Hello,'" Hiram said to the girls.

"Leave them alone," Carole said.

"Just civility," Hiram said.

"What would you know about civility?" she said.

"How is school?" he asked the girls.

"It's their break, Hiram," Carole said. "They haven't been in school for two weeks."

Enough of this shit. "Come on Billie," he said. "Get your sticks; we'll eat out." Billie followed him out of the dining room.

In minutes they were on their way.

In the car, he asked Billie about Tasha and Candice, "You messing with them?"

Billie was shy about sex. Hiram enjoyed teasing him.

"No, Dad."

"Do you like them?"

"They don't talk to me much."

"They're cows. Don't you think?"

Billie didn't respond.

"You're not doing anything with them, are you? Like... you know?"

"It's not that way, Dad."

"You sure?"

"I'm not at the house much. They like it there better by themselves."

"Where are you?"

"At school. And with a friend sometimes. He plays guitar."

The club near the stadium had no sign. The speakeasy-like peephole in the door you opened yourself was never used and there were no guards or bouncers, or even a maître d'. The name "Tritone" in neon green light script waxed and waned in intensity above the bar. They took a table near the deserted bandstand. Billie laid his drumsticks and brushes that he carried in a black-velvet case on the table.

"You been playing with these guys?" Hiram asked. "I've told Ahmad he should let you sit in."

"I know, Dad. But these guys think they're big time."

"So, where you playing?"

"My guitar friend. We're working on a CD."

"You got a studio?"

"He's got a Mac with Garageband. We use his parents' basement."

"How are you going to market it?"

"This is a demo. We're trying to get backing."

"The two of you?"

"We got an electric bass on some tracks. And his girlfriend plays cello."

"In basic blues?"

"Early rock and folk. She's not bad... she's a music major."

They ordered from waitress Sheryl. Hiram knew her from previous visits. He didn't like the size of her nose with dark deep wells for nostrils. She was a little overweight but she had breasts the size of two ripe cantaloupes that enriched his day when she leaned over the table to swipe a cloth over the surface.

"You still in school?" Hiram asked her.

"Naw," she said. "I want to be a masseuse."

Hiram held her gaze for an instant to see if she might be interested but she looked away.

As the band set up on the stage, Hiram waved to get the piano player's attention. Then he held up his Big River harp he took from his side pocket. The piano player flashed a thumbs up.

There were only twenty or so people in the place. It was early.

Hiram finished eating and went to the restroom to clean his teeth with a finger and a paper towel. After the band played an opening number, Hiram approached the bandstand. The piano player stood at the piano and faced the audience. "We have the honor to welcome Dr. McDowell again tonight. A surgeon from the university. He's always welcome here at Tritone."

Hiram mounted the bandstand, whispered to the drummer, shook the hands of the guitarist and the amplified acoustic bass player, and stepped to a standup microphone. They played "Lonely Avenue," in E. The bass player sang. Hiram wailed on harp. Although sparse, the applause was enthusiastic, but Hiram didn't smile. *I deserve more than that!* After "Stormy Monday" in F, the applause was less than for the first number. The band broke and all the members thanked Hiram for the set.

Hiram sat down, dipping his harps in a water glass and wiping them down with a paper napkin.

"Did you ask him?" Billie asked.

"He put you off." Hiram had forgotten to ask. "Maybe later," he said. "Pissed me off, too. You're twice as good as any of them."

Billie swigged on a bottle of beer, disappointment on his face.

"Don't get down," Hiram said. "It will come together for you."

When they got home, Hiram was exhausted from time differences in travel and was asleep in minutes. Carole entered and stood in the dark, barely visible. "Hiram," she said sharply. "Wake up!" The venom in her voice woke him instantly.

"I know about Rima," she said. "Everyone knows."

Shit. Hiram put his hands behind his head, his gaze in the direction of Carole's silhouette.

"I won't have it, Hiram. It's demeaning."

Hiram wasn't alert yet. "I don't get it."

"You won't deny it?"

"What?"

"You're living with this woman."

"How do you figure? I live here."

"How humiliating."

Hiram let silence isolate them from each other. He finally said, "Look Carole. I've never promised fidelity."

"I've accepted your affairs. But I can't tolerate living with another woman. And a woman of color too."

Hiram angered. Carole's sense of possession irritated him. He was who he was. She'd always known that. She had no right to be indignant.

"I love you," he said, straining for sincerity. It was a marriage of convenience, but he did think he loved her at one point before the marriage.

"Stop it," she said.

"Accept it."

"Don't degrade me."

He slipped down in the bed and pulled the covers over him. "I've never even tried to degrade you." *I don't care enough at this point.*

"You love her? Marry her."

"She's a comfort to me when I'm away."

"You admit it? And you won't give her up?"

"It's half way around the world. What difference does it make?"

"I'm your wife!"

"Fine. But I'm not changing."

Carole gasped. *Is she crying?* He couldn't tell for sure.

"We'll go on," he said. "But you need to change your attitude. It's best for both of us. And for the kids."

"And I keep taking care of Billie?"

"If you don't want to, I'll figure something out."

"I don't know if I can face the world thinking people know."

"Few know."

"Liar."

"C'est la vie," he said softly.

Carole hissed. "I'm considering divorce, Hiram."

Hiram turned on his side away from her.

"Did you hear me?"

"Your choice," he said.

Chapter 2

In Hiram's mind, election as Regent to the board of directors of the International College of Surgeons had lifted him far above the sixty thousand plus general surgeons in the world. But for a number of years, he'd known being on the board was not enough; he had to be president. There were things to do in healthcare and education, and ascending to national prominence as president of the International College would give him the authority he needed.

Hiram had flown first class from his latest periodic visit to the foundation hospital he created in Nepal and was first off the connection to Chicago, where he would lead a conference of state leaders on delivery of healthcare to the uninsured. Once he cleared customs in the U.S. concourse, he went straight to the baggage-claim carrousel of DL 4534. He waited fifteen minutes, reading, replying, and deleting emails on his cell phone until deplaned-passengers arrived for their luggage. Hiram looked for Michael O'Leary, MD, MBA, FACS, from San Francisco, a key member of the college's Board of Governors executive committee.

He waved to Michael to get his attention.

"I know what you want. Not the right time, Hiram," Michael said as Hiram approached.

"Wrong, Michael. Perfect time." Hiram led Michael to a second carrousel where there were fewer people. They stood hidden by a six-foot diameter concrete support post painted off-white.

"Look," Hiram began. "I need the votes you can deliver."

"I don't sell votes," Michael said, waiting for the conveyor belt to start.

"What will it take?" Hiram asked. "You deserve better in this organization, Michael. You work hard. You've got the skills."

"I'm offended, Hiram."

"Jesus. This isn't a bribe. I'm building a new direction for the College, putting it back as the world leader in surgery. But I've got to get elected first, and then I've got to have new leadership, new ideas, new staff in the right places. You're integral to that."

"You're offering?"

"Executive director."

"I'd have to resign from the board. You trying to get me off the board, Hiram? Is that what's behind this?

"Never!"

"You've tried that before."

"Goddamn it. Not with you. Hey, you've got experience running executive committees. I want you running the organization. Trust me."

Michael bit his upper lip, a habit when he was thinking. "Academics doesn't hold much excitement for me now," he said.

"Perfect time to change."

"But it's a career risk. I need to think about it."

"Christ. You've been wanting it for a couple years. Don't lie to yourself. This *is* a new career. I'll put you on the President's healthcare task force too. I'll be co-chair in the fall."

"My family," Michael said.

Hiram took Michael's arm to start him walking toward the security exit. "Angie will be proud. And the kids too. You're the right person. Look at the realities. Tom's lousy as director. We need to dump him."

"He's our friend."

"But a shitty director."

"Can you wait a few days?"

Hiram took a deep breath. "I wish. But I need a head count. I've got commitments to make." Hiram paused. "You hail a cab, the offer's gone."

The conveyor for luggage cranked up.

"Well?" Hiram said, looking at Michael.

Michael nodded almost imperceptibly.

"Good choice," Hiram said, concerned with Michael's tentative reaction, his unmistakable lack of enthusiasm. *Why is he so hesitant? It's what he's always wanted.*

"I wish I could trust you," Michael said. He walked to the head of the conveyor and Hiram left without further words.

Hiram hailed a taxi. Michael had a reputation as ambitious and driven, but a straight shooter, honest, never out of season or over the limit. Hiram wasn't sure he could deliver the directorship. *But first I need to get elected,* he thought. *I'll deal with the wrinkles later.*

In the months since their meeting at the airport, Hiram avoided Michael and gave no words of appreciation for Michael's help. Michael swung the seven decisive votes for nomination and Hiram successfully gathered support of the membership. Michael waited expectantly for the announcement of his appointment as executive director.

Chapter 3

The night of Hiram's induction into the College, the auditorium bristled with a formal festivity. Dignitaries sat in black robes in chairs lined in four rows on the stage. As the new president, Hiram stood tall, his hands resting on a flag-draped podium facing the audience, his image gleaming from four giant screens suspended from the auditorium ceiling and projecting to the seven thousand plus surgeons and families in the audience. He thanked family and friends. He introduced new officers and honored colleagues. Few could fault his dynamism, his captaincy, his vision, and Michael could not suppress a wave of envy as Hiram outlined proposed changes in the administrative structure. Michael's heart raced.

Hiram closed his speech: "And finally, it gives me great pleasure to announce that yesterday the new executive director of the College has officially been appointed. His experience as a board member will be invaluable. He is cherished for his academic contributions. He has an MBA and is chair of one of the most influential departments of surgery in the world. Please honor his appointment with a round of applause. Dr. Tom Gardner."

Michael's insides trembled. He'd been passed over. Hiram had welshed on a promise; Michael silently vowed to crush him. He'd have to wait for the opportunities, but he would relish seeing Hiram suffer lifelong.

In the lobby after the meeting, Michael avoided colleagues who would know him. He recognized the attractive middle-aged TV journalist who approached and cornered him near the exit. Paige Sterling. He'd seen one of her TV segments on *Week's End* about excavations of the bones of a medieval king. She was a top news celebrity—fashion conscious, a curt interrogator, and champion of women's rights and minority representation. She stepped up and held out her hand that he shook. She had a firm grasp.

"You're Michael O'Leary. They told me at the information desk."

Michael stared. He disliked aggressive reporters, especially women.

"What's the direction of the College with new leadership?" Paige continued.

"It's not an appropriate question for me, Ms. Sterling. Ask the new President."

"I apologize," she said. "I was told you were, as chair of the executive committee, among those who nominated and supported Dr. McDowell for the presidency." *She can't get an interview with Hiram,* Michael thought. *I'm second best to fill airtime.*

"You've got it wrong," he said. "I'm chair of the executive committee of the Board of Governors."

"But you supported Dr. McDowell?"

"That's confidential," he said.

"I'm still interested in your thoughts for the future. You've been a member of the College for many years."

He wondered if she knew what Hiram really was like. He answered: "The College will support better access to healthcare for all, continued advancement in control and treatment of disease, and address an affordable comprehensive healthcare system."

"Will women play a larger role in the activities of the College?" Paige Sterling asked.

"I'm sure they will. Already the number of women surgeons in specialties and in surgery is increasing."

"I understand there were only 200 women in a total 3300 certified neurosurgeons last year."

"There were only *two* women neurosurgeons in the 1960s. That's a big increase," Michael countered with the pride of being part of an administration that let women into an organization the world saw as an exclusive men's club. "I'm sure it's not that small a representation in other specialties now," he added.

"But my point is still valid, isn't it? Women do not play a big role in surgery."

"It is true of the past. I agree. But a new era is coming. And already women are making significant contributions not only in patient care, but in research and education."

"And what of minority representation? Is that increasing?"

Michael endured a few more questions and then excused himself.

"Here's my card," Ms. Sterling said. "Call me if you ever have anything newsworthy about the College. I'd be glad to help."

You look to destroy, humiliate, expose, and decapitate, Michael thought. *And I'm not the smoking gun. Go for McDowell.* He said nothing.

"Good day," she said.

Chapter 4

For months, Hiram and Carole existed in a tenuous truce that barely masked Carole's anger and Hiram's indifference to her discontent. Hiram stayed to himself and made no attempt to conciliate. Carole avoided him whenever possible and never threatened divorce again when she had the rare opportunity to confront him. *She has too much to lose; as long as she knows that, it will give me peace,* Hiram believed.

On the weekend of Carole's birthday, Hiram had a two-day meeting with the program committee for the college to check out the New Orleans Convention Center as a meeting place for the International College in '08. On the Friday night before returning to Denver, he heard of a jazz club on Napoleon that didn't discourage semi-professionals from sitting in. Fat Frank and his Revelation Blues band was on and Hiram played along. The singer was Maria Petulant (née Porosky in Bedford-Stuyvesant). Glorious she was at thirty-eight, a full figure of midlife that seemed to want to burst out of the white country-print shift with flowers and insects that was tied at the waist with a rope belt. Her black hair hung eight inches below shoulder length and was held back with a wooden clothespin for a country effect. She had dark brown eyes the color of rosewood on the trim of a hand-made guitar, eyes that didn't look away, and smiled with pleasure when looking at Hiram. He knew she would be a great lay and he arranged to sit in with the band the next night, a Saturday, so on Sunday when the band didn't play, he could take Maria to Mangrove Plantation up river for the day. He'd leave early Monday morning for Denver and be back before noon with the time change. He'd miss Carole's birthday but that didn't seem important.

He took Maria to dine at an upriver plantation convention center. She'd bought a new red dress, probably from One Canal, designer-off-the-rack, with a scoop neckline that showed cleavage—it was revealing but a far cry from elegant, if not a little deep-south tacky. After dinner, they went to the suite he'd rented with a river view and a bottle of white wine she liked placed by management on the nightstand. After a little chitchat, they screwed on and off until after midnight. The draperies on the large picture window were drawn back so they could see from the bed the traffic on the river a few hundred yards away just beyond the levee. The ship lights were mostly dim except for a few glaring spots on the bridge. The freighter's nooks and crannies were dark with shadows formed by the pewter glow of a half moon well above the horizon.

Maria poured herself another glass of wine from the almost empty bottle on the nightstand and propped herself up on a pillow. Hiram turned to her, draping his arm over her chest and cupping her breast in his relaxed hand.

"You played well tonight," she said.

"You sang like a mocking bird perched on a honeysuckle vine in summer," Hiram said, smiling and trying to mask his innate sarcasm.

"I want to believe it," she said.

"You aren't from around here."

"I told you."

"I forgot," Hiram said.

"Born in New York. Lived in Louisiana going on twenty-five years now."

"You work mostly here?"

"Yeah. Sometimes Mobile. Rarely Atlanta."

"How'd you start out?"

"Folk. Protest stuff mainly. Then blues. Sang with Professor Blackbeard. Tennessee Red on guitar. Pat Mallory on drums. Tommy Hernandez on bass most of the time. We opened for a year for *Volcanic Eruption* when they did their coast-to-coast tour."

Hiram vaguely remembered the tour. Early rock and roll wasn't strong for him, except as a root for blues riffs.

They stayed silent for a while. Hiram pleasantly relaxed. When she finished her wine, she rolled over and put her arm around him and her head on his shoulder. She smelled of sex and dissipating perfume. The wine on her breath leaked out whiffs of flowers and citrus fruits.

"You got family?" she asked.

"Jesus. Don't mention it. My wife's birthday was last night."

"You forgot?"

"Like being here with you." Hiram smiled.

"Bullshit."

"No. It's a lousy marriage."

"Why's that, baby? You been married too long?"

"Number three. Only a few years. But I don't like her."

"Always?"

"The second month of wedded bliss."

"And you stick with her?"

"She takes care of the kids."

"Where you from?"

"Louisville originally. I'm in Denver now. That's where she lives..."

"You deserve better, honey,"

"I never please her. Never know what she wants."

Maria took her time sipping the last of the wine from the bottle, her empty glass on the floor beside the bed. "She wants love, baby. You ain't got much of that for her."

"Not true."

"Not the sex, baby. Woman wants to be coveted like water to a drowning man."

Hiram's jaw clenched as he rolled over. *I get no sex. And nothing else.* "I give her everything," he said. "I support her two loser kids."

"She just wants you to want her."

"How do you know what she wants?"

"A woman knows," she said, staring at him.

"She couldn't find a better husband," Hiram said.

Maria laughed. "Than you?"

"Fuck off," he said without humor.

"What'd I say?"

"I'm not to blame for her foul moods." He was getting annoyed.

"Every man says that," she said.

"I'm not everyman and I'm not to blame."

"And that drives your wife to depression. That I-ain't-got-no-responsibility-for-how-you-feel attitude. Believe me. I know what it means."

"You don't know shit," Hiram said. Her assertions were out-of-line.

"You're blind as a bat," she retorted. "A woman's nightmare."

Hiram stayed silent as blood pulsed to his head. *What did this marble-brain idiot know? She's a loser and she criticizes me about Carole?* Carole was a bitch. He didn't make her that way. And he didn't like being judged.

"Look. I'm sorry. What pissed you off?" Maria asked, a touch of fear in her voice.

"She's got a drum stick up her ass," he said with finality but with a whiff of conciliation. "Not my fault."

"Why do you feel guilty?"

"Goddamn it," he said. *He wasn't guilty. He had nothing to feel guilty about.* "She's menopausal," he added.

"That doesn't make a difference."

"Bullshit."

"I ain't seen a period in a couple years. I ain't pregnant. And I haven't changed."

"And you're not that great a lay," Hiram said.

"If you care for her at all, help her get through it."

"Not worth the time."

"You're sick," Maria said.

He wanted to spit on her. *What a turd.* But he held back.

"Don't take it out on me!" She got out of the bed, her eyes fearful as if he actually struck her.

"I'm not wrong here," Hiram said.

"Hey. I don't give a damn one way or another," she said, her voice weak.

"You've got a big mouth."

She began to get dressed.

"I thought this night might mean something to you," she said loudly, regaining some self-confidence. "You're a nut case."

"Shut your goddamn mouth."

"Zipped tight, man," she said. "Never again speak to a psycho."

"I'm not crazy."

"You're weird, man. You scare me."

"Get out," he said.

Hiram didn't move even when she was almost dressed.

"Hey, asshole," she said. "Get me back to town."

"Fuck you."

She picked up the phone, told the night man to call her a car.

She waited in an armchair looking at the river. Hiram rolled over occasionally in bed ignoring her. Maria answered the phone. The car was here. She took enough money for fare from Hiram's wallet that was on the dresser... put it in her purse. He'd expected she'd want money and made no move to stop her.

"You're one sick sonofabitch," she said as she closed the door.

Well, he didn't give a damn what she thought. It took him more than an hour to drift into an unsettled sleep but by morning he'd almost forgotten everything Maria said.

Chapter 5

Summer
2000

After his humiliation from Hiram's passing him over for executive director, Michael O'Leary thought only of revenge. He met with Denise Barzee at a bar during an NIH sponsored research meeting in Seattle. It was the first time he'd met her face-to-face, although he'd collaborated with her by phone on a conference call for a project. She'd left Hiram McDowell's lab to take a job in industry a few months ago. This was the opportunity Michael had hoped for.

Denise dressed in a white blouse, a tan skirt, and flats without hose. Her hair was cut short, and she wore heavy black-rimmed myopic glasses. Her life was her career; she never married.

Michael kept the introductions brief. He bought her a glass of wine and ordered a Perrier for himself with a twist. "This is confidential, I would hope. For both of us," he said.

"Your secretary said this was recruiting."

"You don't miss academics?" he asked.

"I like my new job." She fingered some trail mix on the bar, mouthed some, and chewed before she answered. "I do miss academics, actually. Industry's taking iron-fist control over the scientific process in the laboratory. It's more intense than I ever imagined."

"Unethical?"

She paused. "Yes. It's all profit. Any thought of searching for truth be damned."

"But academics has turned mercenary too, even in basic research," Michael said.

"I don't understand."

"Profit. Patents. Researching only what has clear potential for steady income with unlimited growth potential. And government grant support has dried up so labs are dependent on the profiteers."

"I'm discouraged," she said.

"There's a rumor you left Hiram McDowell for more than better pay."

"I have no comments on rumors."

"But you did have your reasons?"

"I had objections. But I was treated fairly."

"You were never given an academic promotion. Ten years plus."

"No different than many."

"But you were deserving. I've checked."

She frowned turning sullen and sipped her wine. "What do you really want, Dr. O'Leary?"

"I'm interested in Hiram McDowell. In the clinical trial that's under way using the drug for suppression of organ rejections. The one that is still in investigative status. There are discrepancies in the published data on the basic scene. Concerns about the side effects. Questions about results in animal studies being transferable to human studies."

"I'm a bench researcher."

"In Hiram's lab. You knew about these concerns."

"It's privileged information."

"It's published. In clinical trials. And there has been a question of deaths."

"Directly related?"

"Highly suspicious."

"I did nothing wrong."

"I'm not accusing, but you don't need to be involved directly. Just being a part of the research and knowing about the data discrepancies that could injure patients is enough to make you culpable."

"I did nothing."

"I'm not asking you for a confession. I just want to know if you think McDowell knew about the errors and ignored them."

Denise paused and remained motionless with her head down and her hands clasped in her lap for many minutes. "Why do you want to know?" she finally said.

"I want to prevent it from happening again."

A waiter approached and Michael ordered another round.

"Not for me," Denise said.

Michael placed the order anyway. "There if you want it," he said.

"What do you want me to do?"

"You have access to the original data. Let us review it."

"What if something is wrong?"

"Something *is* wrong. We want to know if it's intentional."

"We?"

"The ethics committee of the college. Will you do it?"

She shook her head, undecided.

"Don't say no," Michael said.

"I have to think about it."

Before Michael O'Leary left for home two days later, Barzee called and said she'd look into his suspicions. She'd contact him in a few weeks. But it only took two days. She confirmed serious discrepancies in the data used to justify a clinical trial. Memos indicated Hiram McDowell knew about irregularities. She'd send documentation. O'Leary contacted the Health and Human Services' Office of Research Integrity and alerted the dean of Hiram's school of medicine as to his action, as a courtesy on the surface, but really to initiate an internal investigation. He then prepared a full report for the ethics committee.

Chapter 6

Hiram found Billie the easiest child to manage. Ann and Sophie were high maintenance and always needed money, but Billie rarely asked for more than his allowance. Billie had no interest in science or medicine; realistically Billie didn't have the intellect. But Hiram loved his son. Billie's passion was music—pop, rock and roll, jazz, blues. A perfect profession.

Denver
Billie

Billie spent a weekend with stepmother Carole and her girls.

After dinner on Friday night, he looked at classic videos of great drummers, taking notes and marking good segments for repeated study. With sticks and a pad, he worked out some of the patterns.

The next morning at breakfast, Carole said to Billie, "Wash the windows."

"I was going to campus," he said.

"Do the kitchen, the rec room, and the bedrooms."

He knew either the maids or the yardman did such things. "I've never done it before."

Carole scoffed at his hesitancy and said the yardman had the flu and the new maids didn't do windows except on "special occasions." And then only in the kitchen.

She's been fighting with Dad on the phone again.

"Couldn't we wait until the yardman is better?" he asked. *If he is really sick at all.*

"He might not be back. Just do it," she said.

He finished the outside windows in two and a half hours. He was working his way through the inside. He knocked on Tasha's half-open door. "Come in," she called to him. She was still in bed staring at her wall-mounted TV. A rerun of "I Love Lucy" was on with no sound.

"Okay to do the windows?" he asked. She shrugged. She was propped up on two overstuffed pillows. Her shoulders were bare and she had a can of Orange Crush in her left hand. She pulled the coverlet and sheet a few inches higher over her front.

There were only two windows. He opened the drapes and raised the roll-up window shades. The light streamed in and made her wince. She uttered a wet sound of distaste.

She was the younger of the two sisters. Small pouting lips, oversized eyes, and a small nose slightly upturned.

"You'll miss the game."

"I don't like football," she said.

"Not even Colorado?"

"It's dirty."

"I'll do the windows," he said. He didn't care what she thought, really. He finished and was pulling down shades and closing drapes.

"You want to watch the original *Halloween*?" she said, switching to cable and turning on the sound.

"I don't think so, Tasha. But thanks."

"I've got *Rosemary's Baby*." She reached to the nightstand for the disc. The covers slipped down, her plump breasts exposed, only her right nipple visible, a flesh-pink close to pastel. She found and fiddled uselessly trying to get the disc out of a sleeve to make her exposure seem unintentional.

"Maybe some other time," he said awkwardly. Tasha was a lot more woman than he thought. But she seemed desperate and he felt sorry for her.

A week later on a Saturday, the day was sunny and warm and Billie put on bathing trunks and a short sleeve Hawaiian-print sport shirt to lie by the pool on an inflated mattress and listen to drum music.

Tasha came from the house in a red bikini with a towel wrapped around her shoulders. She dropped the towel and lowered herself into the pool, the water line rising slowly over her full hips, darkening the triangles of cloth over her breasts. She stopped herself from going under with her hand on the side of the pool.

She dog paddled to an inflated plastic raft where she lay front down. Her exposure made him uncomfortable—and full of guilt because he wanted to stare—and any desire for a swim was now forgotten.

That night, his father was out of town, Carole was playing bridge with neighbors, Candice had a date, and Tasha had not returned from a mall adventure with girlfriends. He walked the treadmill in one of the garages, then ate warmed over pizza and retired to his room to watch sports, lying on his bed in his boxer shorts. He fell asleep with the TV on and was awakened to the feel of Tasha next to him. She was stroking him with her hand to arousal, freeing him through the slit in his boxer shorts. He didn't speak. He stared at the ceiling, confused as to what he wanted and what he should do. Soon he moaned, involuntarily, his hands grasping the covers beneath him. She took him in, her movements shaking the bed. After she climaxed, she moved up to lay her head on his chest. He held her hesitantly, suddenly buffeted by a wave of shame.

"Don't," he said as she tried to stimulate him again.

She laughed softly.

"Please go," he said. "We'll get caught," he said. He heard the garage door open—Carole probably returning from her bridge game. Tasha hurried back to her room.

He was ashamed. He'd ignored his principles.

The next night Tasha awoke him at 2:00 AM. "Mom's gone for the night," she said. "And Candice went to her boyfriend's. She won't come home if Mom is gone."

He opened the door. She slipped by him, taking off her robe and letting it fall to the floor, crawling head first into his bed, her buttocks jiggling in the dim light from the hall. She turned upright and pulled up the covers. "Don't stand there," she said.

Billie closed the door, his heart beating fast.

After satisfaction, Tasha held him in her arms. "Can I listen to your CD?"

"It won't be finished for a while. I'm recording again next week." At least that was what the guitarist said.

"That's so cool," she said. She tried to make love to him again but he was exhausted and unable to respond.

The next morning, Sunday, he called his dad who picked him up and they went to the Broncos' game.

Tasha wasn't there when he returned to the house. He lost all resistance to her; he couldn't get her out of his mind.

On Tuesday, Billie skipped classes to drive to his friend the guitarist's place; he went to the basement. Had he made a mistake? No one was there. And there was no guitar, no cello, no recording equipment, no bass. His drums were dismantled and stacked without care near the clothes dryer in the laundry room.

He called his friend. Music played in the background. Yes, they were recording today but they were using a studio downtown. Yes, there was a drum in the background... and snare and traps. They'd taken on a new drummer. His friend was sorry not to have let him know. They wouldn't need Billie. They were rerecording the tracks they'd laid down together, using a lot of bongos for some of the numbers. Of course he knew Billie could handle anything, but it was the new drummer's specialty.

Billie rang off and sat on the stair steps for a half hour, his head in his hands, before carrying his drum set to the car.

He went to the house instead of school. Tasha was there. "My band dumped me." She kissed him and led him to his room and their bed. She made gentle love to him. And as they lay savoring the aftermath, she looked beautiful to him and he was proud in the belief that she loved him without reservation.

A month later, Hiram escorted Carole to her department's yearly faculty reception in the Mercedes to match the occasion. She looked attractive in a green knee-length dress with a v-neck and a necklace of double-strand pearls. He wore a required tuxedo with a plaid cummerbund in red and green and a tie to match.

"Billie's depressed, Hiram," Carole said. "His band won't use him anymore."

Hiram frowned. "When?"

"I don't know. Probably weeks ago. He's really hurting."

"How do you know?"

"Tasha told me."

The next day, after finishing his surgery schedule, Hiram took Billie to buy the best set of drums and accessories available, a superior sound system, instruction books, and play-alongs. Hiram called friends of friends, found the best teacher with the best reputation for excellence in the city, and purchased prepaid lessons for Billie.

Two days later, the merchant delivered the equipment, which Carole insisted be installed in the basement away from the living area. Within a couple weeks, Carole told Hiram Billie spent less time at school and more time at the house, days and nights now. He practiced almost ceaselessly at home. And his new teacher had arranged for him to fill in for a high school blues band in Aurora.

"Billie's out of his funk," she announced to Hiram.

Chapter 7

Chicago
Michael O'Leary

The door to the boardroom where the ethics committee of the International College of Surgeons was meeting was closed. Two men in suits sat in two of four armless chairs backed to the wall in a long, wide corridor. Michael nodded to the men and sat. *Why aren't they ready for me?* The chair was too small for his large frame and the edge of a seat cut an uncomfortable line in his hamstrings. The two men were called in. Michael waited.

He reviewed notes from his briefcase. The ethics committee served a judiciary function in addition to its long-range planning and white paper policy-statement duties. He'd known every member of the committee for years as close colleagues; many were stay-with-us-when-you're-in-town friends. *This meeting should go down well,* he thought. *And Hiram should be disciplined. He's a lying bastard.*

Thirty minutes later the door opened and the committee's administrative assistant led Michael into the boardroom. Six committee members and the committee chairman sat in armchairs around an oval table for twelve. Empty chairs had been removed from the table except for a lone straight-back chair opposite the end where the chairman sat. All members stood and Michael shook their hands: the chair Simon, Tom, Leon, Harold, Sylvia, Peavey, Sands. Michael laid folders from his case on the table.

The chair spoke to the purpose of the meeting; the administrative assistant would transcribe minutes. Hiram was accused of scientific misconduct. The committee, in its judiciary function, must determine the validity of the charges and if scientific misconduct had occurred with Hiram's involvement, then make recommendations for disciplinary action against Hiram to be approved by the Board of Regents. The chair noted Michael O'Leary had volunteered to collect and evaluate the evidence in his role as chair of the research committee. "The committee thanks Dr. O'Leary for his work and his presence."

It's a routine start, Michael thought. *Everyone knows I hate the son of a bitch.* That might raise a few pockets of sympathy for Hiram.

Michael presented the evidence. Hiram was principle investigator on a trial that was a double blind study on the effectiveness of a new drug. Four essential papers were published from the lab with Hiram as senior author, papers that established sites of action for the drug and carefully monitored effects and complications in laboratory animals. In the clinical trial, there had been morbidity and mortality that had not been expected. A faculty member had reexamined the published data and found discrepancies in statistical analysis. Serious errors were discovered. The faculty member alerted the Office of Research Integrity. The clinical trial was halted when complications were suspected and the ORI imposed serious restrictions on the lab's activity. On the suspicions alone, the school dismissed two of the researchers. Lawsuits were threatened by patients enrolled in the trial. The situation never reached a national level of exposure because of persistent unrest in the Middle East. But the faculty member, a member of the International College of Surgeons, felt the College should review misconduct and consider action for the College to express its findings and reaction to the situation.

"Good presentation, Michael," the chair said and allowed half an hour for questions from the committee.

"We all know Hiram. It's hard to believe he knew anything about the lab misconduct," Leon said.

"He's driven, obsessive compulsive, probably bipolar..."

"He knows the best after-dinner jokes," Sands said.

"No. I'm serious," Leon countered. "I've known Hiram to always be honest."

"Are there patents involved?" Sylvia asked Michael.

"There are always patents," Harold said.

"Hiram has signed a contract with the drug company which patented aspects of the drug. Hiram's lab director holds two patents on mechanisms developed during scientific investigation. Hiram personally holds three patents on various aspects of the drug and the production process."

"Still, we don't know Hiram knew about misconduct," Tom said. "It's not proven to my satisfaction."

"The lab falsified results," the chair said. "That's clear. The question is: did Hiram know? Was he involved in the falsification? Punishment has already been meted by the school and the ORI to the investigators."

"Hiram's a clinician who built a laboratory by hiring the best PhD he could find and supporting him with competent staff. He would present the basic research questions to be answered, but he wouldn't do bench work."

"It would be easy to verify. I bet he had little to do with the intellectual input into the lab. He doesn't have time."

"Well, he wasn't PI on the clinical trial," Sands said.

"I think he's capable of ignoring truths for financial gain," Sylvia said. "He would think the possibilities of being found out if the drug was found to be highly effective and safe would be minimal. It would be a calculated risk."

"Every chair would do the same," Sands said.

"Well, the ORI believed he had responsibility. He's been barred from applying for federal funding for a decade," Tom said.

"Investigators directly responsible have been dismissed. Journals who published the false data were forced to publish retractions."

"I studied the retractions," Harold said. "I got advice from our statisticians. There is no doubt evil was involved. This was a quest for gold, and scientific truths were sublimated..."

"Falsified!"

"Okay, falsified to initiate a clinical trial the clinicians thought would bring positive results that would allow FDA approval and marketing."

"I still don't think Hiram knew," Sands said. "I've known him too long. I've run the Boston marathon with him. He doesn't cheat in sports."

"How can you say that? You don't really know about his science. What if he used performance-enhancing drugs to win a marathon? You wouldn't know that either."

"He just wouldn't."

"Either way," the chair broke in, "it's off the subject of scientific misconduct."

"It's lying," Sylvia said.

"He's been punished enough by innuendo without proof," Tom said.

"What do you think we should do?" Harold asked Michael.

Michael swallowed. *I've got to say this right.* Any sign that he'd lost objectivity because he really disliked McDowell might cancel any significant action by the committee.

"Most of you know Hiram promised me the position of executive director and never followed through. I don't want that to in any way cloud understanding of Hiram's culpability here. I speak as chair of the research committee committed to carry out my duties regarding a serious incident of misconduct. And I do think Hiram's shown dishonesty. And I think there is almost total belief in those who've investigated that regardless of Hiram's state of knowledge and involvement in the cover-up, he had the responsibility for knowing the truth, and vetting all expressions of data interpretation. He was chair of the department and at times senior author. It was his lab. He was prime investigator on two of the NIH grants awarded the laboratory for this project. He signed the contract with the drug company for the monetization of the research discoveries.

"I believe Hiram should be held responsible. I don't pretend to know to what degree he should be held responsible, but I do not believe the College should be seen to protect one of its own when a serious misconduct has resulted in pain, suffering, and death in a clinical trial."

Deep silence persisted for many seconds.

"I agree," said Tom.

"Me too," said Harold.

"I do think you have personal bias, Michael," Sands said.

"We do not need to vote today," the chair said. "We will allow

Hiram to face the accusations at the next meeting, the 19th of next month. We'll make recommendations after that."

"I don't think he deserves to continue membership in this organization," Tom said.

"He needs to resign as Chairman of the Board," Leon said.

"There is time to make considered decisions," the chair said. "I ask for complete confidentiality. I will also seal the minutes of this discussion until after the board's action, if there is action. Thank you, Michael," the chair said, standing. Other members stood and there were handshakes with Michael and every committee member around the table.

Chapter 8

Hiram was called before the judiciary committee of the International College. He was led by the secretary of the committee into the conference room from the hall where he had been waiting for over an hour. He was directed to sit at the end of the table, away from committee members, in the same chair Michael O'Leary had occupied when he appeared before the ethics committee a few weeks earlier.

The chair started the meeting, noting the date, time, and attending members for the record. "Hiram," the chair said, "we thank you for coming. We know it's a difficult time. We know your feelings for all of us involved must be mixed. But we're eager to hear your story, clarify accusations regarding misconduct, and make a decision on what action we will recommend to the board for disciplinary action, if any."

Hiram shifted almost imperceptibly in his chair as he swallowed unintentionally.

The charges against Hiram were scientific misconduct in the laboratory, but there was also interest in the accusations of "excess improprieties" in his foundation management.

"What happened in the laboratory, Hiram?" the chair asked.

"I take full responsibility. It was my laboratory. I was PI on two NIH grants at the time."

"Data were altered. Data that eventually led to a clinical trial. Complications occurred based on your scientific results."

"The data were altered by a postdoc lead investigator. His involvement has been identified and he has been dismissed. He was reprimanded by the school and denied the privilege to apply for further grants for ten years."

"Not you?"

"Not me."

The chair checked with the meeting recorder to be sure Hiram's denial was in the minutes.

"How did it happen?" the chair asked.

"I trusted him. Assumed his results were valid. He'd worked for me for over twenty years."

"Why now?"

"Money, I think. Some of his funding was from drug companies who pressured him to publish results. And although difficult to prove, there is suspicion that he was remunerated in ways not above board. And I've looked carefully at all his results over the years in my lab. I found two other areas of potential discrepancies, but nothing blatant like the errors now under scrutiny."

"You didn't review the erroneous data yourself?" Urology asked.

"Obviously not thoroughly enough. I had two independent reviews of the statistical analyses and the papers before submission. There were no alerts from those reviewers. Still, my name was senior author on the papers, and I should have taken the responsibility to carefully check."

"An error of oversight?" Thoracic asked.

"Yes," Hiram said.

"And the clinical deaths?"

"No deaths. And the complications could be from the disease, not the treatments."

"Who determined that?"

"Questions were raised both by internal and external review."

"And you agree with those findings? Agree that the scientific mismanagement did not result in clinical complications?"

"I believe that. Yes. The clinical effect of the error was that patients were treated with a regimen that had no effect on their disease process. For that I am deeply sorry."

General Surgery spoke up. "Hiram. There have been charges that you've taken financial advantage of the foundation you've founded. I know we've been focused on scientific misconduct. But the question has been raised by two board members. It's become an issue in our decision for recommendations."

"I don't think that has relevance to the charges at hand," Hiram said.

"I agree," the chair said.

Aaron for General surgery raised a hand for recognition. "Repeatedly, we've stated that financial miscreants should not be considered in the judgment on scientific misconduct. But we've had pressure from members. What's the true nature of these financial mismanagement charges?"

"Aaron," Hiram began, "I've been successful in building a hospital in Nepal, staffing that hospital, developing educational opportunities for US doctors in surgical training. I've negotiated through difficult political opposition, at home and abroad. I've included local physicians and care givers in all developmental aspects of the project. And I did it by hiring managers and fundraisers with connections to those who have money to give to philanthropic causes for health improvement. My effort has been international. And the support has been worldwide."

"And your benefits?"

"I don't understand."

"How did you gain financially? There are rumors."

"All financial arrangements with the foundation are transparent. There is nothing that can be questioned. It's a charity. And very successful," Hiram said.

"Your salary?"

"Varies."

"Half a million?"

"Around that."

Finally it was over. Hiram stood and thanked the committee for their time and understanding. He paused to see what was appropriate. Unless someone started to shake hands, he knew his initiation of a sign of friendship might seem like an effort to influence the group. He waited, then left the room in silence without shaking a single hand and without a single spontaneous thank you from even one committee member. Hiram feared he would be dismissed from the College of Surgeons, the result would be leaked to the public, and it would ruin his career.

The consensus of the committee was that Hiram had made many mistakes, but that every surgeon has some moments in his or her career that might lead to the troubles Hiram found himself in. Although opinion varied, most committee members thought Hiram was not directly responsible for research misconduct. Almost all thought his success at fundraising was beyond reproach without intense independent investigation. The committee members agreed to vote on a reprimand if necessary, but none would vote for dismissal from the college, which would extinguish Hiram's career. Committee members were too close to Hiram's path to success to believe more severe punishment was warranted, or necessary.

Chapter 9

Tasha was pregnant with Billie's child. They had to marry as quickly as possible. Carole never faltered in her love for Tasha and she had to convince Hiram to support them. She did not have resources to help.

Portland, OR
2001

Carole waited in the rooftop lounge of a boutique hotel that overlooked the expressway. She hadn't seen Hiram in weeks, well before she knew of Tasha's condition. This was to be a weekend together. She knew he expected gratitude for this gesture to be with her, but she would not condescend to pandering; she resented being consistently ignored, or even forgotten most of the time, and it was worse now, in their third year of marriage. She *was* his wife but not his friend or companion. Had he loved her? No. But she doubted he had loved anyone except maybe his children in an odd sort of ancestral way. Her value to him? She had filled a need in his perception of how things should be for the public to perceive his family life. And she watched Billie. Not enough scrutiny, Hiram would argue. Well, this was her chance to use her time with him to settle Tasha's pregnancy. She would do it when Hiram arrived here at the hotel from the airport. They'd have dinner tonight. It had to be tonight. Tomorrow, Saturday, he'd be gone climbing Mount Hood with "Peak" Waring, a surgeon from Eugene he'd known since they were in school together at Princeton, while she went to the museum and shopped.

She'd met Peak twice when he'd visited Denver. She found him arrogant and dismissive and was thankful she did not have to be with him for this weekend. Hiram climbed with Peak for training and because Peak paid for all the excursions. Hiram sarcastically chided him for not being a world-class climber—something Carole found ugly and demeaning both for Peak and Hiram. Peak wanted Hiram's admiration so much he laughed excessively at Hiram's degrading, double-entendre teasing. Distasteful behavior for grown men. Peak was a buffoon and a patsy. But if Peak and Hiram got together before she could confront Hiram about Tasha's baby, she'd be ignored and lose any chance of fairness. And talking on Sunday would not be possible. Hiram planned to go to a brunch alone at an off-rate downtown hotel where a blues band played featuring "Flatout Smith" on harmonica. Hiram would sit in and trade a few "fours" as he usually did when he came to Portland. Her cell vibrated a text; Hiram was on his way from the airport.

Hiram ordered a steak medium rare with no sauce, an unadorned baked potato, and extra mixed fresh vegetables steamed al dente on the side. Carole sipped a Manhattan as Hiram ate. She waited until he was served his entre.

"Tasha's pregnant," she said.

With barely a pause and a slight shrug, Hiram said, still eating, "Great. When is she due?"

"It's Billie's."

Hiram put down the blade of his steak knife and the tongs of his fork on the plate still holding the handles. "I don't think so."

"He's the only one."

"You can't be sure with kids nowadays."

"Tasha isn't like that, Hiram."

"Well, it wasn't Billie." Hiram was eating again. "I told him not to get your girls pregnant. Warned him to use protection if he had to have them."

Carole's cheeks flushed with anger. "There is no doubt, Hiram. It can be proven."

"She seduced him, then. Trapped him. She's not that good looking and she saw the opportunity to get herself a man."

"She's attractive and sweet."

"Not sweet. She always treated me like panty shit," Hiram said.

"They made love. A lot. In our house when no one else was there. Billie's going to be a father," she said. "It's a time for joy."

Hiram increased the intensity of his eating. She didn't take her eyes off him but he didn't look at her for more than a minute. "What are you going to do?" she said.

"Do?" Finally Hiram looked to her with cold eyes.

"Support them. It's your grandchild. Billie can't support them."

"Billie will do well. But even so, Billie's got no responsibility for Tasha's mistake."

It's not Tasha's mistake! It's two humans having a baby. Thoughts she wanted to scream to the world but she kept silent.

Hiram continued. "He's got a life ahead of him. He's good musically. I think he's taking computer stuff in college for a career." Hiram wasn't even sure of Billie's major. He just didn't see Billie that often. But he cared.

"Billie should marry her," she said.

"Never. And don't ever think I'm taking care of Tasha anymore."

"She was under age," she said.

Hiram finished his meal in silence. "Take care of it," he finally said. "I'll pay for that."

She felt a void inside her fill quickly with what was becoming a frequent extreme dislike for husband Hiram McDowell.

"I won't do that," she said.

"I'll ask Peak. He'll know someone discrete in Denver."

"It's immoral... illegal."

"Think of it as euthanasia," Hiram said.

"That's repulsive."

"I'm not letting Billie get trapped into some dour future," Hiram said.

Hiram believes all the world exists to serve him. And he'll abort his grandchild to avoid inconvenience.

"Your loving support could create a beautiful future for them," she said. "They're in love."

"I won't do it," he said. "They don't know what love is."

What if I claimed he raped her? she thought. *Of course it's not true. But I could claim it. Seek investigation. Prosecution.*

Hiram stared impassively out a window past her.

She had liked Billie most of the time. But he would never be successful in career or business. Unlike his father, he was kind, and he'd be a great parent, maybe even patch together two families at war with each other.

"And don't think claiming rape will ever stick," Hiram said, knowing what she would think.

"You owe child support at least."

"I know legal experts that could tangle that into oblivion in two hours of fees and nothing ever for you or Tasha," Hiram said.

"This is your grandchild!"

"Bullshit. You'll need proof to convince me."

The waiter cleared the table and Hiram did not look at Carole, nor she at him. Carole spoke when no one could hear. "I'll file for divorce."

"Is that a promise?"

"I will!'

Hiram stood and laid his folded napkin on the table. "Threaten something new," he said. He left without looking at her.

She sat unwilling to move for a while, overwhelmed with anger and hate. He'd used her! Against her better judgment, she'd signed a prenuptial agreement. With divorce she'd get nothing. How could she hold onto the meager assets she had? How would she get Tasha through life as a single mother with modest abilities? She would do it, damn it, to spite Hiram, although he would never think of her again and never feel the hurt she would try to inflict. She'd get DNA confirmation. But it was risky. What if she was wrong about Billie being the father? What if he didn't match? That would close any hope of Hiram, and Billie's, support for Tasha.

She stayed alone that night in the hotel, not knowing where Hiram was. She was not only lonely; she was angry and despondent. Divorce meant nothing to him. He welcomed it. She was sure he'd climb tomorrow. Play with Flatout Smith on Sunday. Never break his routine to work things out with her. And he'd ignore her with purpose to spite her.

She went home to Denver the next day and arrived mid afternoon.

Billie had moved out. In three days all of Hiram's possessions were gone, the house deplete of expensive artwork and valuable furniture. So she kept Tasha isolated not only from Billie, who kept trying to see her, but all the McDowells too. And she filed for divorce. She saw her marriage clearly. She had no love for Hiram; he made her feel useless and unwanted and she hated being around him.

Chapter 10

Chicago
Sophie

Sophie's memory of school—the private girls school in the East—was skewed by the isolation she had felt. With no deviation, she hadn't liked the snobbish girls, and she avoided intimacy. She was cursed with a free-floating, smoldering anger about everything around her—the excesses of personal spending, the unwavering claim to social superiority. Her teachers evaluated her as sullen, curt, and standoffish. And although she never liked being alone, she preferred being alone to having to be with her classmates. She was an average student with a brief scare of failing two required courses. She turned to Hiram for help to pass and made it through with re-exams Hiram demanded and special tutoring he paid for.

Life bloomed for her when she went to art school in Chicago. The school was accredited, although barely from the rumors, and gave a degree with the accumulation of college credits, some of which had to be earned at other colleges with required academic courses.

She started with drawing and painting but realism was difficult for her. She couldn't translate images with any accuracy or dexterity. She tried abstraction, but her dull lines lacked energy and her homogenized colors of tired grays and browns failed to turn any heads.

Learning photography changed Sophie's life. Framing her subjects, awareness of lights and darks, filtered colors to emphasize a mood, recording life in journalistic views, accentuating human forms in portraits that enhanced truths without deceit—all of it excited her. For the last three years of art school, she matured to a professionalism that gave her pride and purpose. She began to open to people, a liberation of caring and trust permitted by her newfound confidence. And she made a friend, Ivana, a girl with a mirrored devotion to photography, whom Sophie loved, and who gave her purpose.

On a Sunday for Ivana's birthday, Sophie took her to the House of Blues Gospel Brunch. On leaving, they walked to The Art Institute of Chicago, critiqued the impressionists, and then discovered a sense of life in antiquity. After a coffee and sandwich in the cafeteria, they walked south down Columbus Street through Grant Park. "Look," Ivana said, pointing two hundred feet away to a man beating a woman with a stone clutched in his right hand.

Sophie broke into a run and Ivana followed.

The woman crumpled to the ground and the man kicked her in the stomach twice with a pointed-toe boot and fled when he saw Sophie and Ivana coming. The woman moaned, bent over and retching. She was bleeding from the nose and mouth and a scalp wound. She was barely conscious.

"I'll call the police," Sophie said to the woman, reaching for her cell phone.

"No," the woman gasped, "no police." She had an accent too slight to pinpoint her origins.

"Call," Ivana said to Sophie as she rolled the woman on her back and supported her head with Sophie's wadded up jacket.

"Who was that man?" Ivana asked the woman.

"No one," the woman muttered.

"You know him, don't you?" Ivana said.

"I'll be all right," the woman answered.

"Is he your boyfriend? Your husband?"

The woman didn't answer and tried to stand up to leave but fell back and curled into a fetal position to ease the pain.

"You have to report him," Sophie said.

The woman shook her head "no."

An EMS vehicle came down Lakeshore with lights flashing and a siren wailing. The police arrived seconds later. The attendants found high pulse and low blood pressure; they suspected internal bleeding when Ivana asked.

The ambulance left with the woman for the hospital and Ivana and Sophie talked to the police for the official report. They described the man and told of the woman's refusal to say who it was.

"Who can understand that?" the cop said. "Common enough. Probably a whore."

"She didn't seem like that," Ivana said.

"A wife then. Some wives seem to thrive on the abuse." *Blatant sexism.*

"Can't something be done?" Sophie asked.

Hospital social services would be contacted to begin an investigation, the cop assured them.

Ivana and Sophie walked to find a bus stop to go back to school. They talked of the woman, and they talked of all the women who were abused physically and mentally in the city. Ivana sensed photography could bring the plight of women in Chicago to the attention of the public. It was a third world existence for many. And Sophie and Ivana needed a graduation project. The school approved a joint project and for months they documented, in a series of images, women in Chicago. They graduated and a New York house published their portfolio that received more than expected critical acclaim.

When Sophie and Ivana graduated, they were Siamese-twin soul mates, and accepted positions at the same studio in New York. They rented rooms uptown on the Westside, and traveled to and from work together sharing cab fare to save money.

The studio work was mostly portraits, usually of the rich and famous. Ivana had the knack for it more than Sophie, but they both gained decent reputations and success. Ivana wanted to do another project based on the success of their Chicago Southside-women collection while in school, to document the plight of women in third world Asian countries and Guatemala, Peru, Nicaragua, Mexico, and Cuba. Ivana was interested in cultures of sexism and degradation of women in general, women who were denied education and forced into labor, even in families with sufficient incomes. They planned the project to completion. Sophie never imagined how happy she could be, how life seemed an expanse of pleasing and rewarding opportunities. Ivana was her best friend. She thought of Ivana as her family, and she felt at peace.

Chapter 11

Hiram sent Sophie a monthly allowance check timed so she could prepay the rent. As what had become their monthly habit, Sophie and her new live-in partner June went to a fine restaurant as a ritual homage to the old man who was off climbing mountains somewhere or politicking in Chicago where he'd been elected President of the International College of Surgeons. On this night, June brought her new client, Ella Robust, who had signed a contract today.

"Is that a pen name?" Sophie asked Ella as they were being led to June and Sophie's usual table.

Ella laughed. "Never use my name. My husband's Polish. Lots of c's, z's and k's."

Sophie smiled but felt no humor.

"June picked it out for me. What do you think?"

Sophie glanced at June.

"No, tell me how it strikes you," Ella said. They took their seats. "It's important. I'll have it for a long time."

"She writes out of this world," June said.

"I don't like it," Sophie said. She glanced away from Ella and June.

"Don't be contrary," June said. For the past few months, June hadn't hesitated to denigrate Sophie in front of others. Sophie held back a retort.

"I write sci-fi murders from a woman's point of view. What would you suggest?" Ella asked Sophie.

"Maybe Peony Galactica," Sophie said after a short pause. Looking back at Ella now she realized Ella wasn't offended.

"Edith's my real name."

"It doesn't sound sci-fi," Sophie said. "More from the time of Plath, or maybe Emily Dickinson."

"Really, Sophie," June said.

"I think she's right," Ella said.

"But Galactica. That's pure cliché," June persisted.

"Sci-fi is cliché," Ella said.

"Galactica is from the Greek," Sophie said. "That adds class. And Peony is feminine."

"Still tacky."

"I don't think so June. Sophie's right," Ella said. "I'd like to change."

"We'll think about it," June said emphatically.

"I don't want to think about it. I like the idea." Ella held her hand up. "Peony Galactica," she said with exaggerated emphasis.

"Yes. Of course," June said angrily. Sophie closed her eyes. "Now, let's order," June said.

That night in bed in the apartment, June showed no need for affection. But Sophie needed her and reached out to touch June's arm. June moved away.

"Can't we forget it?" Sophie whispered.

"We cannot forget it. It's part of a new trend you're on. Always having a better way to do something. I don't like it."

"She asked me."

"Any normal person would have said it was great, no matter what they thought. Why make a big deal about it?"

"I had an idea. I told her. She liked it."

"It's a stupid name, Sophie. Peony Galactica. Shit. I'm in the business. I know what sells."

"Ella Robust?" Sophie turned her back to June. They were silent for many minutes, the air tense between them.

June started laughing.

"What's the matter?" Sophie asked, thinking June was being cruel.

But June rolled over and took Sophie in her arms. "I'm crazy," she said into her ear. "Peony's a good name. At least better than Ella Robust."

Sophie felt a flood of warmth. "I'm glad you like it," she said, relaxing.

"And I love you," June said.

<hr>

Three months later, on one of their check-delivered-from-Hiram celebrations, June invited another new client-author to dinner. They had reservations for Mandarin food at a new restaurant.

"He's a little affected," June said.

"He?" Sophie hated the thought of dinners with male authors.

"Arrogant too. But he's nice enough."

Sophie thought he was bizarre... dyed black hair and a grayish-brown goatee and mustache. It was as if he was trying to look folksy and distinguished at the same time... with the strained flavor of Mark Twain. He looked silly, Sophie thought... ridiculous, really. He wore a linen white sport coat, a red and blue paisley ascot tucked in a white button-down dress shirt, and stressed blue-heather jeans held up by a rope belt with a turquoise and ebony belt buckle.

"Princeton Navarro," June introduced. Sophie wondered if it was a pen name, but was afraid to ask. "Sophie is a photographer," June said.

"How interesting," Princeton said, distracted as he scrutinized two males entering the front door.

"She's quite famous for her studies of women," June said. "A true artist."

"I prefer narrative to visual images," Princeton said. Princeton brought back his gaze to June.

"I think you'd be challenged in describing Sophie's work," June said.

"Oh, I could handle it," he said.

"I do breasts and pudenda," Sophie said to unsettle him a little. She did mostly portraits, never erotica. June gave her a severe glare. But Princeton Navarro didn't seem repulsed or impressed, more disinterested in Sophie and anything anyone else said.

"Princeton's work is fascinating," June said. "Western novels. Exploring how homosexuality wove comradely strength and spirit in the West in the mid 19th century."

That would explain the dress, Sophie thought, struggling not to show any outward interest in what this creep did or who he was.

Princeton Navarro needed only an occasional prompt from June to talk about himself. He'd never graduated from college. He was proud that he was a self-made author. He had independent support, something that fit the moods of meditation he enjoyed immersing himself in. These moods were the source of great images descending on him, he insisted. He could see horses foaming at the mouth, chomping on the bit, the raised tail before defecation. He could hear the hacking smokers' coughs of two cowboys under the stars beneath a cloudless sky, cooking beans in an iron skillet over an open stick-fire.

Sophie moaned inwardly and gave June a hostile stare as she egged Princeton on to his platitudes, spoken, as he drank freely, with an increasingly nasal voice... and with thoughts banal to the extreme.

He invited them back to his penthouse apartment on the Upper East Side. His parents bought it for him. They were generous with their inherited wealth.

"We can't tonight," Sophie said.

"I'd love to," June said. "We'll find you a cab," she said to Sophie. "I can't have you walking back alone tonight."

Sophie returned home defiantly walking alone.

June arrived at the apartment after three AM. Sophie longed to appease June and started to make love but the strong smell of recent sex with a male stopped her. This had happened twice before with June and men. But this time hurt Sophie more. Princeton Navarro wasn't worth it. She turned over and pulled up the coverlet to hide her tears.

———◆———

June moved out of Sophie's place to live with Princeton a month later. He was wealthy beyond either Sophie or June's experience and would soon go to Europe to start working on his new book; he was taking June with him. He was blossoming his career with a new three-volume work on aboriginal sex, yet to be researched, but still well underway as a nonfiction memoir of a fictional outback native. "I've taken a six-month leave of absence," June said. Sophie doubted leave; she thought June had quit or been fired from her editorial job.

"Do you love him?" Sophie asked June.

"I think so."

"Like you loved me?"

"I still love you, honey. It's different. It's an opportunity," June said.

"I don't want you to go."

"Pooh," June said.

"God, he's so weird."

"I've discovered so much good about him," June said. "He's quite intellectual."

"Arrogant."

"Don't be bitchy."

"He is!"

June backed away. "You don't know crap about him."

Sophie held back her need to weep. "Is this it?" she asked.

"I'll give you two hundred dollars for the back rent."

"You owe me twenty-six hundred."

June shrugged.

"You're not coming back?" Sophie asked.

June didn't respond.

"I love you," Sophie said.

June flushed. "Grow up."

"Are you going to marry him?"

June didn't answer. *She doesn't love him. This is security, freedom from the grind of June's time consuming and unrewarding work as a second tier editor where her blunted intellect would never attain recognition. Of course, it will never last. Both will be to blame.* But Sophie couldn't forgive the fact that June thought it *would* last, and that June could care more for Princeton and his money than she did for her.

"I hate you," Sophie said, but her heart still ached.

Chapter 12

On the forty-seventh floor of network corporate headquarters in New York, Paige Sterling opened the windowless oak door to her new boss's temporary office. He was in this space until renovations were complete for his new suite on a top floor. He was alone behind a desk. Perry Rosenthal. She'd never seen him up close. Swarthy. Thick myopic glasses with black rims. Small head on a puny body. Unkempt curly black hair with an oval patch of gray on the back right. He smiled as he motioned her to sit in a wooden armchair in front of the desk and showed crooked teeth with spaces in front. She sat. He stared at her without speaking.

Should I welcome him to his new job as program director, and senior vice-president? But she didn't like his looks or his reputation. He left one network to invade her network that was an industry-leader with better ratings and better pay. Still his gaze did not falter.

"What's with you?" she said, irritated at his conceit. He kept silent. "I don't have to put up with this rudeness," she added.

He laughed thinly. "Relax," he said. "I was thinking. I'm not smooth, but you'll find me easy to get along with."

"Really? At what?"

"Be civil." He was frowning. "I've got to make changes, Paige. Despite what you may think, I don't find it easy."

She remained motionless. Rosenthal's quick ascendancy to top management carried a cloud of rumors about show cancellations and sacking of key on-air personalities like herself.

"Current news segments," he said.

Her heart pounded as her anger flared. *He's going to fire me!* That's what it sounded like. Yes! Of course. There had been rumors. "Twelve years I've been a leader," she said.

"It's not all about you," Rosenthal said. "There will be extensive changes throughout."

"I was the first woman host on *Week's End*."

"Look. I'm making some scheduling changes."

"My segments made *Week's End* what it is."

"I'm taking you off *Week's End* as a host. But I'm not pushing you out!"

Panic shot through Paige. "My contributions have been extraordinary!"

"Goddamn it, Paige. It's not all that. But face reality. You're not what you used to be. You're past your prime. And you didn't make the show. Walter, Tom, Harvey, and Mike made the show. And we're broadcasting to new generations."

"That's sexist denial of my popularity."

Rosenthal shook his head. "You wallow in fantasy."

"My ratings are always up there."

"Never on top."

"Sometimes!"

"Not enough. And your pieces are derogatory to the excess. Your thrust for the jugular offends people."

"I divulge important news."

"With inflammatory details that border on truth and make us all vulnerable for legal action."

"Walter wants me out? Harvey?"

"Everybody wants you out!"

She doubted that was true. "I have a loyal following," she said. She gathered herself. Her future was fogging over. "I've got a contract," she added.

"You got me there. I tried, but I won't break it."

"You tried?"

"Of course. But a buy-out is not good value. And firing a woman is not good politics. I've been on the job ten weeks and I've been accused of whacking staff with a sexist hatchet. Not a good time to add you to that list."

"So you are firing me. Just with slow torture."

"Not now. I'm adjusting your role in contribution to the news cycle."

"Which means?"

"Like I said, no more routine hosting Sunday nights on "*Week's End*." You do short segments when assigned."

"I'm not a rookie."

"It's an opportunity."

"It's demeaning. I'm a celebrity."

"Barely. That food segment on leeks and mushrooms was over-boiled."

I'm not stuffed full of crappy metaphors, she thought. She leaned back and crossed her thin legs. True, they weren't curvaceous like the young competitors straight out of journalism schools. But they weren't that shapeless. And she'd been paying careful attention to her face. She had tight-stretched, wrinkleless skin.

"I can get a job elsewhere. ABC will take me."

"It would be a blessing."

She had no chance at fifty-four of getting a top spot on a hard news program now, especially on a major network. Rosenthal knew it, too. And she was no good at pop culture. But she was on the board of the Whitney Museum of Art, which should give inroads no other journalist had. *My God, on-air time is rarely given to the arts. TV now is all crime, sports, sensationalism, exposé.* And she couldn't bear the thought of interviewing under-clad, over-weight pop artists in six-inch platform shoes. It was depressing. She turned a little more optimistic. Maybe it was time to take on new fields. *Be positive!* Rosenthal was demoting her but he wasn't going to let her go soon; she believed that now.

"I want specials. I've done some memorable ones," she said, pressing for an advantage.

Rosenthal laughed out loud.

"You could have legal complications here," she said.

"Really?"

"Discrimination. Gender. Age."

"You're not a star anymore. And if I replace you, I'll replace you with a woman. "

"You fire the old faithful standbys, your in-house authority will be nonexistent."

"Look. I want you to take over healthcare," he said.

Healthcare! "I don't like doctors," she said.

"It'll make you do better. Put some needed balance into your over-wrought reporting."

"You want me to do research advancements?"

"Do a four-hour Viagra erection as an emergency. How it feels. What to do," he said, but he was laughing.

"Don't degrade my talent. I'm serious."

"Report on the state of the art in healthcare. On unusual advance-ments. Stars in the field. Or doctors' personalities."

"When would I be on?"

"Nightly news."

"From the desk?"

"In the field."

"And the specials?"

"Only shorts."

"A few twelve minute segments on *Week's End?* I don't have to be a host, but I'd be recognized. Maybe every couple weeks. I'll make it good."

"Goddamn it, Paige."

"I keep my staff?"

Rosenthal sighed in submission.

"You won't be sorry," she said. She'd gained some ground. *But God! Healthcare?*

"I'm already sorry," he said.

Chapter 13

Over the next few months Paige produced a number of spots for evening news, some national. Perry had even allowed one for *Week's End,* when he called her in for an emergency meeting.

"You're becoming a poster girl for health," he greeted her.

How clever he thought he was. "What do you want?" she said.

"No, I'm serious. Good work."

How devious. What does he want now? Is he ready to push me out?

"Look, I want you to do an hour-long special after the first of the year on the accomplishments of this doctor, Hiram McDowell," he said. "He's President of the Board of Regents of the International College of Surgeons, and he heads a Department of Surgery in Denver. He climbs high mountains. Runs marathons. He's the founder of a foundation that upfronts a surgery center in Nepal. Beaucoup humanitarian. A super-human hero."

"A doctor isn't exciting news," Paige said.

"The President's chief of staff has officially hinted they'll use him on the President's task force to launch the healthcare initiative for financing the uninsured."

"Who cares about a doctor on a task force?"

"I do. The President does. And all the depressed, hurting, pain-racked citizens without insurance who are waiting for you to make the world care."

"All for political gain and your influence," she said. "Do I get other specials after this? Ones I can choose?"

"We'll see what comes out of the oven." *God. It's like Hansel and Gretel. I hate his metaphors.*

"And I'll be the lead on this McDowell guy? Absolute control."

"Make it good. Impress 'em. Woo 'em. Make 'em awestruck with what they hear."

She'd do it. She'd lost career momentum with her demotion by Rosenthal to healthcare, but she was gaining respect again to spite him. *I've always had the gift.* She'd make this the best special of the year. And if this McDowell guy was the savior for the President's sagging authority, so be it. But she would not do it for Rosenthal and his undercurrent of deals for his own gain. She'd do it for excellence in her profession. To serve her audience.

She stood, keeping her arms to her side to not show the sweat soaked stains she knew were on her dress under her arms. "I'll think about it," she said.

"Yes or no?" Rosenthal said.

She didn't take her eyes off him for many seconds. She nodded.

He waved his hand to dismiss her.

———◆———

Paige led a preliminary weekly meeting of her staff for the McDowell special. Many staff had been working full-time on the project for almost a week; Amara Ude, her new assistant recently appointed by Rosenthal and just starting her career: Victor, her assigned primary photographer with valuable experience with many networks; Condoleezza, her chief writer for nine years; and three techs and gofers. Perry Rosenthal sat in. Paige asked what they had so far.

Condoleezza spoke first. "I've started a file on McDowell's early climbing experiences in the Himalayas. He was part of expeditions that lost six men on an attempt in the eighties. McDowell was injured and his climbing partner died on the descent."

"What's that got to do with this special?" Amara asked with a touch of disdain inappropriate for a newcomer.

"Possibly a lot," Paige said. "Condoleezza found something that borders on extraordinary."

"Reading the accounts from those on that mountain that fatal day is pretty damn revealing," Condoleezza said. "It took luck and guts to make it down. Hiram is mentioned in the memoirs of a Pole and an Argentinean in separate accounts. They were on the mountain trying to survive at the same time."

"I've followed climbers as far as Camp II," Victor said. "The risks are high. Hundreds have died."

"Both memoirs suggest McDowell abandoned his partner."

"There's a point where you have to save yourself. A lot of them believe that."

"We're doing a profile on a famous surgeon," Rosenthal said. "Why are we stuck on a climbing expedition?"

"He's climbed every Nepalese peak above 8,000 meters, some more than twice." Condoleezza said. "It's an important part of who he is."

"It could be related to competency," Paige said.

"More like a quirk," Rosenthal said.

"You've got to be good to survive what he's done."

"Maybe not that unusual anymore," Rosenthal said. "And not related to his health career. Use his philanthropy. All his pro bono work. We're doing this special to assure he remains on that task force for healthcare and the public sees him as a benevolent savior, not just a callous super hero."

I'm in charge, Paige thought. *We need the climbing history to present a balanced portrait.* "We should check out the climbing activity and how it helped him build the foundation and the hospital," she said. "It would strengthen the presentation of his character. "

"He's there a lot, isn't he? In the Himalayas?" Amara asked.

"Four to five times a year," Condoleezza said.

"Has anyone ever been to the clinic?" Amara asked.

"No," Condoleezza said. "It would be great. We could get a sense of the personalities involved. McDowell's leadership style."

"And climbing skills too," Amara said. Paige wondered if she'd been wrong about Amara; she had never shown the slightest interest in McDowell's climbing.

"Well, let's get on it and then move on to other things," Amara said. "We'll have more when I get back from Nepal."

Oh, no. The little minion wants to travel. It's got nothing to do with McDowell.

"On whose authority do you plan to go?" Paige asked, irritated with this surprise announcement from someone who obviously was now reporting primarily to Rosenthal and not to her.

"Perry's," Amara said. Amara looked at Rosenthal who stayed

silent while returning Amara's gaze. Paige waited for Rosenthal to look at her, to let her know she was still in charge. He did not.

"Thanks for being so diligent," Paige said to Amara. *The little witch.* "But you'll be needed here." Paige glanced from Rosenthal to Amara. "I'm going and I'll take Condoleezza and Victor next month. Before climbing season ends."

Condoleezza looked to Paige with surprise. Victor smiled, eager for the photographic opportunities in Nepal.

"I want to document the philanthropic effort. And I'll see about the climbing. I'll oversee the entire operation in Nepal," Paige said with as much emphasis as she could manage without shouting.

"I want to go," Amara looked again at Rosenthal.

"There's no need," Paige said. "The three of us can handle it."

"That's not fair," Amara said, waiting for support from Rosenthal. But he did not respond. Paige smiled inwardly. She'd reestablished herself with impressive healthcare segments to a point where Rosenthal had not been willing to override her authority for the favors of a bimbo newcomer. *Was Amara sleeping with him? That was how he often managed female staff.*

"Is there anything else?" Paige said before ending the meeting. She wondered how the sex with Amara would go tonight. *That little exploiter. She'd fake it like a pro with moans and sighs but with a heart as disinterested as a hermaphrodite to a castrati.*

Paige took Rosenthal aside as they exited. "Don't try to ease me out with that Amara person," she said. Rosenthal laughed. *That's exactly his plan!* She could see that from the humorous glint in his eyes, but he said, "You're paranoid, Paige. Relax."

Relaxing was the one thing she could not do.

Chapter 14

Hiram

Hiram was in New York on foundation business. He worried about Sophie. Sophie said she had broken up with her lesbian friend. She refused to return calls. He was not pleased. When he could arrange free time, he paid a surprise visit to Sophie. He rang Sophie's doorbell several times.

"Open," Hiram said. When he heard no movement inside, he dialed 911 on his cell. "I'm calling the police."

The door opened. Sophie was disheveled in sweats and an extra large black tee shirt with a skull and cross bones on the front. She was shockingly gaunt and trashy looking.

"Get dressed," Hiram said. "I'm taking you out for dinner."

"I don't want to."

"What's wrong with you?"

Sophie burst into tears.

"Where's that June person?"

Sophie moaned.

"She left you for good?"

Sophie sobbed.

Lesbian love, Hiram thought. *Disgusting, really. Can that really be satisfying? Why couldn't a cute talented girl like Sophie find a good looking talented guy? Jesus. And this loser June woman with piss-poor income has to be the worst choice for a partner... and she's living off Sophie's allowance. Sophie's judgment of character isn't the best.*

"Have you been working?" he asked her.

Sophie didn't respond.

"Get dressed," he demanded.

At dinner, Hiram learned the ins and outs of June's defection. Sophie had lost all desire to succeed at anything. She would stare at a television, unable to find something that held her attention. She drank only coffee for breakfast and ate nothing. During the day, she snacked on dried banana and mango packaged snacks. She ate carryout for dinner. Days and nights were indistinguishable for her, she said. Each time she got out of bed, she was determined to work out, but rationalized excuses within minutes. She had no friends now. She took no photos, and she did not accept appointments or go to the studio where she had not worked for weeks. She'd lost weight. She couldn't look into a mirror.

He had never seen her so dejected; where was the vibrant Sophie he knew and loved?

After dinner Hiram insisted they walk.

"I'm tired," Sophie said.

"We'll walk," he said.

It was dusk and they went through the park where the shadows were darkening and the lights on Fifth Avenue were flickering through the trees as they strolled.

"You've got to get it together," Hiram said. *Is she suicidal?* he wondered.

"But I can't just cut off caring for her like that," Sophie said defensively. "You've never had to face that. You've never loved someone the way I love June. And you're a man."

It was a few seconds before he replied. "You're wrong, I think, about never having to face the loss. But I am a man." Hiram smiled.

Sophie didn't respond.

"Your mother. She was dead for me long before she left this world. And I missed her when she left me, missed what she'd been before she got sick."

"You ignored her all those years."

"She wasn't who I married when you knew her, Sophie. You don't have the right or the knowledge to judge me."

"She was your wife. The mother of Billie and me. And she struggled to bring us up without you, for Christ's sake. And she treated Ann as her own!"

"There was a lot you never saw," Hiram said.

"She died because you never cared."

"She died of cancer."

"She gave up. She didn't want to live."

"Damn it. I really did hurt when your mother imploded into herself, believe it or not. I just never could reach her."

"You never tried! Always caught up in your success. You disappeared from her life. And ours."

"What other choices would you have made if you were me?"

"You would have ignored us no matter what had happened between you and mother. It's you. Take some responsibility for mother's decline and the misery of your children."

Was that reasonable? Anger frustrated Hiram. "I am who I am," he finally said. "You're not the first to misunderstand me."

"You're not like most people."

"How can I be faulted for that? I'm not responsible for your misery, for Christ's sake. Why are you whining to me? Maybe I'm not what you think I should be. But you're responsible for your life. And June's dumping on you is not my fault. It's defeatist. And it's wrong. I do care, I'm just not good at expressing it."

"You're one cold son of a bitch," she said.

"Not all the time."

"And you're arrogant and stubborn!"

"Can you think of anything else?" Hiram smiled. Sophie remained stone faced.

They walked in silence. They walked up four steps near 52nd Street. Above the trees the illumination from The Plaza Hotel could be seen—old-fashioned, incandescent glows without the fluorescent harshness of modern displays.

"Time for an after dinner drink?" he asked.

He was hurt by Sophie's detachment from him when she said nothing. *She doesn't understand.*

She was crying. He clutched her arm and turned her to face him. He looked at her until she finally looked up into his eyes.

He took her in his arms and whispered into her ear. "I love you, Soph. Always have. Always will."

In the hotel, they sat in Louis the Sixteenth armchairs around a knee-high coffee table in the bar area.

"You've got to start a project," Hiram said.

"We have a project. Ivana and me. But she's having trouble getting funded. I haven't heard from her in two months."

Hiram absorbed the details. That evening he called his assistant and cancelled all meetings and clinics for three days.

Two days later, he picked up Sophie at her apartment. She looked better. She'd showered. Her leg hair was gone. She'd tried to cut her hair even, but it was still a little scraggly on the ends as if she'd used a razor without looking into a mirror. Sophie and Hiram, with Ivana, went to see Sophie's boss at the photo studio. Within an hour, Hiram had a plan laid out for Sophie and Ivana.

He returned to Denver.

With the backing of Hiram's initial investment, Ivana applied to National Geographic, Endowment for the Arts, and two humanitarian foundations to continue documentation of women in the Far East. Hiram negotiated with the studio to support them during startup with full salaries for half a year, and he would support the other half. In total, they would be generously funded for a time to bring the project to completion. A publisher had already purchased rights, based on their previous work. The first stay would be Turkey. They would live and travel in and around Istanbul with excursions to neighboring countries for three months, then return to assess and plan for the next of three more regions. An apartment had been rented, visas secured, flights booked, and equipment and necessities acquired.

Chapter 15

New York
Paige

Even after her demotion, Paige continued to have an almost universal reputation for due diligence, hard work, and investigative reporting—albeit aggressive and often shot-from-the-hip. And she dedicated herself to discovering the life and times of McDowell. She started her research for the special by attending a Mercy foundation fundraiser where the good doctor McDowell would be the glittering star of a show to pinpoint need, induce sympathy, and loosen bank accounts of people with enough money. The point was to make the attendants harbor a kind of guilt that pleaded to be relieved, and, they subconsciously hoped, a guilt that could be erased only by giving to the foundation... ostentatiously if possible. It was held at the convention center. On the marquee above the multi-door entrance was the foundation slogan, **"Health and Happiness."**

Men still look at me, Paige thought, as she mingled in the crowd while browsing silent auction items. The items were displayed on tables, platforms, pedestals, and hanging from the ceiling, in a room the size of an airplane hangar. And it wasn't just her fame they were staring at. *I still have plenty of glamour. Well, at least some glamour thanks to good facial bone structure and beautiful blue eyes that could never age.* She'd chosen a red silk knee-length cocktail dress with short sleeves and a V-neck. She smiled inwardly when she caught one of the surgeons staring at her. And she *was* an auction item too. Well, to be exact, the pitch was dinner at Le Petite Pois for two with "television star journalist" Paige Sterling. No one had bid on her yet, but it was early.

Other items were impressive too—an Italian vintage sports car that seemed so overpriced that it was unlikely to reach the minimum, a month all-expenses-paid at a chalet near Lucerne, memorabilia from Michael Jackson's father's estate, an Elvis Presley guitar with signed photo of him on stage, a piano used by Horowitz, jewelry valued in the six and seven figures, etchings and prints of Pollack, Magritte, Picasso, Dali, and the like. Those items too had minimums that Paige thought beyond the desires of reasonable human beings, but many of the celebrities in the crowd with unlimited wealth and unlimited need to be admired would succumb to a few extravagances, she was sure. In the giant hall a twelve piece jazz orchestra played. In the smaller auction room to the right of the hall, a string quartet played classical music that entertained guests as they browsed more modest highbrow items: tickets to sold-out shows, dinners for two to twenty guests at exclusive restaurants, museum memberships, season passes to the Mets and Yankees, and other luxuries.

There were eight bars scattered among the rooms, and drinks were also passed and served by an all-male staff of twenty. The main dining room to the left of the giant hall seated over eight hundred. Placed near the center of the room, a platform was readied for the master of ceremonies, an auctioneer for a live auction of hundreds of items, a moderator for the multi-floor to ceiling screen video presentations of the hospital in Nepal. The videos showed the hospital support staff, the healed poor, and the desperately ill seeking treatment who would die without generous support from the crowd tonight. And Hiram would address the crowd.

On every wall space large enough were floor to ceiling photographs with life size figures of Hiram and his staff and patients, and wide-angle panoramic shots of Nepal—the valleys and the mountains.

Hiram's new—mostly ghost-written—memoir extolling his climbing, his rise to the top of his profession, his generosity, his unbounded energy, and his dedication to excellence had a frontispiece of him in cold-weather dress with one arm around a wrinkled but smiling toothless Nepalese woman and his other arm cradling an infant barely visible and half buried in a peasant-woven blanket, the air around them painted with the mist of breath in bitter cold. On the title page of these limited first editions was Hiram's signature and grateful thanks for support in buying the book. A sign said all sales proceeds were for the sick and disabled. The book was paraded around to guests by a picture-perfect feminine specimen in her twenties in a mid-thigh skirt, white fishnet stockings, and gold spike-heels.

The publisher's sales representative, a gray haired motherly looking woman, took Paige's credit card information and looked up from her table. "Would you like to take it with you or shall I send it?"

"Could I leave it here? Pick it up after the party?"

"I can have it delivered to your table, Ms. Sterling, after the dinner presentation."

"Thank you. Please be sure I get it personally. I might forget to look for it."

"Of course. And would you like to meet the co-author?" The woman pointed to her left. "He's coming," she said and whispered, "He comes by every half hour to check on sales."

"I'd like to meet him," Paige said.

The bearded author was young and handsome with an attractive reticence about him. She complimented him on the book and said she looked forward to reading it. She added, "I'd love to have my associate Amara do an interview with you."

"I'd like that," he said.

"Give me your card and I'll set it up."

It would keep Amara busy and it wasn't something of great importance for the special. Probably wouldn't make the cut and would end up on local news.

Hiram was inaccessible the entire evening, always in the center of a crowd. Paige reluctantly admired his attention-getting gesticulations as he told stories of his exploits, his gaze ceaselessly including everyone in the crowd. For a surgeon, he was gifted at engaging a group. And she felt vague discomfort; although he was not physically alluring, she still found his dynamism attractive in a surprising way that she could not dismiss or ignore.

She talked to a senator from western Pennsylvania whose wife, he said proudly, painted scenes in watercolor of rural sheds and unused century-old barns; one of her signed paintings was in the auction. Then she asked the senator, who was a board member, about his trip to visit the Nepal clinic. He'd been impressed beyond his wildest expectations with the facilities, the staff, and especially with Hiram, he said.

"Do you know how much money they expect to raise tonight?" Paige asked, wondering how effective Hiram was in raising the big bucks.

"Over a million. I'd imagine at least half of that from one or two sugar daddy donors."

Paige hesitated to ask too much, but the senator seemed pleased to be speculating from his insider position.

"How much does a shindig like this cost?" she asked.

A cloud of suspicion swept across the senator's face. *He's connected me with my TV reputation. Tightened his scrotum a little too,* she thought with a touch of pride. "Don't have the faintest," he said, squinting slightly, faint wrinkles near his eyes revealing his lie.

Paige knew the standards, even if arbitrary, that served as thresholds for fundraising that the press relied on. Roughly, if a million dollars were raised, the expected return to programs would be $650,000. More than a few ever met these standards. Paige wondered how McDowell's foundation rated among others.

"But at this level, it's always expensive," the senator continued. "It costs money to make money. Deep pocket donors need to be pampered."

Was that really true? Partially, maybe, but as a mandate? Christ, the rental on the facilities must be close to fifty thousand. She guessed the bill for the whole evening to be at least three hundred thousand. That would not factor in the costs of full-time foundation employees—there seemed to be many—and operating expenses. So if the senator would argue that thirty-five percent of the money donated went for party costs, that would be more than reasonable. Sixty-five percent would go to charity. But it was hard to surmise those percentages in this presentation tonight. And the statistics could be adjusted in many ways. What if the gross was four hundred thousand, which Paige thought was probably a more reasonable estimate, if not an over estimate, for six hundred plus guests, even if they were all wealthy beyond comprehension. If the expenses for the evening plus year round expenses were factored in, they could have a seventy-five to twenty-five percent cost to benefit ratio... hardly acceptable. But it could be the opposite too. With huge financial success, say multimillions, even what to most would be excessive fundraising costs could actually be calculated to be more efficient than other penny-pinching organizations with small donor averages. She said her thanks to the senator and expressed her pleasure at being able to talk to him. He looked apprehensive. Had he revealed too much?

Paige wondered if she would have to investigate income, operating expenses, and actual dollars given to charity. Those figures would be hard to accumulate; still she'd need emphasis on the fundraising and the charity. It was another impressive McDowell achievement. She'd put Condoleezza on it.

A few minutes later, she saw—with the lights dimmed and multiple stadium-size screens lowered for simultaneous projection—a superbly filmed overview of the effort in Nepal. The poverty, the smiles of those benefited, the dedicated doctors and staff taking time from their lives to give their expertise to the health of the needy was projected on four screens in the auditorium-size room where dinner would be served. She thought the probable benefits of the fundraising justified almost any production costs. And this might be a shining example that Mc-Dowell's foundation was a super efficient operation that could raise in one night what twenty smaller organizations with fewer resources and eager-but-poor guests with good intentions could acquire in two years of fundraising.

The senator still stood next to her and looked apprehensive. She smiled inwardly.

"A marvelous presentation," Paige said. "A real honor to participate in such a worthwhile event." She meant it.

The senator thanked her with restraint but enthusiastically expressed his pleasure at meeting Paige. *If there's something about fundraising that's not obvious and he hides it, we'll have to check. But I'm impressed.*

Chapter 16

New York
Sophie

"I'm so sorry," Sophie said to Ivana. "I'll miss you."

"Keep in touch. Let me know when you can get away."

Ivana left for Turkey while Sophie dealt with Ann and Robert's family problems in Louisville.

Ann had two children now, Jeremy and Penny. Jeremy had been expelled from the third grade twice now. Penny was in preschool, extroverted but with no real friendships. Ann greeted each day with dread. She feared activities except for church. She turned shy around strangers. Most of the friends she made had drifted off without explanation.

Sophie tried to comfort her. Robert had been spending nights at sports events and movies with guys from work to avoid being at home. That brought Ann to even more acute anxiety.

Sophie took care of the children for two weeks, but Ann couldn't relax and refused to be thought of as neglecting her children by taking a little time off. Sophie's discussions with Robert were long and intense, but Robert, in an aloof but not unkind way, had difficulty in grasping the severity of Ann's condition and he had no rapport with his children. After two weeks, Sophie left. She'd done nothing to make Ann or any of the family's lives better.

Sophie arrived at LaGuardia after 10:00 PM and went straight to her apartment where Ivana's mother had left a day-old recorded phone message. No details. Ivana was dead.

Sophie called. Only Ivana's younger sister was available. "She was murdered," she said. "On the outskirts of Istanbul. We don't know much more. They're hunting down the killers. It's been on the news."

"I didn't know. I was with my sister."

"It's okay."

Sophie was sobbing now. "I couldn't go. If she could have delayed a few weeks, we could have gone together. I didn't want her to go by herself."

"She was eager to get her project started. That's what she said."

"It was our project," Sophie said.

"I know!" Ivana's sister said with impatience.

Sophie put down the phone to blow her nose. She put the phone on speaker. "I'll give you my cell number. Let me know when you know more."

She rang off and lay down on her sofa, her arm draped across her eyes. Her heart was empty. Her best friend, who was to be married after the project was completed to a musician who adored her, was gone.

As sorrow increased and imagined images of Ivana's murder decreased with time, Sophie wondered if she could finish the project on her own. In Ivana's name and memory? It was on Ivana's talent and energy that the project ever got funded after her father's initial gift. *Can I do it?*

That night she finally fell into a light sleep. She awoke with a start hours later. She had to keep active. She would complete the project. After all, the travel plans were made and the finances were budgeted. She didn't have Ivana's language skills, but she would manage.

She began to make arrangements, looking at the itinerary they had worked out with such detail and excitement. Her equipment could be collected and checked and ready in a few days. She would do it even though Ivana couldn't be there! And it was going to be good, the way Ivana would have done it.

But then anxiety gripped her. She had to convince the foundation's backers she could succeed alone. She had to work out strategies. She'd make appointments with those key backers so she could continue. And for the first time in years, she closed her eyes and prayed to God to let her be successful... to do what was right for Ivana.

Chapter 17

Hiram listened to Sophie's plans. It was ridiculous. Dangerous. And it would do nothing for her career, her life. "No," he said. There was no way he would let her go.

When required, Sophie could turn stubborn. No one could stop her! Not even her father. Hiram considered financial, and even physical restraint, but knew Sophie was clever enough to eventually circumvent any plan to prevent her going he put in place. Besides, for the first time in her life, she would be financially independent from him for more than a year. She'd have to sacrifice, budget, do without, but she had enough to refuse his help. She wanted to see herself as independent. He was okay with that, pleased in fact. It was good for her.

Two weeks later, Sophie called Hiram in tears. The foundation would not let her go on her own. They would not be responsible for another death of a single woman. She was desperately looking for someone to join her. But there were no photographers.

"Let it go, Sophie," Hiram said.

"I'm not going to do that. I don't need you for this if I can find someone," Sophie said. "And I will!"

We'll see what comes of that, Hiram mused.

Billie called three days later. "Hey, Dad. I'm going to Asia with Sophie."

"Absolutely not," Hiram said. "You'll finish college."

"I failed two courses."

"Retake them."

"They're going to expel me."

"Well, you're not going with Sophie. It's naïve to even consider it."

"You go to all parts of the world all the time."

"Not the same, Billie."

"We'll be safe if we're careful. And a woman traveling with a man has protection. Sophie looked up the State Department statistics. And she'll avoid any countries with political unrest that might threaten foreigners."

"Forget it, Billie."

Billie's silence told Hiram he too was determined. Determination to this degree was new for Billie, and as he had felt with Sophie's resolve, Hiram felt a little pride. At least Billie had a vision of something to accomplish.

Hiram called Sophie. He had made contacts, he told her, and he could make arrangements for her to have a home base at his foundation hospital in Nepal where she'd be safe. She could then make excursions into the areas she sought to document and return to Nepal between trips. It would prevent her from wandering place to place tied to an agenda that couldn't be easily changed if she faced unpredictable dangers.

"And Billie. Can he go?"

"I don't like it."

"He's a traveling companion I can trust."

Hiram considered Sophie's request a stroke of luck for Billie. Billie's life in Denver was falling apart anyway. Carole had a restraining order on him to keep him away from Tasha and his son Earl, and Billie had been arrested when he defied the order. Sporadically Billie played late night in bands. He was into marijuana. School held no interest for him. There was not one thing he seemed to want to accomplish. And after his tryst with Tasha, he rarely went out with girls. Hiram knew this trip was for the best—a Godsend for a son without direction—and a chance for Billie to help Sophie follow a dream that would help assuage her guilt.

On past habit, Hiram wouldn't give into Sophie without some resistance that he considered instructive, but since he had already decided to let Billie go, there was no reason to keep Sophie in agony. To Hiram's continued surprise, Billie now seemed motivated and increasingly excited to travel with Sophie.

Chapter 18

Late one night, well after midnight, Robert, Ann's husband, returned home from New York where he'd spent time with lawyers. He tiptoed in the darkness to their bed. Ann had not slept. She sat straight up.

"It's Jeremy," Ann said. "I'm terrified."

In the dark Ann felt for a tissue in a box on the bedside stand and wiped her eyes. She took Robert's hand under the cover when he slipped into bed. "I'm tired, Ann," he said.

"Was it bad?" she asked.

"I could be indicted." He turned his back to her and pretended to sleep.

She tried to sleep. She thought about the dead puppy in the swimming pool, under water legs splayed, belly down, eyes open. She moaned at the memory of the burial behind the garage with two Popsicle sticks for a cross among the turtle, the gerbil, the parrot, and Harry the cat. She cried softly.

Robert turned. "What now?"

"Jeremy killed the puppy. Penny found it. She saw him."

"Step back from it, baby. It's not that serious. Do you really know what happened?"

She didn't for sure. Penny said Jeremy held it by the neck under the water. She'd thought that was true. But now she was unsure.

"I don't," she said.

"Penny's lied a lot these days," Robert said. "Just let it go. He's probably innocent. It must have been an accident."

"But he's capable. He's mean, Robert. He shoots birds with his BB gun. They never die right away. He brings them into the yard to watch them. Sometimes it takes hours."

"Did you ask him about the puppy? One on one?" Robert asked.

"I did. Of course. He got angry. Then sullen. He never admitted to it. And he doesn't deny."

"I don't think he's violent," Robert said.

"He's hit me with a T-Ball bat. Threatened me with a poker from the fireplace. He cut me today. With his pen knife."

"Go to sleep. I'll talk to him this weekend," Robert said. "I'm taking him hunting."

"I wish I'd never had children," she said.

Why couldn't Robert just comfort me? A hug, no matter how brief. She felt so alone, so vulnerable, so permeated with fear that never abated. But Robert turned on his side away from her again. "See a psychiatrist," he said.

"He won't go to a psychiatrist."

"Not him. You" Robert said.

She sobbed. "I'm not crazy."

A void swept into Ann followed by desperation.

"Relax," Robert said. He always seemed irritated with her failure as a mother. He blamed at least some of Jeremy's problems on her weaknesses, her never taking a firm stand, her reluctance to demand better behavior. He'd never said it out loud, but that's what he thought, she was sure. And he felt smarter than she, and intolerant of her lack of success in anything.

———◆———

The psychiatrist said little to Ann in the first session. He sat so she couldn't see his face, but at times his responses seemed tangentially distracted, unrelated to her as if he were paging through a girly magazine, or maybe a gourmet magazine like the one she'd seen on the coffee table in the waiting room. He definitely thought she was at fault for her depression, that it was something in her.

"I can't manage the children," she said, "especially Jeremy."

"What do you think is the cause of his rebellion?"

"He's just violent. I don't know why."

"I see. Tell me about it."

"Our neighbor, Mrs. Sandhurst, her schnauzer died."

"You suspected Jeremy?"

"I saw it dead. Its skin charred off. The whole neighborhood saw. Its lips were gone, its teeth exposed in some eternal snarl. I can't get it out of my mind. I get nauseated thinking about it."

"And Jeremy did it?"

"Yes. I think so."

"But you have no proof."

"Jeremy hated that dog," she said.

"Did you accuse him?"

"He said I was always accusing him."

"What did your husband do?"

"He didn't like the dog either," Ann said. "He said, 'that woman should have kept the damn thing locked up. It bit someone, didn't it?' he said. 'It was always yelping.'"

"Did he think Jeremy did it?"

"He thinks Jeremy can do no wrong most of the time. He said, 'You can't believe Jeremy is involved. He never goes to the park by Mrs. Sanhurst's house.'"

"How do you feel about your husband?"

"Oh, I love him very much," Ann said quickly with no hesitation. "He tries to be a good husband and father."

"What about Jeremy?"

"I love him. Of course I love him."

"Isn't he hard to love? I mean, he sounds difficult to be around."

"He's very smart. Sometimes he can be a joy to be around."

"And the other times?"

"He's sullen. Withdrawn. Quick to anger." She paused. "Mean, too."

"How is he at school?"

"He acts out sometimes in his classes. He gets sent home often. But he gets really good grades. Effortlessly."

After the session, the psychiatrist placed Ann on medications—tranquilizers to dull the anxiety and antidepressants to return her energy and reduce her fears. She would refill the prescriptions well before the prescribed date, calling the doctor to call the pharmacist. She was miserable, but needed the drugs for mind and soul alterations.

———◆———

In the next session a week later, Ann blurted to the psychiatrist as soon as she arrived, "I want to get out. Leave them. I don't do either of them any good." She'd have to look over her shoulder from the couch to see him sitting out of her view with his legs crossed at the ankles and stretched out. He didn't speak as he waited for her to continue.

"Of course I can't leave them. Sometimes I want to kill myself." She didn't like this session. He seemed disinterested, supercilious.

She sat up and looked at him. The psychiatrist's naturally heavy-looking eyelids widened slightly. "Why do you say that?" he asked finally.

Ann stared with disbelief. It wasn't hard to figure out! She settled back into a more comfortable position.

"There is more to this than the children," the psychiatrist said.

Ann saw no reason to respond. She'd told him about Robert. How distant he'd become. Rarely spending time at home. Blaming her for all the problems with Jeremy. "You've always preferred Penny over Jeremy," Robert had said more than once. "It pits one against the other." Well, now she knew Robert wasn't brimming with love for either Jeremy or Penny... for anyone really... and she now doubted that he even liked himself with all his troubles.

The psychiatrist waited. Despite herself, she felt a tension rise inside her. The psychiatrist was manipulating her. The silence became uncomfortable.

"I'm afraid," she said, "or I would kill myself." She said it to shock him. She'd thought about it, but she would never do it. It was against God. She sensed no reaction in him, even without looking at him.

"We all carry secrets that affect our lives," he said. "What are you carrying? What is it that you can't share with anyone?"

She was irked by the childlike superficiality of his demeanor. He made her angry again.

"Something you need to get out," he said.

That was prying. She didn't like his pompous emersion today. But he was perceptive. She'd give him that. She did have something—true or not—she had kept hidden. And it did make her treat Jeremy differently. Jeremy didn't seem like any person she'd known. And he didn't have any traits she could relate to her or Robert's families. Jeremy's disregard for other human beings for example. His rage at the smallest provocations.

Well, she'd had sex in a moment of weakness. Within months after her marriage, she was vulnerable and insecure and Robert seemed to look through her most of the time. He showed no passion or satisfaction from their lovemaking. She'd flirted with a barely competent plumber called to fix a poorly functioning water heater. He was quick to arousal and had taken her standing up against the front-loading washer in the basement. He'd said nothing after and left after she'd written a check to cover his invoice. The timing was right. And she would always wonder, but she'd never take action to prove or disprove Jeremy's real father, afraid what the knowledge would do to her either way. She would never tell anyone. It would serve no purpose.

"How are you feeling now? Right at this very moment?" the psychiatrist asked. "I sense hostility. Irritation. Is it toward me? Or something else?"

Her distaste for this insensitive treatment erupted. This mundane, crass, useless questioning by a human being, whom she thought probably wasn't handling life any better than she.

"I hate this," she said.

"You still have half an hour."

She stood and took her coat from a coat tree near the door.

The psychiatrist didn't stand. "I really think you should talk it out," he said. "Not hold back."

"And maybe I think it won't make one damn bit of difference one way or another," she said. But she felt inadequate now, unable to think without indicating out of control feelings that exhausted her. She walked out.

"You finished so soon?" Robert asked when she entered the waiting room. He stood and went into the doctor's office. He was back in minutes.

"He refused to talk to me!" Robert said. "Said you were beyond his help."

Secretly she was glad. She didn't want collusion of two males against her.

Chapter 19

Hiram traveled with Sophie and Billie to Kathmandu and set them up with their own furnished apartments on the top floor of a three-story complex near the hospital. The apartments were leased by the foundation for visiting doctors and dignitaries in a safe upscale area—those VIPs who were felt to be potentially too important for fundraising efforts stayed in the rooms available on the hospital grounds.

Rima, a nurse coordinator and Hiram's companion in Nepal, met Sophie, Billie, and Hiram at the airport. Rima nestled into Hiram's outstretched arms with affection intensified by their long absences apart. It was clear Hiram stayed with Rima while he was in Kathmandu. Sophie glanced a questioning look at Billie. Had he known about this?

Sophie took a few days to settle into her apartment after Hiram left and then, with Rima's help, planned her first photographic excursion with the hospital staff on one of their periodic trips to villages in the countryside. On an ideal day, the sun made its ascent behind the snow-covered mountains and the morning light in the valley seemed weighted with dusk from the previous night. Within minutes, the sun drew burning lava-glowing halos into the sky that laid spectral earthly shadows vibrant with night blue-black.

Sophie had been ready for more than an hour when Rima came with a driver and two vans, the second with staff and equipment from the hospital. They left Kathmandu on the road to Tatopani. Rima explained she and the staff would vaccinate and distribute antibiotics for pneumonias and iron supplements for anemia throughout the rural areas. Sophie expected to photograph in the villages while the work was going on. This was her first excursion, practice for extending her travels with Billie, but without Rima, who must meet her care-giving responsibilities. Sophie gasped. The van barely missed a heavy-duty Chinese truck the color of granite and the shape of half a train boxcar coming head on; horns blew and neither vehicle braked. Instead both swerved in contrasting unity, avoiding collisions with seemingly impossible maneuvers. Rima looked to Sophie and Sophie managed a weak smile. If Billie was affected by a road with little pavement, no markings, unyielding traffic, and covered with nonchalant humans, chickens, goats, and debris, Sophie could not tell. She thought of Ivana in Turkey before she was killed, wondered what her feelings were at that moment, and when she first arrived. Ivana would not be one to be afraid, and Sophie felt shame for her petty fears.

Sophie took her camera from her bag, checked the settings, and began taking pictures of the traffic, which was hard to frame through the windshield. But each shot was filled with random humans and animals skirting among trash and rubble and the ever-threatening vehicles—even in the rural areas, where all of civilization seemed to exist writhing on snake-width curves of the never-straight road.

No one spoke over the clanks and groans of the van; rocks pelted the undercarriage; the engine backfired; and it was almost impossible to understand even a shout. When they stopped, the driver spoke no more than twelve words of English, four of which seemed to mean "don't." Rima had an accent and often-fractured syntax, but was understandable and, with her soft vowels and crisp consonants, she was a pleasure to listen to.

Two hours later the van arrived at a village. Sophie thought of it as a refugee camp with makeshift housing... no electricity, and water gathered from a nearby stream draining from the mountains. But remnants of generations cluttered the landscape. Rima met the others from the other van and they set about their examinations and treatments in a lean-to, open in front and on the sides. Monsoon season had started, and a gentle misty rain enveloped the city—not unpleasant or aggravating. Rima and her team were expected and more than fifty people, mainly women with children and the elderly, stood, squatted, sat, or lay waiting their turns patiently. Although Sophie could see no semblance of a line, or even a system for identifying who might be next.

Sophie snapped pictures. Billie carried her gear—two other cameras and an assortment of lenses and batteries in a backpack. Rima came to them both.

"Come," she said. "There is a girl I want you to meet. She is special in mind and I think have great, ah... I think you say 'promise.' But she is away and I must take you to her."

Sophie and Billie followed Rima maybe two hundred yards through the village. At one point there was a two-foot metal statue surrounded by concrete block, the statue and concrete splashed with dried and still wet blood. Sophie pointed with a questioning look.

"It is of Kali," Rima said. "Shiva's companion who slays evil." Rima did not slow down and Sophie ran to catch up to her. "Sacrifices?" Sophie asked. Rima nodded but said no more.

In another hundred yards, they came to a shed with a low door and no windows. The floor was dirt. Four goats lay near the back wall. At the side a girl sat with her back against the wall, her knees up with her arms resting on them, her skirts covering her legs. She had a plastic bottle with water by her side. Sophie took pictures.

Rima talked to the girl in quick spurts. The girl stared with brown eyes dark as a hillside cave, and a faint smile on her thin lips. She shook her head twice and her night-black hair, covered in a red bandanna, fell over her left shoulder. Her hand gathered the strands and stroked them absently.

"This is Shristi," Rima said. The girl looked from Sophie to Billie and smiled. "She is very smart, and I want her come work for you while you in Kathmandu."

"Work for us?"

"She clean, cook, buy food, run errands. She learn English word, help you translate."

"We don't need help," Sophie said, acutely aware of Billie gazing whenever he could at the stunning beauty of the girl.

"No. It is right."

"We would pay, of course," Sophie said.

"No. Foundation pay. And Shristi deserves the... "

"Opportunity?"

"... chance to do better."

Rima looked long into Sophie's eyes, and Sophie knew Rima's caring and hope to give Shristi a better life. "It is right," Rima said.

Sophie nodded, and Rima spoke to Shristi who stood up. Sophie took pictures.

"She is ready," Rima said.

"She lives here? In the goat shed?" Billie asked.

"Oh, no," Rima said. "Not live. It is chaupadi."

"I thought that was illegal," Sophie said.

"Many village practice old ways."

The four of them went back to the lean-to clinic. "Shristi will wait here until we go back," Rima said. "You make photograph."

Sophie started her photography.

"What is chaupadi?" Billie asked Sophie.

"In some places, women are banned from the home during their periods. They are not allowed to touch kitchen utensils, share the same water source, go to school, or sleep inside the home during their periods. They sleep where they can, sometimes even in the open."

Billie closed his eyes briefly to emphasize his wonder at the customs in this country. "She is beautiful," he said.

"I got some really good shots, even as we went in," Sophie said.

"A goat shed," Billie said under his breath.

Chapter 20

Sophie received a letter from her editor.

Dear Sophie—
We've enjoyed what you've sent us. Great potential. And the girl with
the goats! Incredibly moving.

I know you're documenting the plight of women, which is devastating
from what you've done so far. But there is so much done that I feel—
as do all of us at Veridian House—there is a need to put the work in
context, not only with the environment, but also by contrasting genders
and age groups. You've done a few children with the women, that's
good, but more and maybe some contrast with the men too. And we
think most of your work is Hindi. What about the Buddhist and Muslim
cultures that envelope Nepal? Is there something to be learned there
without losing your emphasis on the state of women in general, and
even enhancing the effect on the viewer?

Please keep us abreast of your progress. Will you be able to make the
six-month deadline?

Regards to your father.

Sincerely,
Emile Prendergast
Editor-in-Chief

Sophie responded by email.

> Dear Mr. Prendergast—
>
> Thank you for your letter. Nice to hear from you. I was, however,
> concerned with the tone. Do you feel I'm not meeting your expecta-
> tions? Are your suggestions an either-or for publication? And as far
> as expansion of subject matter, I thought you set a strict limit on the
> number of photographs you'd take. Do your suggestions mean I have
> no limits? I already have thousands of great images that I think would fit
> well into the scope of a larger book.
>
> With best regards,
>
> Sophie

◆

Sophie walked from her apartment to Billie's place at the other end
of the building. As always, the door was unlocked and she entered
without knocking.

Sophie stared at the cloister-tidy apartment. For the first time
ever, the bed, visible through a doorless portal in the bedroom, had
the edges of the covers cornered with hospital precision… and not a
wrinkle. The open door to the bathroom showed towels folded and
hung on the racks, a pristine white bath mat next to the tub, and a
slip cover over the toilet seat with an embroidered bird in flight. The
kitchenette had cleared counters, and the two chairs were lined up
perfectly with the small wooden table. To one side of the living room,
Billie worked near a table in a straight-backed chair, carving a block
of light-grained laminated wood maybe a foot and a half square at the
base and two feet high. The shape of a human head was emerging.

Billie worked on his lap, sanding the wood block. He acciden-
tally knocked a drumstick, one of many, from the table in front of
him. He picked it up. He had carved and finished the drum sticks
from traditional and exotic woods, and now shipped finished products
back to the states where now a number of stores took special orders

and displayed his three most popular standard sizes and weights. He'd started carving scenes too, when Sophie didn't need him he worked on variations of Hindu masks, reliefs of distant mountains stained and painted with majestic snowcaps and caressing cloud layers.

Shristi had made the difference in Billie's domestic efficiency, arriving daily, seven days a week. No one knew how Shristi came to work and exactly how she got from the house of a distant cousin she stayed with in the outskirts of Kathmandu. Then Rima found an abandoned, but functional motor scooter for Shristi and advanced her money for fuel. Shristi's English improved from the intensity she applied to learning. She was always seeking the right word, seeking the best pronunciation. And when she worked, Sophie had begun to talk to Shristi about the photography and about America. And Sophie asked Shristi about her dreams, which were sadly limited because of the void of opportunities in the village, and in Nepal altogether.

"Bro," she said. "Got word from the editor to expand. Need time in Tibet. Maybe even China. I'll set up for a month or two."

Billie said nothing.

"You all right with that?" she said.

Billie shrugged, "Sure."

Oh, my. He doesn't want to be away because of Shristi.

As Sophie was about to leave, Shristi came in with produce from the market in her arms. She went straight to the kitchenette as she greeted Sophie and Billie and returned carrying a chair back from the kitchen to sit near the table slightly to the front left of Billie. Billie turned his attention to creating Shristi's image. Silently Sophie watched with admiration at the precision with which he handled his tools. He repeatedly looked to Shristi's face for guidance in shaping her emerging image in the wood block. It was his first attempt at sculpture of a human head.

———◆———

Shristi visited daily to clean Sophie's apartment. Always at the same time, she came and left. Sophie began to look forward to her soft steps in the hall, her shy entrance, her greeting that sounded like the gentle breeze through the leaves of a tree.

As she worked, Shristi frequently looked to Sophie. "How you say?" she asked, pointing to an object.

"Bowl," Sophie said.

Shristi tried to imitate but the response was unrecognizable, yet sounded more pleasant, and always more beautiful with Shristi's lyrical voice, Sophie thought. Shristi laughed with embarrassment and Sophie smiled encouragement and spoke again. "Bowl." And after many tries, Shristi quickly improved, faster than anyone could expect. And Sophie often touched her gently and said, "Very good, Shristi. Very good." And Shristi smiled self-consciously. With Sophie's encouragement, Shristi added ten to fifteen new words a day... nouns at first, then simple verb forms. And then modifiers. And Sophie read in English to Shristi, keeping her longer than she should, she knew, because Shristi had other work but Sophie enjoyed being with Shristi so much she could not stop keeping her as long as she could.

Chapter 21

Sophie

In response to her editor's demands, Sophie and Billie travel to photograph a funeral.

Above the stone steps that form the bank of the river, level ground is paved in stone and a dead man's younger sons add wood to the funeral pyre upon it. A few feet away, the wife, dressed in red, leaning back on her knees, her arms outstretched, wails with the sharp tones of a scream. Sophie stands on the opposite riverbank taking pictures. Billie is steadying the tripod and shooing two monkeys that deliberately annoy them from a perch on one of two stone pillars. A few yards away, an emaciated man in only a loincloth with a gray beard sits with legs crossed meditating. His body is off-white with some sort of dried covering with sequins caught in it. He puffs weed occasionally.

"I don't like that guy," Billie says.

"Sadhu. A holy man."

"I know. But he looks like a zombie."

"Ash or chalk, I think. Maybe paint."

"I wish he wouldn't look at us."

"Hold the tripod!"

Billie stabilizes the tripod and Sophie focused her lenses across the river where the sons of the dead man—who is now wrapped in orange cloth covered with flowers, his head and bare feet exposed—slide the corpse on a bamboo stretcher feet first until the body is half submerged in the river. Three times they complete the ritual emersions.

The first son bathes fully submerged. Then the body is carried again to the flat ground above the river steps and placed on a funeral pyre under which wood logs crisscross in a pyramidal stack. The first son ignites the pyre, and when the flesh is charred, the crowd of relatives and family that have gathered slowly disperse. Flames turn muscle and bone to ash.

Sophie changes lenses often and, after many wide-angle views, trains in on faces of the men. Only a few women are in the crowd above. She sees an older woman, presumably the mother, grieving. The woman wails but the sound dissipates as it floats across the river.

"How much longer?" Billie asks.

"You don't like it?"

"Creepy."

"We stay until the deceased's ashes are swept into the river."

"We've got to get back before dark."

"Find the driver. Ask him how long we've got."

With Billie gone for a few minutes, Sophie takes another camera from Billie's backpack and frames shots of the Sadhu from various angles. She drops a generous number of coins into his outstretched hand when she is finished. He smiles a tooth-gapped grin.

Billie returns, collapses the tripod, caps lenses, and begins packing.

Sophie slaps him from behind on the side of his head. "What the shit are you doing?"

"We're not going back in the dark. And we're not sleeping out here," Billie says.

"I'm not here to miss opportunities."

Billie grabs her arm and draws her close to him, face to face. He is taller and for the first time she can ever remember she shrinks under the shadow of his imposing stature.

"We're not here to die, Sophie. You're my sister and we're not taking risks."

She steps back, her breath caught at his assertiveness. *Where is docile Billie?* She'd brought him to be a compliant companion. This is almost domineering. "Cool it," she says without her usual authority.

But he steps forward to within inches of her to intimidate. "Get your stuff," he says. "I'll meet you at the van."

A few minutes later, without a word, Sophie gets into the van and they start back to Kathmandu late in the day, and already lengthening shadows partially obscure wrecks, overturned trucks, barely visible potholes deep enough to swallow a goat, wandering sacred cows, pedestrians, and hairpin curves with no barriers to prevent unguarded drops from cliff edges thousands of feet high. Sophie silently seethes. She's been denied shots of a lifetime. "We could have made it," she says.

"The driver won't drive after dark," Billie whispers to Sophie. "His brother got killed in a nighttime bus accident."

"We could drive ourselves."

"Grow up," Billie says.

———◆———

On Tuesday morning, Sophie went to Billie's apartment to show him the edits from the funeral shots the previous day. She thought they were spectacular. Billie was at his carving table, working on two mountains in bas-relief. The apartment was cluttered with discarded clothing and his bed was unmade. On the floor, surrounded in wood chips, was the now obvious head carving of Shristi.

"It's a mess," Sophie said, sweeping her hand to indicate the apartment.

"You're not my mother."

Why had he become so hostile? "Who would want to be your mother?"

"I don't want *you* to be my mother. Just know that you're not."

"Hey. I came to show you the photos."

"Busy," he said.

Sophie took a few deep breaths. *What is going on?* "What's wrong?" she finally said. "Was it the funeral? The drive?" True, his tone had offended her, mostly, and his arrogant defiance of her supremacy as an older sister. She couldn't help but resent that.

"It's not that."

"You were right, Billie. It was a risk. I was wrong." *An apology!*

Billie kept working. Sophie felt the despair in his silence. His emotions emanated from the heart and she was shocked by their depth and intensity. It was more than the altercation at the funeral. And it was more than Billie's unexpected disrespect for her, more than his refusal to accept her apology.

His jaw clenched.

"Screw it," she said, turning to leave.

"Shristi's not been here," he said faintly. "Is she still doing your place?"

So it was Shristi. Sophie thought for a second. "Yes," she said. Her place was spotless yesterday and for every day since Shristi started. "How long has it been?" she asked.

"Five days."

"Maybe she's sick," Sophie said.

"But working for you?"

His logic was right. "You'll have to go it on your own," she said, seeing it was not what he had wanted to hear.

"Is it the money?" he asked. "I thought the foundation paid her."

"I don't think it could be money. That's not Shristi. And Rima would have told me."

"I'll pay her. How do I find her?"

"Rima will know. I'll ask her."

"Go see her today," Billie said.

"I'm working the market today."

"Jesus, Sophie. You could talk to Rima and work the market. It's not that big a deal."

Billie got up and went into the bathroom, drawing the barely-opaque hanging curtain over the doorless opening behind him.

Sophie left, her irritation mixed with disbelief at the change in her brother in the last few days. Was it only Shristi? Or was it being away from home? Or living in a bizarre land with few friends and little to do?

Rima was busy with patients and Sophie waited for over an hour. Rima took Sophie to the corner of the clinic where supplies were stored so they could hear.

"It is very good to see you, Sophie. It's been too long. Is your father well?" Rima said.

"You don't hear from him?"

"Only just before he arrive here."

"And you're all right with that? He's been gone a month."

"Yes," Rima said.

Sophie had always been curious. "Do you miss him when he's gone?"

"Of course."

"You're not married?" Sophie asked.

"I never marry. I go to school."

Sophie studied Rima briefly. A giving woman with a beautiful soul from another culture who still made a difference in a sexist culture where men, and most women too, considered women to be barely more than domestic animals. She wanted to ask Rima if she loved Hiram. But she could not. And Rima would not know what love meant to Americans... other than what might be seen in movies and on what television was available, and that was hardly representative of selfless love between two humans in a way Nepalese women would never experience or understand.

"Shristi stopped going to my brother's to work."

"It take time, but I find someone to help out."

"Is it money? He is willing to pay."

"It is not money. The foundation is generous. You're father is much respected."

"Why not Shristi? She really suits us both."

"It is not right now. I want best for Shristi. She smart and school best to give her life she deserve."

"What's that got to do with Billie?"

"He looks at her with gaze like moonlight."

"She is beautiful to look at."

"No. It is much more. She sits so he can carve the wood."

"She helps him?"

"No. He make *her* in wood. She is like, how do you say, the same thing?"

"His model."

"Yes. His model. And he looks at her sometimes with desire like waterfall, and she is afraid."

"He would never hurt her."

"Oh, no? She is afraid like she want to like him too."

"She loves Billie?"

"She simple girl with much chance... more than most. Her family no like her with white man's child. To be mother would keep her from school. It not easy to be mother."

"Billie wouldn't do that to her."

"He think like that. I see it."

"Rima. He would not do that!"

Rima looked away. "Not what your father say. Your brother make baby with girl. He tell me girl at fault. Billie leave her."

"Never!"

"It is what I know."

Rima's unshakeable honesty and Billie's opportunities with Shristi convinced Sophie Rima's worries were justified.

"Did he pay her for modeling?" Sophie asked.

"Yes. He give her money every time. At first I think that good for her."

Sophie sighed. "Thanks, Rima," she said and gave Rima a hug that Rima did not return.

——◆——

Sophie entered Billie's place without knocking. He was half asleep on the bed, dressed but without socks and shoes. Sophie stopped in the opening to the room. "I spoke to Rima. They know about Tasha?"

"They couldn't." Billie sat up on the edge of the bed blinking his eyes.

"Our father told Rima."

Billie stared without comprehension.

"You can't deny it," Sophie said.

He still didn't seem to know what Sophie was talking about.

"I talked to Rima. She's afraid you're trying to woo Shristi."

"None of your business, Sophie."

"Are you?"

"Of course not."

"Did you try?"

Billie said nothing.

"Rima knows how you feel. Shristi thought you desired her. That you paid her to model for a purpose. And you looked at her funny like men do."

"Aw, for Christ's sake."

"Did you ask Shristi to stay at night?"

Billie remained silent.

Guilty! "What about Tasha?"

"Dad wouldn't tell about Tasha."

"He told Rima. I think he tells her whatever is on his mind. He can trust her. Probably one of the few in this world he can trust."

"I wish he hadn't."

"Do you like that he lives with her when he's here?" Sophie asked.

"I don't know. I guess it's all right."

"Even when mom was alive?"

"Since we were kids, probably."

"I wonder if he has children by her?" Sophie mused.

"I don't know. I don't think so," Billie said. "How do you feel about Rima?"

"He's had so many women. Maybe this is the one he really cares for."

"And you think that's okay?"

"He'd never admit it, but he needs love, Billie," Sophie said. "Real love."

"It's nothing about love. He needs sex," Billie said.

"Because that's how you feel about Shristi? Isn't it? You can't stay away?" Billie's eyes revealed his repressed desire for Shristi.

"Rima would put no demands on him," Billie said, with more insight than Sophie thought him capable of. "She would accept him for who he is."

"And what about Tasha? What did she do for you?"

"I can't see her. Carole will never let me."

"Tasha didn't marry, did she?"

Billie hesitated. "I don't know for sure. I don't think so."

"My God. She's the mother of your child. You don't know?"

He shrugged. "She won't answer my emails," he admitted. "I think she still lives with her mother. She came to me, you know. But she wasn't a whore. I liked her."

Sophie shook her head. "Oh, sure. Typical male. She comes to you. Forces your limp dick into her virgin vagina while you're eating

SpaghettiOs and Reese's Peanut Butter Cups in bed watching sports on TV. Gets pregnant. And you never speak up?"

"Dad talked to Carole. He refused to let me see Tasha again after that. Carole wanted us to get married before the baby came."

"That's reasonable in my moral world," Sophie said.

"Dad wouldn't listen to her. He said it wasn't mine but Carole said she could get DNA proof. Dad then said I'd been trapped. That was when he sent me to Cal State for a semester. He gave Carole money for child support in a lump sum and gave her the house."

"When did all this happen?"

"The years before you went to New York. Before Dad divorced. You were the one who refused to even see Carole after you left for Chicago."

"And it's yours, isn't it?" Sophie asked. Billie looked down and away and his silence told her he was the father. "You can't feel good about this, Billie," she said after a few seconds. "Your little secret."

Billie stayed quiet and looked away.

"Does Ann know?" Sophie asked. Ann, deep in religion, always odd about her tolerance of sexual improprieties, wouldn't approve. She would see it as mortal sin.

"I don't think so," Billie said.

Sophie was through talking about Tasha... or Shristi. "We leave soon for Tibet. Be sure you're ready."

"I'm ready."

"God, I hope you don't have designs on Shristi. I couldn't take that."

Billie swore. "Are you jealous?" he asked. "You look at her funny."

"Not jealous. Concerned about your behavior."

"You like her," Billie said as a matter of fact.

"Very much."

"Not that. You know what I mean."

"I don't."

"It's not like Tasha and me, is it? That kind of love between girls?"

"Shristi's a child. Don't be thinking she's a woman," Sophie said.

Sophie looked for the carving of Shristi. But it was cut down into smaller, various-size pieces to be reworked for other images. "What happened to your masterpiece?" she said, immediately sorry for her sarcasm.

Billie didn't answer but she could see sorrow in his eyes. *He really loves her.* "I didn't mean anything," she said. He slumped as if defeated. She left quickly, upset she'd been so mean.

Chapter 22

Nepal
Paige

Paige turned out the light clamped to the headboard on the single bed with a thin mattress. The cold seeped through the poorly constructed window and she adjusted the flimsy hotel blanket but couldn't stay warm. Silver moonlight streamed in with a crisp, cold glow. Over the pajamas she already had on, Paige added a sweater and sweat pants from her bags. She was exhausted from the hours of travel to Nepal but after lying in the semi darkness for hours listening to breezes that bristled outside and the movements of hotel guests in neighboring rooms, sleep would still not come.

In the morning, she went to see the hospital. Condoleezza and Victor had arrived two days before. Condoleezza was waiting at the front entrance.

"Victor's filming background material in the morning light," Condoleezza said without greeting.

"What have you found?" Paige asked.

"McDowell will meet with you now."

"Anything I should know?"

"I get a sense he's only a small cog in the operating mechanism. There is an administrative staff of over twenty and a very competent CEO."

"You expected…"

"McDowell in fatigues operating with light from a campfire on a plank supported by two saw horses, and near-death patients waiting patiently in a line that stretched for a quarter of a mile."

Paige smiled. "We need to find the patients. Talk to them."

"I'll do it," Condoleezza said.

Paige was greeted by Hiram who rose from the modest armless wooden chair behind the small kneehole desk in his cramped office.

"Paige Sterling!" he said, extending his hand.

"Dr. McDowell."

"Hiram, please."

They sat down separated by a silence, both searching for opening words.

"I'd like to thank you..." Paige began. This was the first time she'd seen McDowell up close in person.

"You're fatigued after the trip?" McDowell interrupted.

"Wiped out," Paige said.

"Where are you staying?"

"Crowne Plaza."

"My God. We can't have that."

"Really. It's not that bad."

"I wish I'd known," Hiram said. "Excuse me for a moment." He left and was back in three minutes. "We'll move you into the foundation condominium rooms we lease."

"My staff..." Paige began. She briefly thought about conflict of interest.

"We've already arranged for rooms for them in the south wing of the hospital. They can also eat in the cafeteria. Not great food but dependable."

"Maybe I should call the hotel..."

"I've taken care of everything. All your things will be in your room within the hour. I've put you on the same floor as my daughter Sophie and near to my son Billie's place, so if you need anything, feel free to knock on their doors at anytime of the day or night."

"Thank you. Of course we'll reimburse..."

"Never. You're our guests."

He was more charming than she would have imagined, even if she'd ever thought about it. As they'd done their research, she'd begun to think of him as almost robotic... ceaselessly moving without fatigue... and inaccessible. But she seemed to be wrong.

She asked about the hospital and the foundation, told him what they'd like to document over the next few days and asked permission to talk to personnel and film the surroundings.

He agreed to everything. "I've arranged a trip to one of the villages for you and your staff day after tomorrow," he said. "It's a weekly trip for my staff. You can see the work of the Mercy Foundation in action."

"Is that Rima?" How curious she was about the relationship between Rima and McDowell. But she didn't want to offend him so early in her visit. The trip was exactly what Paige hoped to see and she expressed her thanks.

"Will you be working with your staff?" she asked.

"I can't. I'll be climbing in a few days. But I wondered if you'd like to trek with the expedition to the glacier. We'll be moving on to reach the mountain. But I can take an extra guide and porters for you to come back the next day. Gorgeous scenery."

"Will we see the mountain?"

"Not the one I'll climb. It will take thirteen to fourteen days to reach the base and acclimatize. It's in Tibet."

"I didn't bring hiking gear."

"Dress warmly. We'll have jackets, boots, and equipment for you. Take any of your friends you would like. They'll provide company for you on the way back."

She liked being involved, but wondered about her conditioning. She'd hiked occasionally in national parks and on country roads. How would she fare trekking in Nepal all day for two days?

"Do I have to be in shape?" she asked.

"We'll drive to meet the expedition, and the Range Rover will pick you up when you come back to our starting point. You'll like it," he said.

McDowell showed her the operating rooms, the clinics, the wards. He introduced her to key personnel and spent some time praising Rima. She organized much of his schedule when he was in Nepal, he said. Then he handed Paige over to key administrative personnel who showed her the cafeteria, explained the hours, and encouraged her, Condoleezza, and Victor to use the foundation facilities whenever they needed. Then they toured the compound and the staff facilities.

At day's end the receptionist at the hospital walked with Paige the few hundred yards to her new rooms. Paige looked carefully, but she saw nothing threatening on the walk and felt comfortable that there would be no danger alone, even at night. She was slightly ashamed of her caution reflex bred by so many years living in Manhattan.

The sitting room was comfortable with a sofa, a table and chairs. Her bedroom held only a single bed, with little room for other furniture. A small doorless closet next to the bathroom had all her clothes neatly hung. Her bags were on racks, her toiletries arranged on a shelf under a bathroom mirror. When she checked, nothing was missing.

The two-hour trip to the village in vans with scantly upholstered seats left her sore where metal supports rubbed her back and legs. On the trip, she sat in the back with Sophie. Near the city, it was difficult to talk, but as they reached the country roads, the shouts and curses, blowing horns, and bleating animals receded to a constant thrum. The van shifted constantly but in higher gears that made less noise. Paige leaned to Sophie. "You like it here?" she asked.

"I do... yes," Sophie said. Sophie was a pretty girl with delicate features and very dark brown eyes that fixated for extended times on things, as if absorbing details. She was not unfriendly, but Paige did not feel a warmth about her. Paige wondered if everyone felt the same about Sophie.

"Is life here difficult?" Paige asked.

"Not really," Sophie said. "It's living with the poverty that's difficult. Lives are incredibly hard here. And they don't need to be."

They rode without speaking for a while.

"Why are you here?" Sophie asked.

"We're doing a documentary special on your father."

"I know. But why him? And why come here?"

"Your father is rumored to be in consideration for an important presidential task force. We want the public to know him. And his work here is widely admired. We came to document all that he's done."

Sophie turned her head to look out the window, watching Nepal country and civilization pass by outside. Suddenly, she gripped Paige's arm. "Look," Sophie said. The van had slowed to maneuver through a series of deep potholes in a segment of unpaved road. Sophie pointed to a refuse pile near a small stream a few yards from the road. A dark skinned emaciated woman in a ragged, filthy dress and bare feet held a naked infant on her hip. She was standing in trash, discarded carcasses, wet cardboard scraps, wagon and car parts, tree branches, and mud and metal cans amidst Styrofoam fragments; she drank from a soup can she picked up, and then placed the rim to the infant's mouth. The baby turned her head away. A male toddler without clothes and a small girl in a ripped dirty-gray dress that was once white foraged through the rubble a few feet from the woman, their arms up to the elbows in slop and excrement.

"That makes it hard to be here," Sophie said. "Filth, disease, ignorance."

Paige shared Sophie's feelings. The scene was inhuman and distressing, and Paige felt pain in her chest for the injustice of it all, and she felt guilt that she was so privileged. The future for the woman and her children was unimaginable.

"I'm documenting the plight of women," Sophie said. "Trying to bring recognition of how desperate their lives are... without hope."

"Without family support?"

"Victims of rampant, often violent, sexism. It makes me sick."

The van sped up and they were quickly around a curve, climbing on a narrow single-lane road with two-way traffic. At times they were close to canyon and cliff drops where the base could not be seen from the van. Paige intensely planned what she would do to survive if the van went over the edge. But she would only live a few seconds, long enough to feel the fall of thousands of feet and to hear the instant impact of van on rock and then the end. She was terrified until they reached the relative safety of the village.

Before dawn the next day, they motored to the start point to meet with porters and guides and buy last minute supplies. The expedition had seven climbers, twelve porters, two native guides. A Sherpa who had climbed often with McDowell allowed an interview by Paige about McDowell as a climber and a companion on the mountain. She got no sense of enthusiasm or admiration for McDowell from the small, squat man who spoke only broken English. But she was sure he had no personal dislike and he would treat all foreigners the same way. For him, McDowell seemed another foreign climber who was simply a source of income for his family.

Condoleezza wasn't thrilled about hiking and stayed behind to gather financial and patient confirmation at the hospital, but Victor came with Paige with cameras to shoot footage of Hiram on the trail. He would shoot an interview segment with McDowell and Paige with a background washed with a setting sun before they ate in the evening.

After two hours on the trail, Paige had to stop and place a borrowed bandage on a blister on her heel. Soon she began to limp slightly. She kept her eyes down, afraid to trip on a loose rock or an icy spot, and she only glimpsed rarely at the mountains and the valley. As they slowly gained in altitude near six thousand feet, her fingers, even inside her more than sufficiently warm gloves, felt numb with cold, especially on the hand that held the walking stick. She quickly felt miserable enough to wish she hadn't come, despite the vast land-scapes and soaring peaks around her. She wanted to rest and she began to dread sleeping in the open; her imagination saw a sleepless night with penetrating cold and unidentifiable ominous sounds.

In the evening, on a campstool a porter provided, Paige sat around a fire made for her. Most of the climbers were already preparing various sized tents for sleeping. They all would be on the move two hours before sunrise.

McDowell came to her and sat cross-legged on the iced ground beside her. "Enjoy the day?" he asked.

"I'm too out of shape."

"Do this for a couple weeks and you'd be ready to climb mountains," McDowell said.

"Doesn't the altitude get to you?"

"Most of us take acetazolamide. Many carry oxygen for the higher altitudes. And above 10,000 feet we ascend slowly, day by day, in small, 2,000 to 3,000 feet increments. We sleep at lower altitudes when possible."

"Don't you worry about the dangers? What was it like on the tragic expedition in the eighties?" He was slightly below her and she looked down on him. He was looking into the fire, choked to speechless.

"That was terrible," he finally said.

"Was it mountain sickness?"

"Partially, of course. Most suffered from the lack of oxygen. But it was a horrendous storm on descent. Surprised us."

"Your partner died."

McDowell looked away. She couldn't see his eyes. "Woolf," he said.

"Was there anything that could have been done to save him? I've read they have rescue teams?"

"Limited rescue near the summit. Helicopters can't fly above 16,000. And the rescue operations from base camps couldn't move with the weather the way it was."

"After you summitted, you saw Woolf as you descended?"

"He was almost dead."

"From sickness?"

"And fatigue."

"Did the weather clear?"

"It was near zero visibility and forty below when I last saw him."

"And he was alive when you had to leave him?"

"Barely. He asked me if I'd made the summit. He was pleased. As I would have been for him."

"Looking back on it, was there anything you wish you could have done to save him?"

He frowned with irritation. She could see he was offended. She'd gone too far, or at least worded her question with a little too much aggression. *But damn it. He left the guy.*

"Everyone on the expedition followed accepted emergency protocols. We were trapped by one of the worst storms ever remembered."

"So many died," Paige said.

McDowell seemed to retreat within himself at the question. "From many causes." His eyes were moist. He wiped his eyes with a gloved hand. "I'm sorry," he said.

"I understand," Paige said. But she couldn't tell how sincere McDowell's emotions were.

"I see Woolf's family at least once a year," McDowell said. "Those who survived get together over the years. Woolf was a good man."

Paige said nothing; McDowell seemed to need silence. He was a complex man.

After a few minutes McDowell stood and said good night. He asked if she needed anything before he left. She sat for many minutes until the fire began to die and then moved to her tent that a guide had carefully laid out for her. She didn't understand McDowell. And she couldn't grasp his contribution to the world as a physician. He seemed busy with so many unrelated things. And she needed to feel better about him to produce a special the way Rosenthal wanted—to boost McDowell to national prominence.

Paige spent seven days in Nepal. She was tired and coughing from the flu when she returned to New York. The humanitarian effort was impressive and deserved to be recognized. She'd learned a lot about McDowell, but felt there was still much uncovered.

Chapter 23

The time has come for the scheduled trip to Tibet. On the last few days in Nepal, she and Billie attend the festival of Dashain to photograph. Billie stays close to Sophie, afraid to lose her in the crowds of celebrating families. Sophie is jubilant with the colorful costumes, the happy smiling faces of the women, the joy in the laughter of the children. Sophie has difficulty getting distance from the crowds for wide-angle shots in the square. She frequently calls for a different lens, which Billie, from having assisted for so long now, instinctively has ready.

Rima, who spent much time with them for so long, is with her family today, some of whom have come from other parts of Nepal and the world to celebrate. Sophie sees children on swings at the corner of the square, their headdresses sparkling in the sun. She reaches in Billie's backpack for a Canon 800 mm telephoto lens and attaches it to her camera. She stops to frame and focus.

Billie surveys the faces in the crowd. Proud faces of parents, harried faces of elder children creased with worry and responsibility, ecstatic faces of children basking in the finest costumes families can afford and dancing to music and playing with new friends or brothers or sisters.

"Which way is the temple?" Sophie asks Billie; she is eager to document the intensity of the worshipers. Sophie has no sense of direction, and she is so focused on humanity that she rarely remembers architecture or geological details. He points to the east. He holds Sophie still as she begins to move. Less than twenty feet away is the slim figure of Shristi, garnished in a gown shimmering with red and gold, a tiara on her head, and a splash of red on her forehead. She is at once demure and beautiful. She looks down when she knows Billie is looking at her.

"Don't think about it," Sophie says.

Shristi holds the hands of two of her sisters, one on each side of her.

Billie gives Sophie the backpack and walks to face Shristi, whose head remains bowed, her eyes down. She looks up when Billie says, "I miss you, Shristi." But Shristi's English is not yet good enough to know what emotions hide in the tones of his simple words yet he sees from her gaze that she shares his feelings. Billie places his hand over his heart and then points to Shristi. Soft moisture floods her eyes. She shares his pain at their being apart.

Billie kneels down to each of the children, greeting them, trying to make them smile in their apprehension of having a foreigner so close to them. Billie stands and bows slightly as Shristi gazes into his eyes without reservation. How he misses Shristi's daily presence, her quiet kindnesses, her modest beauty. For a few seconds they are lost in each other in ways their separation has intensified. Both know the feelings of the other; and both ache with the need to be together again.

Sophie grabs Billie's arm and turns him around. He does not resist and they begin heading to the temple.

"Don't fall in love with the impossible," Sophie says.

"Don't start..."

"Listen..."

"Just shut up."

"You're thinking you can figure out some way to take her home when we go back."

Billie's jaw clenches.

"It's impossible. You know that. Even if you could finagle the arrangements, what would you do with her? Keep her in a storeroom? Can you imagine her trying to fit into Denver? Limited language skills. No friends. Unable to easily contact family. Wondering if she would be a nurse now like Rima if she'd stayed in Nepal."

Sophie won't admit to herself that she wants Shristi to go back with them. She tries to ignore the lurking worry of Shristi sharing Billie's passion. It would only provoke sorrow. She could never act— or reveal—her caring for Shristi. It was kinder to keep her here, immersed in the reality of a predictable future than to be consumed by the perils of immigration to a new land, totally dependent on the immature Billie, and so close to Sophie's caring and desire. Sophie's heart would never be the same, whatever happened.

"It's not like that," Billie says testily.

"Bullshit," Sophie says.

Billie will not speak. His aching heart floods his mind with images of Shristi.

"Rima was right to keep you from chasing after her."

"Jesus, Sophie. Just be quiet."

"Can't stand the truth?"

"I don't like you telling me what you think the truth is."

With her jumble of feelings, Sophie can't know the truth. And Billie doesn't know his truths either.

Billie might not be good for Shristi. And it isn't just about screwing, although he yearns to hold Shristi in his arms. Billie sees Shristi as a woman without guile, without rancor. She holds no envy or jealousy... Sophie is sure of that. To Billie, Shristi is a calm sea with no submerged creatures that can destroy and devour. He never thinks that any touch of evil could exist in Shristi's calm beauty. She seems vulnerable in her trusting of him, a trust he knows he could never bear to break. To court her would bring anxieties and worries into her existence... she does not deserve them. And if he arouses desires in her, the pleasures will be replaced immediately with the greatest anguish. Sophie is sure Billie knows all this without thinking about it.

"Take the pack," Sophie says, kneeling to take a shot of worshippers entering the temple with offerings. Billie smiles at Shristi and her sisters beside her, her nieces behind her, and says goodbye before turning away.

With Shristi out of sight, Billie says he wants to be gone from Nepal. He will never be able to live here without feeling her loss. Returning here is not something he will ever voluntarily do again.

Thank God they will be off to Tibet soon after the festival; it might be a few days, but they'll be gone. Billie says he wants to go back to the States without returning to Kathmandu. Sophie knows his feelings.

Chapter 24

New York

Paige arrived an hour early to be sure she sat at the head of the table in this post-Nepal production meeting. She was apprehensive over the obvious increasing bond between Amara Ude and Perry Rosenthal and she wouldn't let Amara take away a choice seat at the table for impact over crucial decisions.

At the top of the hour, seven staff members, including Condoleezza and Victor the photographer, plus Rosenthal and Amara, began to arrive. Paige opened the meeting but Rosenthal immediately asked Amara, "Where are we?"

"We're still in discovery stages," Paige said, immediately blocking Amara's response.

"Let me hear what specifically needs to be done?" Rosenthal stood to walk to a white board and picked up a black marking pencil, looking around the table.

"The script needs to be finalized," Condoleezza said. "We're close. We need to make decisions on what and what not to include."

Rosenthal wrote: "1) Script."

"I need to storyboard the Nepal trip," Victor said. "It's not coherent. I need input on the priorities."

Rosenthal wrote: "2) Storyboard."

"What was the real purpose of Nepal?" Rosenthal asked Paige. "Does the climbing stuff do anything for the health impact of the segment overall? Why would it make McDowell the president's go to man on healthcare?"

"The climbing is important. It's tied in with his foundation activity," Paige said. "We're not just an ad agency for the President and staff, we're journalists with responsibilities to our viewers. Nepal is about climbing and healthcare, a big part of McDowell's career and his success. We were shown the results."

"But there's too much about poverty and sickness," Amara said. "McDowell's our subject. Not wretched poverty and people barely surviving."

"The poverty is heart wrenching. And McDowell makes changes for the better," Condoleezza said.

"I've seen the raw footage," Rosenthal said. "The interviews. McDowell's presence in Nepal was less than selfless. He went there to fund his expensive climbs. Keep that out of it. Make it all about healthcare."

"I have an interview with the author of the memoir. McDowell was a hero saving a child. We could promote that," Amara said. "And that could at least introduce his activity in Nepal."

"That's good thinking," Rosenthal said.

"He's made a lot of money fundraising," Condoleezza said.

"It's impressive," Amara agreed.

"But we can't even determine if he's salaried or what expenses were covered."

"You've got an obligation to delve into that," Rosenthal said.

"We're painting a portrait of a man who will be in leadership positions," Paige said. "Good journalism demands a balanced report, not salary to expose."

"Have you any facts of misdoing? All I hear is innuendo," Rosenthal said.

"I think we should determine the facts before we decide to dismiss them," Amara said with self-importance.

"Spend time on it," Rosenthal said, "But remember, we have a deadline."

Rosenthal wrote: "3) Research."

"Perry's right," Amara said, smiling at Rosenthal and then looking at the group. "We can promote his Presidency of the Board of Regents for the International College of Surgeons."

Rosenthal wrote on the board: "4) Timeline."

Condoleezza looks agitated, Paige thinks. *She is a topnotch journalist!*

She sees the Nepal trip as essential to an honest portrait of McDowell, even though she thinks it's inefficient and mismanaged from a financial viewpoint. And she doesn't like what she sees as McDowell's arrogant superiority over those around him. "The foundation is big-business and even from a cursory examination it's profiting from raising money for a charity," Paige said.

"Look at the whole operation," Condoleezza said. "Their operating expenses yearly are in high eight figures, maybe more. It's above the national average. We really need to expose the excess."

"The foundation funds the charity," Paige said. "We should emphasize the source. There were thousands of lives saved, weren't there? It's not pretty. We found specific documented healthcare benefits only in the hundreds from the records we could access. And useful follow up on care results is damn near impossible. We know only what the foundation and McDowell release about the benefits to the poor and sick."

"But the surgeries they must do!" Amara said. "That has to be verifiable."

"Not so easy," Condoleezza said. "The records are spotty, and hard to find."

"They do preventive health too. Vaccines. Education. I know that," Amara said.

"I'm not saying they don't do a lot, and that the benefits are not to be admired easily," Condoleezza said. "But there is no reliable record of the scope of the benefits available and the benefits actually received, or an estimate of value to the recipients that we can compare to their fundraising results. No comprehensive data. And the organization lives high on the hog."

"So you think it's a bogus effort?" Rosenthal said.

"Not bogus, not illegal," Condoleezza said. "Just loosely run and profitable to levels we'll never document."

"What does McDowell have to do with it?" Amara said.

"He founded the organization so he could climb mountains," Condoleezza said.

"You can't prove that," Rosenthal said.

"Maybe not document, but pretty clear," Condoleezza said. "The math is suggestive. What they bring in from government support, tax exemptions, donations, grants, and sales compared to the ratio of what they spend on charity, what they spend on themselves, and what happens to surpluses is not standard for good organizations. From my estimates, less than 40% of their gross income goes to the needy, if that much."

"Well, we're not doing a special on charity operations," Rosenthal said. "This is McDowell. A leader in healthcare! Emphasize the good. The President wants him."

"You spin this and it could come back to bite us," Condoleezza said.

"We've got to be honest," Paige said.

"It's impossible to report everything. It's our job and prerogative to pick and choose," Amara said.

"But not cover up," Paige said.

"If you're leaving out a balanced presentation for a positive political effect, it's not admirable," Condoleezza said.

"It's what we do," Rosenthal said. "What do you really think, Amara?"

Paige glanced at Condoleezza and looked away, ashamed she was so afraid to lose even her weakened status in the organization. *I should speak out for what is right*, she thought, *for balanced, objective journalism with no spin. But this special has a political purpose. That's common and not illegal. And every human has two sides. Even more. And how to know what is right to present, wrong to leave out, or prudent to ignore is what we deal with in every special we produce. And Rosenthal's the boss. He's making the decisions here and having Amara implement his wishes. It's suicide to buck him now. He has too much at stake.*

Amara spoke before Paige had the chance to articulate her thoughts. "I wouldn't suggest any hint of wrongdoing in fundraising unless there is solid proof," Amara said. "Exclusion of suspicions is right and what we should do; it's honest journalism," Amara said. *But it isn't honest reporting of McDowell's character*, Paige thought with a pang of remorse. She could not look at Condoleezza.

"Exclusion of important facts for political gain is not what we should be about," Condoleezza persisted. Condoleezza was an admirable colleague. Honest and unafraid.

"Crazy," said Rosenthal. "And that's not what we're doing."

"I agree," said Amara.

"McDowell's name will soon be a household word," Rosenthal continued. "I did make commitments. And the timing is important. We need to get this out, and without innuendoes. There is nothing wrong with that."

"5) NOTHING POLITICALLY DAMAGING" Rosenthal printed on the board.

Less than two weeks later, Rosenthal called Paige in. She sat in the chair in front of his desk.

"The President's chief of staff called; The White House confirmed they're putting McDowell before congress for confirmation for Secretary of Health and Human Services."

"Is he really qualified?"

"We have three weeks."

"I need to get legal started. I have Condoleezza vetting. I want to do a couple focus groups."

"I've changed my mind, Paige. This piece has to be the best."

"It will be."

"You're not going exactly in the direction I wanted."

"My attitude is fair reporting with truth and balance. And we need to support McDowell's nomination."

"I don't like your balance. I'm putting Amara in charge."

"What's in charge? What does that mean?"

"She's the lead."

"She's a babe in the woods."

"I don't believe that," Rosenthal said.

"She'll be on air too? In place of me?"

"Yes, and she has full control of content."

"She'll be doing the editing?"

"Totally, and without you looking over her shoulder."

"I'm healthcare!"

"This is Amara's."

"That's wrong," Paige said. "You know it's wrong." She told herself she knew this would happen. But it didn't ease the pain. "You're making a mistake," she said.

"I made a mistake a long time ago. I should have let you go."

Chapter 25

Paige's condo on 72nd near 5th

Paige greeted Condoleezza at the door.

"It's time?" Condoleezza asked.

"A few minutes. Red wine do you?" Paige asked.

In minutes they were settled in Paige's common room in separate armchairs looking at a wall-mounted fifty-inch TV.

"How's it going with Rosenthal?" Paige asked, using the remote to find a channel but with the remote on "mute."

"You know he's still fucking that Amara twerp. It's lasted longer than with his usual bimbos."

"I suspected."

"He's such an asshole. Wait till you see what they put together."

"Your script?"

"None of it. Little twinkle eyes did it. I see her in my nightmares. Little Miss Muffet sitting nude on Rosenthal's prong-inflated lap in some ridiculous satin covered sofa in his bedroom. I bet they watched porn flicks with 3-D glasses on, and he never read the transcript even once. The prick."

The special came on. Hiram McDowell. "Good Evening," Amara said, sitting in a director's chair with her legs crossed, her skirt hem two and 3/8's inches above her knee, an open leather folder on her lap, but obviously staring at the teleprompter. "I'm Amara Ude. Tonight we examine the astounding career of Hiram McDowell, the President's nomination for Secretary of Health and Human Services. It's a story of hardship, determination, persistence, devotion, caring, precision, and accomplishment. Hiram McDowell... "

"It's all fluff, isn't it?" Paige said.

"What else would you expect?"

"He's not a saint."

"Maybe he'll make a good Secretary of Health and Human Services," Condoleezza proposed.

"Not if he needs to stay in one place for more than a few days."

"Well, maybe moth-eaten integrity and spotty family devotion don't count as deterrents to cabinet members' appointments. And he can accrue ideas from a mountain top in Nepal."

Amara narrated scenes from early years in Louisville, teaching in Denver, the International College of Surgeons in Chicago, the foundation headquarters in New York and then brief scenes of the hospital in Nepal. Before the end, Amara introduced the author who collaborated on Hiram's memoir. She'd ignored an interview Paige had produced for the special and made no reference to it.

"You won't believe this," Condoleezza said, directing Paige to look at the screen.

Amara asked the author about the earthquake. "It was in the spring?"

"The beginning of April, 1976."

"7.5 on the Richter scale."

"Villages destroyed. Hundreds dead."

"And Dr. McDowell, working alone, saved a life still in the womb of a mother dying from injuries."

"A wall fell on her, crushing her legs. Dr. McDowell heard her cries as he and his team were searching the rubble."

A panoramic view of an earthquake scene from the air was shown for seven seconds while they spoke.

"Alone, away from other searches nearby, using only a Swiss Army Knife and strips of cloth he ripped from his shirt, he delivered her baby."

"Alive?"

"Yes. By C-Section."

"And the mother died?"

"She died just before the delivery."

"And the child, alive today?"

"In school in Kathmandu, thanks to the generosity of Dr. McDowell."

There was a picture of Dr. McDowell sitting in the center of a circle of young children. One child was on his knee.

"Is that the child?" Amara asked.

"Yes. I believe so," the author said.

"It must have been a pleasure working with Dr. McDowell."

"I feel blessed I had the opportunity to interview him."

Amara began her closing.

"That's not the picture of the man we would have presented," Paige said.

"Nothing of any depth," Condoleezza replied.

"Sentimental rubbish. Nothing to let anyone believe he won't make at least an adequate Secretary of Health and Human Services."

"And nothing to believe he has any special skills or traits to do any better than the guy that rotates your tires every six months."

"And I don't have a car," Paige said.

Condoleezza laughed.

◆

On the west coast, twenty-seven hundred miles away, Michael O'Leary turned to his wife. "Turn it off, please." The credits of Amara's special faded. "It can't be true," Michael said.

"What's that?" his wife asked.

"Listen," Michael said, dialing the number of a New York Times reporter-friend on his cell.

His wife listened to the one-sided phone conversation, the voice on the other end of the phone barely audible.

"Jason?" O'Leary said when he connected. "Did you see that special on McDowell?"

"Most of it."

"Well, that story about delivering the baby from the dead mother in the earthquake zone. It can't be true."

"Why not?"

"At the beginning of April that year, Hiram was in Chicago getting ready for a board meeting. His longtime secretary at the college was being honored at a special dinner."

"So?"

"Hiram was not in Nepal the first few days of April."

"They made a mistake on the date."

"It's in the book. Hold for a minute." Michael turned to his wife. "Get Hiram's book for me, please." Michael thumbed through the pages. "Yes. It's here. It says 1976. There's an earthquake photo. It's not dated."

"How do you know about Hiram in Chicago?"

"Well, this was his administrative secretary. She was good. And when she retired after her 25th year, the board gave this dinner and party and Hiram made the presentation. He tied it into an April fool's joke. A bad joke about one doctor pushing his cloned identical-self doctor to his death from a tall building for being rude and sexually inappropriate to patients and the doctor was arrested for making an 'obscene clone fall.' Not many of us forgot that."

"It doesn't make sense. Why would he lie?"

"Look. McDowell is capable of making things up for gain. He's not malicious, but he is ambitious. I would believe saving the kid might be a true story sometime in his career. Most surgeons have similar dramatic experiences. But I'm sure it didn't happen at the time he says it happened in his memoir," Michael said. "Maybe it's within the poetic license of the co-author. I don't know. But I think they should be held accountable to truth. That's all."

"I agree. I'll look into it. Who was the moderator of the TV session?"

"Amara something."

Michael hung up.

"Hiram didn't save that baby?" his wife asked.

"Not when the co-author and the book said he did."

"Maybe some other time?"

"That's probably right. But knowing Hiram's marketing fervor, it could have been fantasy based on a collection of memories real and imagined of some other event. I hope not."

"Will he be Secretary of Health?"

"Probably. I doubt anything will come of this. Even if Hiram lied to the author, the courts are leaning to no illegality of falsehood in memoir. But one thing I'm sure of, he doesn't deserve a cabinet post. Not only for this. For many other nefarious reasons."

Chapter 26

Washington
Museum of Natural History
Sophie

The President presented Hiram as the new nominee for Secretary for Health and Human Services in the Rose Garden on a Thursday and family members were invited. Most of the family arrived the weekend before. They stayed at the Willard. All had planned to visit the sites of Washington but Penny got sick and Ann stayed with her at the hotel when Robert, Sophie and Jeremy went to explore the museums. They went first to the National Museum of American History.

Sophie, Robert, and Jeremy came to a locomotive with six massive driving wheels on each side and with carriages of smaller wheels in front and back.

"Are you interested in engines?" Sophie asked Jeremy.

"It's a locomotive," he said sullenly. He pointed to the sign: "Southern Railway" and "1401."

"Jeremy had a train set in the basement. O-gauge," Robert said.

"Do you still have it?" Sophie asked.

Jeremy shrugged.

"He destroyed it," Robert said. "$12,000."

"I didn't."

"Don't lie."

"It stopped working."

"Because you hammered it with a bat."

Sophie touched Jeremy's arm. "Do you know how this locomotive works?"

"Steam."

"How do they make the steam?"

"Heat the water with coal," he said impatiently.

"It must have taken a lot of coal and water."

"Fourteen thousand gallons of water and sixteen tons of coal to go 150 miles."

"It could go a lot farther than that," Robert said.

"Why is it green?" Sophie asked.

"It was a feature of the Southern Railway," Jeremy said. "My engine was black with steel wheels."

"Was your engine steam?"

"Electric. I had a steam model engine. But it wasn't a train."

"This carried the body of President Lincoln," Robert said. "I'll meet you at the flag. I want a picture," he said as he turned to separate from them.

"This locomotive was made about 1926," Jeremy whispered to Sophie as his father walked away. "One like it did pull the body of President Roosevelt when he died. From Georgia. But not President Lincoln."

"Teddy?"

"FDR."

"Thank you, Jeremy."

"You're welcome," he said.

At the presentation two days later, the family—without the children—sat on the front row of folding chairs in the Rose Garden of the White House as the President introduced Hiram as the new Secretary of Health and Human Services. Hiram had insisted Ann not bring Jeremy or Penny.

——◆——

After prolonged deliberation, the University informally and clandestinely put Hiram on probation based on medical research misconduct, handled by a private one-on-one talk with Hiram by the chancellor. Hiram would take severe actions against responsible staff and make public his solutions to correct any perceived problems or harms of the misconduct. He would remain chair, since most believed he was not directly involved in deceit; the school would continue to promote the image of Hiram as the world famous surgeon he was and who had been duped by trusted members of his staff.

Within the month, he received a letter from the Mercy Foundation. He'd been unanimously supported for another term as president of the board. He was thanked for his contributions to the foundation. By phone, the executive director, a woman Hiram had never liked, called to ask him to help lead the independent investigations of finances and reorganization of the foundations' administration structure and change in personnel. Hiram thought his agreement to cooperate was generous and gracious. But he planned to temper his influence in case discrepancies were revealed. He was unaware of wrongdoing, and if irregularities existed, he believed he had no involvement. He documented reasons and explanations for things he thought might come under question. He consulted his personal lawyer to lay a carefully orchestrated paper trail that would exonerate him from any wrongdoing if investigations ever produced accusations and indictments.

Chapter 27

The President's staff pushed for rapid confirmation for Hiram. The politics of healthcare had turned volatile and confrontational under the present Secretary. Hiram would be a change both parties yearned for. He was without political baggage and had strong credentials in delivery of healthcare, education, and healthcare financing. With less than a week to go, he was prepped and coached by seven individual experts for days. Today was his final session before the confirmation vote of congress.

This practice session was held in the boardroom of a firm of a lawyer-consultant to the President's staff in a building with a modest exterior but with an interior of overpriced art and flagrant decorative excess that outrageously inflated rental fees. Hiram sat in the middle of one side of a rectangular table for twelve. His three mentors sat opposite. Antonio Marchetti, whose office this was, was dressed in a burgundy and grey pinstripe suit, a deep blue stay-collar shirt, and a salmon colored tie with paisley designs. His shoes were capped and spit-polished to a reflective shine. The other male lawyer, Crease Horn (Buddy), dressed in faded jeans with a leather belt and brass buckle inlaid with turquoise, a white shirt with an open collar, and a chrome-studded light blue denim vest stitched at the bottom and held together in front with rawhide. He had a jeweled pin with diamonds and rubies and sapphires in the shape of an American flag about the size of a credit card pinned on the upper left. A small, overweight woman with short-cut black hair was a speech coach. She held a digital recorder that she'd use for immediate and later-studied feedback to document what Hiram said and how he said it. She had on a cherry red suit with a knee length skirt, an off-white blouse, and a jacket with two buttons and wide angular lapels. Maybella Hernandez.

Hiram listened to general instructions. Each coach reviewed the basics in their specific areas of expertise. Look at the senators. Remove all signs of nervousness. Pause before answering and know what you're going to say. Don't get angry. Don't be defensive. Bridge from the question asked to a question you want to answer. Don't be negative. Review all the updated notes on every senator you'll be given the night before and again before the hearing. Be honest; if you can't be, say you'll have to review the facts, or you can't say at the moment but you can provide that information later, or that you don't have enough information available to you (but don't do that too often, you could look incompetent.). After four hours of practice questions and answers, consultants said he was ready. Maybella stayed late to go over some details of his delivery, using her recorded data as reference of what he needed to improve.

Hiram was exhausted and concerned that he didn't know how the consultants felt about his testimony. They weren't like, "You nailed it doc!" It was more like they couldn't do anymore to improve him, and they weren't sure how it would come out.

"What do you think might go wrong?" Hiram asked Maybella after the others had left and she had finished her delivery instructions.

"You get angry," she said. "Most of those dudes in congress are lawyers, everyone expert at destroying witnesses on the stand."

"I've seen it in expert witness testimony," Hiram said.

"You ever lose it as a witness consultant?"

"Almost a couple of times. But never completely."

"What about those times you did lose it, if even a little? How did they attack you?"

"Mainly attacking my credentials—schooling, intelligence. That I was being paid for testimony and making it look dirty and dishonest."

"Don't let 'em get to you. Think of it as a duel of swords. Deflect their gambits and thrust back," she said. "But be firm and gentle. You seem to have a tendency to yell."

Chapter 28

Three weeks later, Condoleezza came to Paige's office. Paige led Condoleezza down the hall to the coffee machine for privacy.

"Did you see Amara's apology on *Week's End* last night?" Condoleezza asked.

Paige said, "No."

"Here. I've got a video clip on my mobile."

Amara sat alone in front of a backdrop of Nepal. "She's using our material," Paige said. The supporting images were shots of Victor's when Paige and Condoleezza were in Nepal.

Condoleezza propped up her cell phone screen. Amara looked youthful, successful and savvy. She began. "Dear loyal fans of *Week's End*. Recently we did a special on Dr. Hiram McDowell, his philanthropic activity in Nepal, and his new memoir about his experiences in raising the quality and availability of care in Nepal and neighboring countries. Since the airing, we've been made aware of discrepancies in accounts related to his memoir. I assure you *I* was not aware. The book has been withdrawn from the market."

"Do you know details?" Paige asked.

"Nobody can verify McDowell's saving the child from earthquake rubble that Amara described on the special. Remember? She had the ghostwriter read from the biography and patched in a response from McDowell from another interview. McDowell was never in Nepal during any earthquake that anyone can prove."

"He could have the date wrong."

"They couldn't even find the child. They could have photographed any child. Amara didn't vet the book."

"She trusted the publishers to vet the facts."

"She and Rosenthal. Rosenthal would have approved what she did."

"Unbelieveable."

"That wasn't the real crisis, Paige. Lying in the memoir is common enough. But McDowell's publisher, Fornham and Mitchem, is owned by the same parent company that owns the network.

"Jesus, a real conflict of interest. Do you think Amara knew about the ownership?" Paige asked.

"Possibly. But Perry must have known."

"You're right, of course he knew. That's why he added the interview about the book to the special in the first place. Book-sale profits boosted for a sagging publishing business. They were pressed too by the short time to the confirmation hearing. They had to cut corners. Do you think McDowell's confirmation will be affected?"

"He's already blamed the error on the author. I doubt he'll suffer."

"I just don't understand human beings sometimes. Why lie when you've got so much truth to validate your worth?"

"Has Rosenthal contacted you about going back on air? He's demoted Amara. She'll bounce back, of course, but right now she's got her tail between her legs."

"What's she doing?"

"She's back to local news for local affiliates for a while. The sex must not have been good enough to keep her on top."

"He should have fired her long ago."

"It still could be good for you," Condoleezza said.

"No. Even if he gave me my old job back, I'm not eager to go back to healthcare journalism."

"Where will you go?"

"Maybe I'll do something entirely different."

"A Julia Child stint? Cooking for celebrity singles. Weekly on cable?"

Paige laughed.

Chapter 29

Ann

The dark living room felt alien. Ann was exhausted. She stared at the turned-off TV across the room. And she stayed still, as if movement would bring danger and make her even more afraid of she knew not what. Fears consumed her now, fears so pervasive she feared having to live. She could barely remember joy or contentment, peace and caring. Jeremy was expelled again from school. Robert rarely spoke to her. Penny was a spoiled, mean child constantly demanding. Her life was repairing the broken, watching TV reruns to avoid despair, arguing without persuasion, feeling without love, dreading the future.

The garage door went up. She could hear it, feel the vibrations. The engine died. The car door closed. A key pierced the lock of the kitchen door. Robert's steps pounded the floor. The lights flared with the sound of the wall switch activation.

"Shit," Robert said.

Ann closed her eyes without looking at her husband.

"Why are you sitting in the dark?" he asked.

She broke into sobs. She had screamed at Jeremy again. He wouldn't sleep. He played killer video games with earphones on loud. He had to hide his hyperactivity and he kept his music—quick, loud, and annoying—at full volume. She wanted to hit him, hurt him. She couldn't stand his disobedience just to be as rebellious as he could. About everything!

"I can't take it tonight, Ann. I just can't do it."

Ann stopped crying. She stared at him.

"It's over," Robert said. "I could be going to jail."

My God. She knew nothing about Robert's business really. How could this happen? What about the family? How would she take care of the kids? She was completely alienated from her father now, after the wedding.

"Don't stonewall me," he said.

She didn't care.

"We'll be broke," he said.

In so many ways, she thought. "What about the money Daddy gives us," she finally said.

"I don't know. It's a fraction of what it used to be."

"And your family, Robert?" Ann said, her voice choked with tears. "They've got money. "

"They won't help."

"They have to."

"You know they can't."

"The inheritance?"

"They won't share that."

"How could you do this?"

"I didn't try to do this," Robert said.

"It didn't just happen to anyone. What happened?"

"I was keeping you in the manner you've always demanded."

"I've never demanded. And Daddy took care of us. He never complained."

Robert came to her, leaned over, and kissed her. "I'm sorry, baby. I screwed up." He straightened back up. "I love you," he said. "I'm so sorry." When she didn't respond he kissed her on the forehead and went to bed.

Ann stayed on the sofa, brought her feet up, lay on her back, her head half propped on the armrest. The lights stayed on. She did not sleep. Before dawn, Penny came to her to demand breakfast and went to Jeremy's room to pester him awake.

———◆———

In the afternoon of the same day, Hiram, in Denver, took a call from Sophie in New York.

"Robert's been indicted on security fraud," she said. "Ann's not doing well."

"I don't get it," Hiram said. "He makes good money."

"Embezzlement too, I think. Ann is hysterical and fuzzy on the details."

"I'll call her," Hiram said.

"She expects you to bail him out."

"I don't think I can do that. I don't like him. And I don't have enough anymore."

"We've got to help Ann," Sophie said.

Hiram remained silent.

"Well, she's still your daughter and my half-sister and I'm going to spend time with her. She sounds suicidal. I don't think you can ignore her."

"I told you I'd try to call her," he said.

"Robert could go to jail, couldn't he?"

"You go back to her. Get Billie over there too. He's good with the children," Hiram said, hanging up.

Chapter 30

Louisville
Paige

After prolonged scrutiny, Hiram's pluses seemed to outweigh his negatives and the senate approved his confirmation. Three days later, Paige entered the lobby of the downtown Marriott and tipped the bellman twenty dollars for two bags delivered to her suite. Although never excessively wealthy like so many of her male cohorts, she still enjoyed exploiting her celebrity status even after being demoted. She spent lavishly at times and enhanced her image whenever she had the chance. Besides, she was, thank God, still on an expense account for this assignment from Perry Rosenthal.

Ten minutes later she met Condoleezza and a camera crew in the lobby. Crews from two other networks were in various parts of the hotel. Condoleezza said, "We'll start at the school. The chief investigator will wait for us."

That was good. Get the demographics of the tragedy, and then start to investigate sources and witnesses. Rosenthal had been the one to send Paige, and she assumed the goal was to bring as much insight as to the causes as possible for a twenty-minute segment perfected and wrapped up in the next seventy-two hours for a timely Sunday-night, prime-time broadcast. Let the locals and other networks describe the dead and document the grief.

All admittance to the crime scene area was restricted and the police had set up an area for journalists in a storage room of a nearby furniture store. During introductions and a briefing, the investigator, in his early fifties, seemed small-town and slow-witted. But his information would be invaluable as breaking news recorded at the scene. It would also provide an intro for the in-depth segments, and he was more than willing to be filmed. They'd have to patch voiceover quotes; he wouldn't be good for audio in a visual segment; he was un-imaginative and wandered off topic.

"What do you know about the victims?" Paige asked, holding a microphone up to the investigator's mouth.

"Twelve dead," he said. "Five others taken to the hospital. I don't know their condition."

"All children?"

"Not all. I don't know exactly. The search for more victims will take time."

Paige glanced at a child's body—partially covered on a gurney and so small there was barely enough to show a presence—being rolled to a flashing EMS vehicle. Parents and onlookers were being held behind a barricade of wooden restraints and yellow crime scene tape. Survivors were being led out to mothers and fathers, neighbors and acquaintances, distraught with terror and relief.

"Who was the shooter?" Paige asked. Pain suddenly burned in the investigator's eyes. She wondered if a child of his might be one of the victims. Great stuff after all. She signaled one of the cameramen with a slight hand gesture to get a close-up.

"He took his own life, from initial reports. Not confirmed," the investigator said.

"He was a student here?"

"I don't know."

"Were there other shooters?"

"Unlikely."

She felt a potential for incompetency of local police to deal with mass killings. God, there had been enough of them that authorities should be prepared. But police response was not the focus of her segment. She would record but not dwell on the grief, focusing more on motives and desires and reactions of anger, despair, and revenge. She pressed on with her questioning. The shooter was a young boy. He was sure of that. He was not sure how the shooter died, but there was no longer danger of immediate killings.

Paige interviewed a few local bystanders; no one in the school at the time would be available... they were being held in the recreational indoor play area. Paige called Perry Rosenthal.

"I want you live on the six o'clock national news," he said.

"I can't do it. This is emerging news for the locals for immediate release. We're better journalists than scraping for the sensational. We need to explore the causes."

"Just do it. "

"It's a crime. Not healthcare. Why me?"

"You were available?"

"This is the third mass school murder this year. There are issues. Societal violence. A youth culture brought up on violent video games. The decline of family structure. Parental neglect. Lack of gun control. School preparedness. I'm here. I've got an opportunity to investigate these issues for what could be a whizz-bang segment. We could air it in three or four weeks, still with the freshness of the horror of it all, but with enough distance and enough impact to suggest actions."

"Look. Just report the killings. The shooter."

"How do you know so much?"

"We know it's a male about eleven."

"No one knows that here."

"I trust my sources," he said.

"All the more need for carefully considered, in-depth coverage then."

"The kid needs to be punished... if he lives. Don't contribute to letting him get off."

"I'll be objective. You just approve the plan and the timeline. Send my usual crew. And stop worrying. I've never let you down."

"Don't tone down the horror of it, Paige. Frame it for what it is. Mass murder. Inhuman. He's an evil kid."

"Why isn't kewpie-doll here for the sensational stuff?" She meant Amara who was always worming her way back into Rosenthal's good graces.

"She would be. We broke up two weeks ago."

"I'm not good with on-the-scene crime. I'll stick with finding out the influences, use the locals for coverage of the immediate. I won't turn this into political advantage for the network." She would explore possible causes of this specific tragedy, without unfairly targeting one that might easily be ballooned into politically correct accusations. It's easy to try to influence the populace when they're collectively fresh from grieving a tragedy like this. They had to investigate this case, try to understand the shooter, and find significant influences. *Of course he's mentally ill,* she thought, *but there is more to it than that.*

Condoleezza joined Paige thirty minutes later.

"Well, Rosenthal thinks there needs to be tighter gun control," Condoleezza finally said.

"He wanted us to do on-scene coverage. I refused."

"He told me. He wants to focus on gun control. A hot topic for the administration and ripe for a news segment."

"Doesn't any reasonable human want gun control? But really. Is that the solution?" *Does that answer these questions in this case? Gun control is an issue. But it's not right for us to use this tragedy to motivate political action. That's not what we should be about. We're journalists. We want to find the most supportable and reasonable explanation for this action, and only then can we contribute to preventing the violence around us.*

"I'll do what's right. Not just pragmatic politics," Paige said.

Condoleezza held up a folder. "I've got the name of two of the victims. A woman and her daughter found shot in Oakland Estates. Almost surely connected. The shooter shot himself but is on life support and expected to live. The mother is critical, apparently at least one bullet in the brain."

"Who is she?"

"Ann Patchett. McDowell's older daughter."

"My God."

"And Perry assigned you and me because he thought we'd have an inside into the McDowell family, didn't he?"

"Undoubtedly. Or he would have given it to Amara as a plum to woo her back for a few of her best faked climaxes."

"The bastard."

Jeremy, in an outburst of insanity, had killed twelve people, including Penny, seriously wounded his mother when he shot her with a 22 rifle, and then sat on his bed, placed one of his father's shotguns with the stock on the floor and barrel under his chin, and pushed down on the trigger. The blast blew most of his face off but he could breathe and lived to be placed on life support at the Louisville hospital.

The McDowells circled their wagons and tried to cope as best they could. Media attention was intense and constant… for weeks. Paige Sterling and her staff prepared a special on violence in schools and painstakingly particularized the McDowell family and the influence Paige thought they had had on Jeremy's action. And she pinpointed, with emphasis, Hiram McDowell, the neglectful father.

Chapter 31

Sophie picked up Hiram at the Louisville Airport. He had hired a private jet from Denver before picking up Billie at a nearby motel on the way to Penny's funeral. Ann was still in the hospital heavily sedated and barely conscious from brain swelling and on assisted breathing while her lung wound healed.

"It's best," Sophie said to her father in the passenger's seat. He did not respond.

"I don't think she knew we were there," Billie said from the backseat.

"I'm sure she does," Sophie said.

"It's hard for me to see her like this," Hiram said.

"Just talk to her. Tell her stories," Sophie said.

Hiram shook his head. "I'm no good at that."

"She knows you're there. I feel her responding when I talk to her."

"I don't think so," Hiram said.

"Maybe it's better she doesn't know about Jeremy for a while," Sophie said.

"Wouldn't she remember Jeremy?" Billie asked his father. "It must have been horrible."

"If she saw him. But if he shot her first before she had a chance to see him, she wouldn't know, and if she did see him, she might block it out."

"Who's going to tell her?" Billie said. "Somebody's going to have to tell her."

"We'll cross that bridge when we come to it," Hiram said. "What's new on Jeremy?" he asked.

"No change," Sophie answered. "No one knows if he's conscious.

He was unresponsive to any stimuli. They've got him heavily drugged to prevent internal swelling of the brain."

"How could he miss?" Billie asked. "He put a loaded shotgun barrel under his chin while sitting on his bed and pressed down on the trigger."

"How do you feel about it?" Hiram asked Sophie.

"I wonder if we could have prevented it," Sophie said. "I never suspected."

"But the suicide?" Hiram asked.

"I don't know."

"Does a try at suicide absolve him from the killings as a show of remorse?"

"I'm not religious now."

"What do you feel?"

Sophie paused. "Anger mostly."

"He was never right in the head," Hiram said, his own anger surging.

"Troubled," she said.

"A lot more than that," Hiram said.

Chapter 32

A week after the murders, Ann remained in critical condition. The rest of the family arrived at the cemetery for Penny's burial service.

A hundred plus mourners clustered around the graveside service for Penny. Many distant and near-distant relatives attended who were so far removed from the McDowell family, they had to introduce themselves to each other. There were teachers from Penny's school and dignitaries involved in sorting out the details and trying to explain the motives. The press had been excluded from entry but had a van with an antenna on the street outside the cemetery wall. The minister's words were sparse; Penny had a short life and an unjust death and it was hard to be extemporaneously upbeat about the significance of her death or her impact on the future of the living. He tried to expound on philosophical generalizations about her unjust death contributing to expanded understanding of mankind, but it came off inept in thought and delivery.

Sophie saw an attractive young woman with a pretty face, short hair, and a full figure that was trim. She was obviously uncomfortable in these surroundings with this crowd, avoiding contact with those around her. She wore a black designer dress that fit her well. *Tasha! How she's changed for the better. She must have come alone from Denver.*

Tasha could not have seen Penny more than once or twice in life. Sophie had not seen Tasha's mother Carole many more times than that. Her father and Carole had been divorced for years now with little interaction between them. She nudged Billie and nodded in Tasha's direction. "Tasha," she whispered. Billie said nothing.

At the end of the service, there was a chance to approach the casket. Tasha was among the first to pay her respects. "Don't you want to talk to her?" Sophie asked Billie. "She came a long way." Billie walked to the casket after Tasha had moved away. But Sophie was persistent when he returned. "Talk to her," she insisted.

With Billie hesitantly at her side, Sophie approached Tasha before she left for the exit to the street. "How nice to see you," Sophie said. "I'm Sophie..."

"I remember," Tasha said.

"It was kind of you to come."

"It must be very hard for the family," Tasha said.

"It is not easy," Sophie admitted. Billie avoided Tasha's gaze.

"Is your mother well?" Sophie asked Tasha.

"She couldn't come."

"And your sister?"

"Well, thank you. How are you Billie?" Tasha asked, turning to Billie and putting her hand on his arm. He let her hand stay for many seconds before he moved so she had to withdraw it.

And that is why she is here, Sophie thought. *Not just that her son is part of the McDowell family, a fact never admitted but definitely known by all. Tasha was here to see Billie. She still loved him. Her child was not an accident.* "Did you bring, Earl?" Billie asked.

"Mother thought he should stay home. He's in preschool," Tasha said.

"And you?" Sophie said. "What are you doing?"

"I'm a hostess at a sit-down restaurant in Boulder."

Sophie looked to Billie for him to say something but he said nothing, still staring at Tasha. *He can't find words,* she thought. *He's overcome.*

Sophie said her goodbyes and asked Tasha if she had a ride. Sophie wanted Billie to spend time with Tasha. But it was not to be. She'd come alone by rental car and had to get to the airport. Sophie and Billie stood together as Tasha left.

"You weren't very friendly," Sophie said.

Billie said nothing.

"She's very attractive," Sophie said.

Billie still didn't speak; he was still watching Tasha as she stopped at a car and looked for keys.

"Wait here," Sophie said and left Billie to hurry to Tasha. "Please keep in touch," Sophie said. "Could you give us your address and phone? We want to know what you're doing."

"Of course," Tasha said, taking out a pen from her shoulder bag and tearing off the back page of a magazine to write on. "I live with my mother," she said.

"Thank you again for coming," Sophie said, taking the page and folding it.

She went back to Billie. "She's very nice," she said. She handed the address and phone number to him. "You keep this," she said.

"I think Carole still has a restraining order on me."

"Not now. They're not forever. And Tasha wouldn't have come if she thought it would be difficult for you. She's not that kind of person."

After the funeral, Hiram closed the Louisville mansion, sent all valuable possessions to New York auction houses that would accept them, started procedures to get the house on the National Historic Register in preparation for sale.

Sophie stayed with Ann as often as she could. Ann had recovered enough to regain function in her partially paralyzed right hand. She limped when walking, dragging her right foot with the toe pointing out. She had difficulty relating to others. Her speech was garbled at times and she became frustrated when others couldn't understand.

Sophie had pleaded with her father to hire a fulltime companion for Ann. Ann couldn't be left alone when Robert was away. And Sophie wanted to get back to NY, back to her career. She'd been away for two weeks. Hiram hadn't responded yet. He was having financial difficulties. His income was reduced, and he was liquidating assets to avoid confiscation by debtors.

Hiram spent many weeks in Chicago, developing his projects with the International College of Surgeons. The uproar over his false portrayal of his activities in his book and criticism over his exposed misuse of charitable funds refused to go away. Michael O'Leary, after again presenting additional evidence of Hiram's wrongdoing to the ethics committee, convinced committee members to recommend Hiram's dismissal from the college for a full vote. Three weeks later at the board meeting, after minimal discussion, Hiram was asked to consider resigning his presidency. It was more than a request. But he was not dismissed from the college. Michael O'Leary would be appointed interim chair of the board until the regular annual election occurred in February. Most members felt he was the best candidate to fill the position.

Billie persisted in seeing his son Earl despite the objections of his ex-stepmother, Carole. He obstinately dated a happy Tasha, who helped him spend time with Earl away from her mother.

Chapter 33

Billie and Tasha married in the ballroom of a ski lodge in Aspen. Neither had any church connections but they hired a minister from an Episcopal church in Denver. A few days after the wedding, Sophie flew to Louisville to be with Ann. Ann wasn't functioning well enough on her own to travel easily, and Robert was not supportive enough now to be dependable when Ann needed him.

Ann was at the extended care facility with Jeremy when Sophie landed and Sophie went to see her. Ann was in Jeremy's room, sitting beside a hospital bed with metal side rails. Foam cushions to keep pressure off stasis ulcers supported Jeremy's legs. His thin arms by his sides had a faint bluish cast against the white sheets. His face, in various stages of healing and repair, was almost unrecognizable as human. His orbits were tiny caves with skin grafted to cover bone, but no remnants of eyes or lids.

Without a lower jaw and nose, scar tissue left irregular surfaces where a mouth should be. He breathed through a tracheotomy. Monitors and respirators were clustered at the head of the bed.

Ann stood and hugged Sophie. Ann had been crying when Sophie entered. Now she sobbed.

"How is he doing?" Sophie whispered.

Ann let Sophie go and stood back. She had dark half-circles under her eyes. Her skin was loose and hung in folds on her neck. Her lips were cracked from drying. Her hair was cut short and unevenly. Faded brown strands that once had been lustrous were now streaked with gray.

"How can I know?" Ann said.

"What do the doctors say?"

"He's got brain waves. He seems to respond to loud sounds. Maybe he hears. But that's all."

"But you talk to him?"

"What's the use?"

"Look," said Sophie, "you take a break. I'll stay here for a while."

"Don't you want to come to the house?"

"I'll be over later. I'll spend time with Jeremy."

"Robert can come to get you."

"I'll take a taxi, thanks. I'll call to tell you I'm coming."

After Ann left, Sophie lowered Jeremy's bed and let down the side rail. She pulled up a metal straight back chair and pulled up the sheets to cover Jeremy's paralyzed arms and legs. She put her hand on his cold hand.

"Jeremy. If you can hear me, try to let me know. Do anything. Wiggle something. Try to make a sound. A turn of the head. Anything you can think of. I'll be looking but might miss something so if you can, do whatever you can over and over.

"We love you. We want to know if you hear us. We want to do things that will make you happy. I've brought a portable radio. I'll tune it to NPR. If you can hear it, I hope it makes you comfortable.

"I always remember the happy times with you. You are such a bright and capable guy. You make me happy and proud to be your aunt.

"I'm going to touch you in a lot of places on your legs and arms and look to see if there is anything you can do to let me know you feel something."

Sophie applied pinpricks and pressure touches. There were no responses she could detect. She used hot towels and a washcloth with ice cubes. There was no response.

"Good," she said. "I didn't see anything but I know you'd try if you could. So we'll do this again many times before I leave.

"I'm doing really well with my first photography book. Not too sure if the second will get published. But I'm sort of famous. And your

Uncle Billie got married to Tasha. He is really happy to be close to his little boy, Earl. Your dad hasn't found..."

Did his head move? Just the slightest jerk?

"Did you just move your head, Jeremy. If you did, try again."

She waited. She repeated the instructions twice but saw no movement.

"I thought I saw something, so keep trying. I'd love to confirm it."

Sophie got up and went to her shoulder bag near the lounge chair in the room. She'd picked up a Harry Potter book in an airport bookstore. She sat in her chair close to the bed, placed the book on her crossed leg, and opened to the beginning: "Mr. and Mrs. Dursley, of number four, Privet Drive, were proud to say that they were perfectly normal, thank you very much. They were the last people you'd expect to be involved in anything strange or mysterious, because they just didn't hold with such nonsense..."

She read three chapters, closed the book, and leaned close to Jeremy's ear. "We'll continue soon," she said. She'd seen no signs of movement, but she was sure his color improved from the chalky blue-white she'd seen when she first arrived.

She called the nurse and waited until the monitors and alarms were in place for the night before taking a taxi to Ann and Robert's.

Chapter 34

Hiram visited for a day in Louisville from Denver, where he spent most of his time. He was no longer a part of the International College of Surgeons in Chicago or the foundation in New York. Jeremy had been readmitted to acute care at the hospital for treatment for aspiration pneumonia the day before. From the airport Hiram went to Jeremy's room. Sophie sat with Jeremy, letting Ann rest at home where she knitted in silence, unable to tolerate television or company.

Sophie stood when her father entered. "Where's Ann?" he asked.

"She needed some time to herself. She's not doing well."

Jeremy coughed, and Sophie moved to the bed and adjusted an oxygen tube that fed the permanent tracheotomy tube in his neck, then suctioned the mouth cavity.

"Does he understand anything now?" Hiram asked.

"I don't know. I think he does. At times he seems attentive when you talk to him."

Hiram walked to the bed. "How could you do this?" he said to Jeremy's unresponsive, flaccid form.

"Jesus, Dad," Sophie said.

He's ruined a family, Hiram thought *He's imprisoned his mother in guilt and hate. He demands total attention of others, never able to give. As a human he's beyond comprehension.* Hiram looked at Jeremy's mangled head. He could not know if Jeremy understood. If his brain even functioned on a cognitive level. He examined with the intensity of a skilled surgeon the partially-scarred, half-healed, motionless face damaged from the shotgun blasting up from under the jaw. There were no clues to Jeremy's emotional states—even if they were there—that anyone could depend on.

"What if he can hear you?" Sophie asked, disliking Hiram's lack of compassion in talking so bluntly.

He looked at Sophie. "I hope to God he can hear me. He should be put out of his misery."

"He's a child. Your grandchild. He must be suffering," she said.

"How do we know what he thinks? He's never tried to communicate." Hiram said.

"I do think he tries sometimes. He has spasmodic jerks."

"Reflex. Not conscious."

"Music seems to calm him at times when he might be agitated. Something changes. Some alteration of consciousness."

Hiram leaned against the bed. "He doesn't see, smell, taste, feel, or hear," Hiram said. Sophie still sat in the plastic upholstered hospital armchair.

"He might hear, maybe feel," she said.

"He doesn't respond to stimuli," Hiram said testing again with pinches on Jeremy's skin.

"I think he moves his head when the music is his favorite."

"He's never going to be human," Hiram said.

"Ann tries to love him," Sophie said. "But she hates everything he's done. She mourns for the victims. I don't think she'll survive."

"If he ever improves, how can she take care of him? Can she understand him any better than we do?" Hiram asked. "When do the doctors think he might be released to the family?"

"I don't know. He needs fulltime nursing. How long will insurance last?"

"How would she take care of him when she runs out of insurance?" Hiram said. "Especially if he's not strong enough to be released from long-term constant care. We don't have many resources anymore."

"I don't think they can release him the way he is," Sophie said. "But I don't know. Ann can't stand to be around him. Still she comes here early every day that she can. When the day nurse comes, she won't leave him. She stays to late afternoon. Just sits here. She can't read. Her eye movement isn't quite recovered. She's crushed with guilt."

"For what, for Christ's sake."

"She never thought she was a good parent."

"That's not what causes mass murder."

"Maybe it's the video game violence, easy access to guns."

"He went insane. Some inner evil," Hiram said. "I always thought he was a little off, but I never thought he was a killer."

"He could be very kind, at times," Sophie said.

"You liked him?"

"I did at times. And I don't hate him now. If he still has a life, he must be so alone, so afraid."

"This could go on forever," Hiram said, moving away from the bed. "Clear this pneumonia and he'll be right back, suspended between living and dead with vital signs forever stable and electrical evidence of brain activity. And he'll be sucking the life out of all those around him."

Sophie said nothing.

Hiram slid an aluminum side chair to the corner of the room. He stepped up on the seat, reached up, and shoved the tube-shaped eight-inch security video camera off center.

Sophie stood up. She looked at her father frowning... not understanding. "What are you doing?"

"Quiet. Sit down," Hiram said. Sophie stayed standing. Hiram waited, listening, then he went to open the door, surveyed up and down the hall. "No one's coming," he said.

Hiram moved the few feet to Jeremy and gripped his arm.

"It hurts him," Sophie said.

Hiram did not loosen his grip. "He's not alert enough to hurt," he said.

"He's in there!" she insisted.

"Listen carefully," Hiram said. "Go outside the door. Lean against the wall. Wait until I call you."

"Why?"

"Just do it. He's choking."

"He looks peaceful," Sophie said.

"The secretions are building up. It's not for you to see. But I may need help. Stay outside the door."

"Shouldn't I buzz the nurse?"

"Just stay outside the door and wait, Sophie. I'll handle it."

Sophie moved to pick up the suction tube but Hiram held her back.

"Do exactly what I told you. This is one time I won't let you disobey me. Now go."

"I don't get it."

"Sophie!" Hiram shoved Sophie toward the door.

Sophie did as she was told. She waited outside watching the second hand on the wall clock... four minutes. She heard nothing through the door until Hiram called. She opened the door.

"Run for help," Hiram said. "He's suffocating."

"Use the call button."

"I said run. I can't find it."

In minutes personnel and equipment had arrived in Jeremy's room to begin resuscitation. Sophie leaned against a sidewall as far from the work of the emergency team as she could be, while still remaining in the room. Jeremy was dead. She was horrified. Still Hiram worked feverishly with other personnel to revive him. But he *was* dead.

The presence of death frightened her.

Chapter 35

Nurse Katrina Offel was born, raised, and schooled in Belgium and came to America when she married her American-born husband, who was now comfortable with savings from success in sales for a farm machinery parts distributer. Nurse Offel trained in Detroit for nursing. She was on duty the day Jeremy died.

As was routine in hospital deaths, the week after Jeremy's death Nurse Offel reviewed the tapes from two wide-angle security cameras in Jeremy's room. She reviewed all the videos for the time Jeremy was in the hospital until after his death. On the afternoon of the death, she clearly saw Sophie arriving and sitting with the patient. She fast-forwarded expecting to see the death. There was no sound on these monitors. The grandfather arrived and he talked to his daughter. Then the camera angle jerked away from the center of the room to focus at an awkward angle on the sink and the open bathroom door, misdirecting the view from the patient. There was no movement on the video for many minutes until an anesthetist on the emergency team she knew went to the sink briefly to wash hands. Nothing else was visualized. She fast forwarded to about three hours later. The camera was moved again to focus on room center. There is an LPN tucking fresh linens on the bed. A janitor in scrubs is mopping the corner of the room with a squeegee mop. The entire episode was not on video. The monitors were at the nursing station but mounted under the counter, a poor choice or someone might have seen the misdirected camera.

She reviewed images from the second monitor. It took a few minutes to find the segment. The lens focused on the back of Hiram standing at the bed. The patient was motionless but the grandfather seemed to be working, his hands in front but not visible, near the boy's head.

Nurse Offel mentioned the observation of the one misdirected camera. The chief nurse asked the doctor on duty the night of the death about it, showed him the video on fast forward. He didn't see an obvious reason for the misdirection until he studied the second camera's video. He took the videos to the chair of the quality assurance committee for an opinion as to what they interpreted and whether it had any significance. The next day, the video was presented to the risk-management manager, who couldn't explain but thought it should be investigated. A lawyer contacted by risk management for advice found the video curious enough to report it to the authorities. He felt that the video showed the possibility of intentional interference with respiration. He asked for vital sign monitor records but they were not available; they were erased after twenty-four hours.

An investigator arrived and agreed that there were odd circumstances. The video was sent for laboratory scrutiny with contrast enhancement and magnification. The investigator seized other videos in other rooms and from the halls. Just after the time of camera misdirection, maybe a minute or minute and a half, a young woman came out of the room and leaned against the wall, her head down. She barely moved for more than four minutes, then ran to the door, opened it. She did not go in but listened through the crack in the door for many seconds. She seemed to say something. She then ran down the hall to the nurses' station. Personnel came into view on the run toward the dead boy's closed door.

Sophie visibly grieved Jeremy's death. Hiram seemed matter of fact and left the next day for Denver to see patients.

Nurse Offel, as a dedicated caregiver, had long been opposed to euthanasia or taking the life of a living creature in any way. She knew Jeremy's injuries and health status well, knew he was brain injured but with measured electrical evidence of not being brain dead. She believed he was physically strong enough and could be kept alive indefinitely. His pneumonia was acute due to staphylococcus but not resistant to most antibiotics and recovery had been expected to begin in twenty-four hours with complete recovery in a few days. She was aware of prolife groups eager to suppress the acceptance of assisted suicide in America, where the criminality was debated, inconsistent laws for and against were in place, and the court cases that had been tried had stimulated strict, but varying, requirements in the few states that had legalized assisted suicide. The death had been classified as asphyxiation due to complications from his pneumonia. But with her suspicions, her anger mounted that a doctor could have taken a life for any reason. Dr. McDowell may have wanted revenge for the heinous crime that ruined his family, or he may have wanted euthanasia—though no one could know what the boy wanted. But neither were right in the eyes of God, and neither were legal in nurse Offel's mind, although she was well aware of the legal controversies. She reported her suspicions to authorities and now investigators were in the hospital daily. She felt a rising anger at her certainty that the boy's death had not been due to complications from risks associated with the patient's injuries. She contacted the nearest right-to-life group with any substance in Chicago. They listened eagerly to the circumstances and then came to Louisville to fact find and quickly claimed criminal intent against Hiram McDowell. With clever reporting, they could rekindle an issue of anti-euthanasia or pro-life, which had lost intensity over the last year.

——◆——

An investigative team was formed by local police. All hospital personnel were interviewed. The doctor Hiram McDowell was in Denver and wouldn't be available until Jeremy's burial. The boy's aunt, Sophie McDowell, had been contacted at the dead boy's mother's house. She had refused to be interviewed. Detectives would have to arrest her to talk to her and they didn't have anything specific enough to charge her with. Why was she hesitant to speak about the death if nothing was wrong? It pointed to guilt.

As the investigation proceeded, detailed analysis of the recording from the diverted camera that was active during the death clearly showed in the mirror over the sink that motion at the bedside could be seen but was not well defined. The video was sent for expert analysis in Indianapolis. Days of work clarified the images of Hiram McDowell working over Jeremy at the bedside at the time of death. It was clear McDowell was not resuscitating the boy, but the angle was not precise enough to reveal McDowell's actual actions. Still suspicions were heightened when it was clear that McDowell called to his daughter in the hall, his manner calm but deliberate, and then he hesitated in a pensive pose for thirty seconds before positioning the boy for resuscitation. At no time did McDowell take action to prevent the asphyxia that was the cause of death. And the evidence would be suggestive that he caused the asphyxia and death. And except for two brief periods of less than two or three seconds, McDowell was always in the mirrored frame recorded on the video.

Chapter 36

Sophie still worked in New York for the studio. She'd stayed with Ann and Robert when Hiram was arrested. She would be a key witness in the trial for the murder of Jeremy. The prosecutors asked her to testify and threatened subpoena if she didn't cooperate. Hiram's defense team expected her to testify for Hiram and wanted to depose her as soon as possible as a witness for the defense. Sophie agonized over the decision. She would testify only to the facts of what she knew about the day of Jeremy's death. *But I think my father might have done it... for Jeremy, for all of us,* she thought, *but suspicions shouldn't condemn him.* If her father had taken a life—although the defense was trying to make that as unclear as possible—she would make no assumptions, offer no conclusions, no matter how many times she was asked.

Sophie would stay with Ann and Robert while they awaited trial developments too. National attention had made trial preparations intense. Billie came from Denver. Robert had been convicted on multiple charges. He served a six-month sentence and would be under probation for years. He was selling BMWs at a Louisville dealer and spending as little time with Ann and her extended recovery as possible. Ann walked now with a limp, and spoke with slurred speech and aggravating pauses while searching for thoughts. She often seemed to want to say something but could not think of what it was or how to express it. She had recovered enough to care for herself and do basic house work.

The trial took three weeks.

Paige wrote an Op Ed based on her nationally televised segment on McDowell after the murders. Perry Rosenthal had uncharacteristically supported her over Amara and approved her effort.

DOCTOR CONVICTED OF 2ND DEGREE MURDER OF DISABLED GRANDSON: EUTHANASIA DEFENSE DENIED.
by Paige Sterling

The high court convicted Dr. Hiram McDowell of second-degree murder in the death of his disabled grandson, who was accused of mass murder in a school two years ago. Dr. McDowell pleaded not guilty. The McDowell defense rested on the claim that Dr. McDowell was not guilty of murder, but assisted the suicide of his grandson, Jeremy, during a hospital admission for nondrug-resistant pneumonia. His grandson was severely physically and mentally disabled after a self-inflicted suicide bullet to the head within an hour after he allegedly systematically shot to death ten children and two adults, including his sister. At the time of his death, he was on life support. Initially, Dr. McDowell denied any complicity in the boy's death but video circumstantial evidence convinced the court otherwise.

The legal status of assisted suicide is not consistent throughout different states. But the court, in its best judgment based on extensive criminal and state and federal investigative evidence, determined that the action taken by Dr. McDowell did not match even the basic guidelines for euthanasia in those states where it is legal with strict guidelines. Right to life groups feared an acquittal of Dr. McDowell would lead to court rulings and state and federal laws that fostered an unconstitutional right to assist in the death of a patient who desired death. The court agreed, in one of the infrequent jury trials involving a euthanasia defense that assisted suicide could be non-criminal under certain circumstances, but this case was clearly death to an invalid without consent or indication. That the victim was an alleged mass murderer could not be admitted or considered during trial or deliberations. The appeal process is complete;

McDowell could face more than 50 years imprisonment. He will be sentenced on the last Thursday of the month.

A physician has been convicted of murder. Just or not, we've failed to uncover the slightest understanding of why his grandson killed so many innocent children and adults. So many causes are proposed that promote anger from those who have economic or personal interests, yet there is no consensus and no call to action from legislators or the public on the influence of: lack of gun control; violence in our society glorified by TV, film, video gamers; the deterioration of the traditional family; apathy to the quality and availability of mental health care; genetic predisposition. We've convicted a grandfather of murder and a reasonably punishable motive has never been uncovered. Revenge? Compassion? Love? Hate? And we've made no advance on understanding the cause or what is just in the punishment of any mass murderer, much less a child. Worse, there remains little outrage to demand a change in our society. The horror dissipates, the anguish of the victims and their families recedes, and our focus drifts until the next unforgiveable act again occurs. That is our shame—a crime to the living—this tolerance of inaction to prevent tragic violent victimization of innocents in the future.

PART TWO

Chapter 37

A jury convicted Hiram; he was sentenced to twenty-five years for second-degree murder. He had little hope for successful appeals. Without a future, and with the misery of relentless solitude, despair hovered. Life was cruel and unfair; his anger mounted. Loathing for those who had ruined his life persisted; revenge inflamed him day and night. In dark moments, fleeting thoughts of suicide frightened him but he stayed sane by keeping physically and mentally active.

On the 216th day of his incarceration, while in the prison exercise-yard, an inmate shoved a makeshift wire knife into his chest puncturing his lung. An accomplice knocked him unconscious and he almost died. During his two-month recovery, he knew survival in prison would be impossible. He wasn't perfect but he didn't deserve this fate and he began to focus only on escape.

He escaped a year and seven months into his sentence, a few weeks after he was assigned to work in the prison infirmary. He walked from dawn to dusk covering twenty-five plus miles a day. On his seventeenth day of freedom, he returned cautiously to Louisville to obtain cash, then took a city bus to the interstate bus terminal and headed south to Memphis, calculating he would be on a bus to Nashville, by the next day. From Nashville he bused to Indianapolis. Two days later, he was headed for Carbondale where he switched transportation to take a train to Chicago. He traveled on the cheapest coach fares, where passengers would have the least interest in him and he'd have the lowest chance of recognition. He bought supplies: a water purifier, a GPS system that could not be tracked, a flannel shirt, jeans, a jacket, hiking boots, a backpack, and two changes of underwear. From Chicago he went north and west, avoiding civilization, heading for wilderness, where, because of his climbing and trekking experience, he would be comfortable to survive with minimal human contact.

———◆———

Hiram passed through South Dakota into Wyoming, Idaho and Montana. In sparsely populated states he purchased supplies only in chain stores, avoiding convenience stores and family-run groceries where strangers were remembered and talked about. Except for obtaining supplies, he planned to see no one for four months. When climbing and trekking, he'd seen men lose coherence to their thoughts, seen them lose the will to go on, and sometimes accept the out-stretched arms of death to relieve them of mental and physical pain... and the fear of what was next. He would not let himself deteriorate. He set up a daily routine: a minimum of one and a half hours of con-ditioning upper and lower body, core, arms and legs. He took long walks, climbing when he had the opportunity... for his enjoyment. He packed mostly dried fruits and vegetables for sustenance. He drank only purified water. He had first aid supplies and meticulously looked for scratches or abrasions on his body that might be a source of infection and treated them. He lived off the land to keep purchase of supplies to a minimum. He couldn't easily obtain or risk firearms, and so he hunted with a knife, trapped, and fished.

He carried two paperback books taken soon after his escape from a free table in front of a going-out-of-business bookstore—Aristotle's *Poetics* and Plato's *The Republic* in one volume, and the tales of Jack London. He would reread them until he could replace them. He had paper and two mechanical pencils, and for at least an hour every day he recorded details of his past and present.

He regularly designed new projects: on an open road, he'd measure his walking and running pace, count his steps, time his progress, and compare improvement; in deep wilderness, he'd create a living space, often only a few cubic feet, with essential materials within arms reach. He prioritized his needs: concealment, safety from elements and predators, and a view to scan for intruders who might enter his surroundings. He started to outline mental conversations with himself on healthcare delivery, politics, health research needs, medical ethics. But as weeks passed, isolation gradually robbed him of positive thoughts and realistic desires, and he counted the days until he thought the risk would be low to move to more populous environments.

Chapter 38

Two months after Hiram's escape and without any success in capture by authorities, Paige was determined to be the journalist credited for Hiram's return to prison. Based on her TV coverage of McDowell, she convinced a publisher to buy the rights to a McDowell biography. To scoop the competition and assure maximum sales, she had to talk to McDowell to verify details of the trial, imprisonment, and escape. She was sure that Sophie, as McDowell's favorite child, would be his most likely contact. She had to gain Sophie's trust. After multiple calls by Paige, Sophie agreed to see her.

It was hot in New York. Sophie's window air conditioner wasn't working well and they sat in the common room of Sophie's apartment house. Sophie guided Paige to two chairs at a folding card table as far away as possible from an older man in Bermuda shorts and a Jets tee shirt, sitting in a pale green plastic lounge chair and reading a hard-cover John Grisham book. Sophie brought two Diet Cokes from the rear of the room where a brown compact refrigerator sat next to a sink and a microwave on a tiled counter. Definitely a step down from where Sophie used to live.

"Have you heard from your father?" Paige asked.

Sophie shook her head no. *Is she lying?* Paige couldn't tell. *But probably not.* Sophie seemed honest in a straightforward, nondevious way.

"He'll hide in the wilderness, I would think," Sophie said when asked. "He can tolerate isolation."

He would not go back to Nepal now, Paige thought. *Hiram would stand out. Besides, how would he get out of the country without being detected?*

For a few seconds Sophie seemed lost in thought.

"How is Ann?" Paige asked.

Sophie gave a slight wince. *Ann can't be doing well. Could anyone in her circumstances?*

"I saw Ann last weekend," Sophie said. "Robert has a job and she's home alone during the day now. It's hard for her but she seems to be adjusting."

"Does she have friends?"

"She goes to church a lot. Not just the services, but group sessions. I went to one with her. She's often too incoherent with her speech impediment to contribute much, and she cries a lot. She hasn't recovered well from brain damage but the other wounds have healed pretty well. She walks without a walker now."

"Does she hate Jeremy?" Paige asked gently, cautious not to provoke.

"She's grieving for Penny, and all the other victims. I think she feels responsible."

"Not Jeremy?"

"She thinks she's to blame. At least partially," Sophie said.

"For what?"

"She thinks she didn't bring him up well."

"It can't be her fault."

"She won't believe that. I think it's a way of punishing herself to relieve her grief."

"Has anyone heard from your father?"

"No."

"But you've asked?"

"Billie said he'd heard nothing and Ann just cried. I don't think she'd heard either."

"How do Ann and Robert manage expenses?"

"They live with fear of bankruptcy from the debts due to lawyers and hospitals looming over them. They can't get money from her trust unless Dad will release it. He said he'd try to do it from jail but he left before arrangements could be made. Bankers won't act on releasing funds without permission or probate, and a lot of lawyers are fighting to be first in line to be paid before family.

"How are you doing for money?"

"I had to sell the condo. Work has slumped a little but I have enough. I send what I can to Ann and Robert."

"And Billie?"

"He's working in the music shop and making his drumsticks to sell. He sends money to Ann occasionally but it's barely enough. He has Tasha and Earl to take care of."

Paige asked about Sophie's future plans.

"Portraits aren't in demand much these days. I don't know what will happen."

A good person, Paige thought. *Does she deserve a father like Hiram McDowell?*

Chapter 39

New York
Sophie

Sophie fell asleep after reading in bed with the light on when the front door chimes to her apartment rang. She slipped on her slippers, pulled down her nightgown, and went to the door.

The chimes rang for the third time. She looked through the peephole but saw nothing. Probably a hand over the opening. She stepped back.

"Open up, Sophie. I know you're there."

Sophie hesitated indecisively. Did she know this person? She did not want to be rude, but she was afraid. New York was not safe.

"Open!" the voice said.

"Who is it?" Sophie asked.

"It's me. June, for Christ's sake."

It was June. The voice had changed but it was June from two years ago. Sophie had forgiven June and it had helped to forget her. Still hearing June again brought strong anxiety.

"What do you want?" Sophie asked.

"Just open the goddamn door."

"No!"

"I'll camp out here until you do. I've got nowhere to go."

"I don't want you here."

"Open up. After all I've done for you."

You've done nothing. How could I have loved you? Sophie thought.

June pounded the door with the heel of her shoe.

"Stop," Sophie said.

A male neighbor opened a door down the hall. "Knock it off."

"Fuck you," June said.

"I'll call the police," the neighbor yelled back.

A woman neighbor shouted: "Make her stop, Sophie!"

"Is that what you want?" June said through the door. Sophie's heart pounded faster.

"Call the police," the woman neighbor yelled.

Sophie's fear made her indecisive. She dreaded a scene but most of all she dreaded arguing with June. She had to act. She undid the latch and the security chain. June opened the door before Sophie could pull on the handle and entered dragging two luggage bags behind her.

"Unacceptable," the female neighbor said and slammed her door. June parked her bags near the bedroom door before moving to the two-seat sofa where she sprawled out, her back slanted on the cushions so her head was thrown back, her legs stretched out in front of her.

"God, you're stubborn," June said.

"What happened?"

"He threw me out."

"Princeton Navarro?"

"The jerk," June said.

"Are you still married?"

"He never married me. I was his consort to the Europe he tried completely unsuccessfully to conquer. He ran with a pack of queers. I spent months alone. We've had sex twice always in threesomes with another man."

Why come to me? "You can't stay here."

"I need a place," June said. "I've got no money." June had never paid the back-rent she owed. "I called my old boss but they don't have any positions. Maybe Taylor and Rankings will take me for copy-editing. I'll go tomorrow. But I've got to rest and press a pant suit. And get cleaned up. God, the flight was a disaster."

"Not here," Sophie said. *I'll never again share a bed with you. Or my life.*

"I'll sleep here on the couch." June went to the bathroom. Sophie didn't move. June used the toilet, flushed; she started the water for a bath.

Sophie opened the bathroom door. "Stop," she said.

"For Christ's sake, Sophie. Grow up."

"I've got to leave early tomorrow."

"Be quiet when you leave. And put a spare key on the kitchen counter."

"I don't have a spare key," Sophie lied and felt bad about her dishonesty... and even worse about her weakness in confronting June.

Chapter 40

Sophie cried. She sat side-by-side next to Paige on a high-back wooden bench at a table for four at the restaurant "Schnitzel." Clientele were sparse at five o'clock.

"I can't stay long," Sophie said. "I'm so sorry."

"What's wrong?" Paige asked. This was one of Paige's planned meetings to continue friendship with Sophie, still the most likely link to Hiram McDowell.

"I've got to find a place to stay. I've been locked out," Sophie said.

Paige took her hand. "I don't understand."

"This woman I knew a couple years ago shows up and moves in. I don't want her."

"How did she get in?"

"Late at night. She threatened to make a scene." Sophie sobbed briefly. "Next morning I went to work telling her to leave. But she stayed, moved in. She's been there three weeks. She says she's looking for a job, but I don't think so. I sleep on the couch. She never leaves the apartment. She drinks wine and beer and eats my food. And she's taken money. I've tried to get her out. Yesterday she put new locks on the door."

"She sounds horrid," Paige said.

Paige weighed the situation. She had a spare bedroom and she liked Sophie. And having Sophie close would be good company, as well as give her more of a chance of knowing when Sophie finally talked to her father.

"Let's eat. We'll talk it over," Paige said.

"I'm not hungry. And I need to find out what legally I can do to evict her from my place before it goes too far."

"Come home with me then," Paige said. "I'll cook something light. I can make some calls to legal council I know as to what's the best way to proceed."

Paige hired a lawyer and helped in every way for Sophie to continue to work and get as much justice as possible in getting her apartment back. June claimed her right to stay in the apartment was based on her previous relationship with Sophie. June twisted a possible eviction into a squatters-rights issue involving the building's owner. Sophie still couldn't access her possessions that she thought were being sold by June. Sophie claimed theft but June insisted all Sophie's possessions were gifts, which tied up all those concerned into wrangling over semantics and related law in small claims court.

Sophie stayed with Paige the three months it took to dislodge June. Paige never heard Sophie talking to her father.

Chapter 41

Montana

Hiram

After many months in wilderness, Hiram was grateful for his years of climbing and trekking experience in harsh natural surroundings. He felt the most safety while camping above five thousand feet in dense cover to not be visible from the air. Air searches had been stopped, he was sure, but he could not allow a random sighting from a low flying aircraft. He hunted and fished and he only occasionally needed store-bought supplies.

With rare human contact, he began to talk to himself out loud almost continuously, sometimes answering back in an unfamiliar voice. The fear of depression and disorientation loomed even though he continued a stringent daily regimen of four hours of walking, running, and additional resistance exercise for every major muscle.

But he was always angry, like lava in an active volcano. Sometimes it erupted in explosive violent behavior—after a minor inconvenience or a disturbing memory—with an all-consuming presence that extinguished thoughts and gave him fast heart rates and cold sweats. The world was unjust, and he hated those responsible for his misery: Michael O'Leary, Paige Sterling, his coauthor for misrepresenting the truth, the board of Directors at the foundation for withdrawing support, the College of Surgeons, his wives.

Anger consumed other emotions. He was never happy, or pleased, and thought, in dark moments, about a fading will to live. He convinced himself he missed no one that he once thought he loved and he remembered former friends and acquaintances for revenge, always with an eye for an eye. To grasp some feeling of momentum in making a new life, he reorganized his plans for survival at least weekly: never be recognized as Hiram McDowell, nominated for Secretary of Health and Human Services; stay away from places where people might remember him; move facilely among stratas of society—homeless, working poor, and middle class, but avoid upper classes where former acquaintances might recognize him; never leave evidence of his identity or past; never be arrested, stopped or questioned where fingerprints or photos might be compared to files or circulated; never trust anyone with the slightest knowledge of who he was; establish multiple identities for use when needed; until a new identity is firmly established, use no credit cards, checks, deposit or savings accounts or apply for benefits; look for the safest place for a permanent residence where he could live with normalcy and community involvement without constant fear of apprehension.

He wrote daily for mental stability. He believed the bulk of undeserved attacks on him needed complete recall to teach the world what can happen to an innocent man.

Chapter 42

Hiram found a safe cave formed by a rock overhang that was protective from elements. The cave, buried in dense foliage, was invisible from a hundred feet. The fallen tree trunks and dried limbs and branches that were scattered around would alert him to movement with sound. But he'd come to one of those times when he needed human contact, no matter how brief. He needed fuel for his camping stove and more water purifier and he could always use dried and canned fruit, jerky, soup, and nuts.

Seven miles from the cave, three buildings at the crossing of a county road and a paved logging road were the first sign of human existence. There was a convenience store with gas pumps, a single-room white clapboard church with a steeple, and a flat-roof store building with the word "BOOKS" on a windowless weathered oak door.

Hiram entered the book store. Books on recessed shelves lined the side walls except the back wall where a metal double door occupied most of the windowless, whitewashed concrete space. The door was padlocked with chains through two bolted curved handles. Four armless wooden ladder-back chairs haphazardly surrounded a circular oak table in the middle of the room with books and papers scattered over the surface. A vintage computer sat to one side. To the right was a boxy wooden desk, where a wizened woman with steel gray hair sat with her head down. She was still except for her chest moving with her breathing; she seemed asleep. He walked to the shelves. He found no system of display; he searched for alphabetizing, but it wasn't by author or title that he could see. He drifted toward a cluster of paperbacks mixed with hardbound titles with faded, torn, and ragged-edged dust covers. No tags or plaques indicated grouping by content. Because he traveled light, bulky, heavy books did not suit him. But he spotted a Penguin Classic—Emanuel Kant's *Critique of Pure Reason*. He turned pages. He began reading "Of the Division of Transcendental Logic into Transcendental Analytic and Dialectic." Difficult to comprehend, but damn it, he should be able to understand the contribution basic philosophy has made to culture. *I'll work on it.*

The woman was still asleep and shifted only slightly in position. Hiram sat in one of the empty chairs at the table and read more. After a few pages, the woman spoke in a raspy accented voice. To Hiram, it sounded low class, maybe rooted in the Midwest. Her head was up but her lids drooped.

"Find something you like?" she asked.

"Don't see the prices."

"Look on the front flyleaf. In pencil. Someone else put ink in there. If a price ain't there, then it's a loaner. This here is more library than store. And I get books for folks on loan from the county library in Watertown. Glad to find something for you. I go by usually on a Tuesday. This place closed, of course."

There was no price on the front flyleaf. On the back was marked "50¢." "I'll just buy this," he said.

The woman leaned forward still sitting in her chair but with her feet solidly on the floor. She had cold, sharp blue eyes. "That the Kant?"

Hiram nodded.

"You won't like that much."

Shit. I'm not here for a consultation about what to read. "I'll take it," he said.

"I won't sell it to you. You're not going to like it."

Damn it. "Don't tell me what I'm going to like."

"I own the book. Why you trying to read philosophy? Them thoughts are as brittle as a dead-wood branch."

Hiram didn't want to say he was looking for meaning in his ruined life. He needed to explore the thoughts of great minds in the past. He was trying to answer the question of why life had chosen to torture him. *I'm innocent, for Christ sake,* he thought for the umpteenth time that day. *My God, I'm living alone in nature without seeing a human for weeks at a time... my past tracking me like a starving bear.* He had plenty of time to read.

"Just sell me the book," he said.

The woman stood up, stooped a little. She remained defiant.

Hiram's anger flared, and he didn't know why. This woman had a bookstore, or library, or something in between, and he'd found a book that interested him, and she was denying him his will. He didn't like that; he couldn't stand arbitrarily unreasonable people. "I'll pay more," he said. "Five dollars, do it?"

"No," she said.

"You've got another edition on that shelf near the door. I can see it from here. Sell me that one."

"No."

"Why not?"

The woman toddled to Hiram with determination and took the book from his hand.

"This is ridiculous," Hiram said.

The woman pointed to the door.

"You're kicking me out?" he said. *It's a sexist thing. She hates white males.*

She set her jaw, drew her crooked finger back then jutted it forward again pointing to the door again.

Hiram didn't like the possibility that he might lose. He took a deep breath. "Look," he said. "I've gotten off on the wrong foot. I've said something. Or you don't like my looks. But I'd like to know why so I can make amends."

The woman laughed. "You're out of control. So wedded to power you can't think straight."

"That's bullshit. You can't know me. I've got no power, now. None at all."

"You think you do."

"I've got nothing, woman."

"You're a materialist that lost his material... I'm sure. But you're right. You don't have anything of value inside, anything that might fill you with joy at living," she said.

"Is that what you dream at that church up the street?"

"That church closed. God left this part of the country decades ago."

Hiram resented the woman. She was physically bland with her age and unkempt looks. "Loan me this book then. I'll bring it back."

"No."

"I'm honest."

"I believe you try to be sometimes," she said. "But that ain't good enough."

Hiram's anger surged again. "Give me a break."

"I'm trying to tell you something. You're looking for answers. You're a mess. And that book will not help. I won't let you have it."

"And you're the one to punish me by not selling me that book? You hate men." But he had heard a change in the quality of her English that said she had education. And English well spoken seemed to add authority of truth to her words.

The woman went back to her seat behind the desk. "Think what you want," she said.

"You're insane," he said.

"You're not a shining example of straight thinking. Stop thinking about yourself."

"I'm not thinking about myself!"

"You're upset about not having your way. Like a little baby. Pull yourself together."

This was the first person he'd talked to in weeks and she was nuts.

Hiram shouldered his pack of supplies and walked out the door without looking back. The muscles in his face were tight, and his heart was still beating fast and strong from his rage at the woman's ramblings. She wanted to provoke him for no reason. He didn't really care about the book; he cared about being denied.

He was back in his cave in three and a half hours. He wasn't hungry and ate only dried banana chips.

For days after his visit to the bookstore, Hiram shortened and often ignored his routines. In a world of recriminations and recurring purges of anger, his encounter with the old woman had seemed odd at first, and he tried to dismiss the memory of her and the disdain she'd shown for him. But he kept thinking about her. She wasn't crazy. Weird maybe. And he objected to her criticism. He'd done nothing wrong but live his life as best he could. He'd done nothing serious enough to be so severely punished as he had been. And then to be reprimanded by a woman nobody. So why? And he was trying to regain a life worth living as soon as he could maintain the security of an established new identity.

And what did the woman care about a book by Kant being loaned or sold to him? What was that all about? It wasn't about the book. She wanted to be in control. He'd seen enough of that sort of hostile feminism in his life. Bitch. Some loser stuck in the wilderness. He needed to ignore her but he couldn't stop wondering why she attacked him. She had some brains. Damn it. He had to go back to the woman, to stop his wondering about her motives.

The door was locked. The store interior was dark. A piece of notebook paper was tacked to the doorframe at eye level. A note written in Magic Marker said, "GONE FOR DAY." Any store closed during normal business hours irritated the shit out of him. Goddamn it! What kind of business was this? Everything about this woman turned into painful blisters that wouldn't stop hurting. Jesus.

He trekked back to his hole among the rocks.

The next day he left before dawn, unable to sleep more than a few hours due to his fear of noises in the forest, of the patter of a rain shower, of his own light-sleep snorts. He was losing confidence in his chances of normalcy. His imagination injected him with trepidation.

He arrived at the crossroads just after first light the next day. The convenience store was open but he could not risk a pointless encounter there. He walked off the road for two hours and returned. The door to the book store was closed but unlocked. Inside he smelled the same dry decay and felt the motionless silence as he did before. The woman wasn't visible. The door to the back room behind the desk was closed.

He browsed, but he was agitated, his mind occupied with how to engage the woman in conversation.

He searched for paperbacks that would be practical for carrying when he moved on. He skimmed over titles of health and self-improvement, of history. He picked up a biography of Lincoln but it was too thick to be a book he carried with him.

The woman came into the room and sat in her chair. The coarse smell of fresh-brewed coffee seeped through the room. Without looking at her, he waited for a greeting or an offer to join her but she said nothing. He continued to browse, now distracted by her silence. She was provoking him. Finally he turned. She was unchanged, wearing the same dress with a high-necked frilly collar, buttons down the front and long sleeves.

"Good morning," he said.

She raised her coffee mug in a sham greeting, quickly setting it down in front of her, her eyes never leaving his face. Papers and books and a variety of broken pencils and uncapped pens cluttered the desk.

"Busy day?" he asked, unable to suppress sarcasm.

That stimulated her to look at a daily planner that she leafed through—looking at only two pages—and then sat back. She didn't respond. She was looking at a book she'd retrieved from the corner of the desk.

"Can you help me?" he said with exasperation. He felt alone, washed with self-pity. He needed something from her. Some indication she cared.

"With what?" she asked.

He paused. He didn't know how she could help him. She seemed unwilling to admit she remembered him. He blurted out the first thing he could think of. "A book." He added more hesitantly. "I was here before."

She laughed. "Got plenty of them. Look for yourself."

"Can't you recommend something?"

"Don't know as I can."

"Isn't that your purpose?"

"Don't think about it much. But I don't think so." She was back talking in her uneducated, country-born accent.

"Well, I need something to pass the time. What do you like to read?" Hiram asked.

"That's personal, and I don't think I know you well enough to make it your business. You ain't thinking 'bout the Kant book again, are you? I remember you had some burning yearning for that."

"Why didn't you let me have it? I don't understand and frankly, it's been bothering me."

"I don't hanker to take advantage of folks like you. Folks walking in the wrong direction in life."

"That's stupid."

"Say what you want. It's the truth you can't see." She took a sip of coffee with exaggerated slowness.

He took three steps closer to the desk. "What truth?" He couldn't fathom why this woman's thoughts meant so much to him. It was his being in the wild so long. He'd lost reasonable judgment about a person's value. He would have never said more than "Hello" to her in the old days. "Don't just sit there accusing me," he said. "I'm not a nobody."

"You want to talk?" she asked.

"Well, yes. I do." What other choices did he have? He'd failed to find a competent companion. He wanted someone else, but this was all he had at the moment!

"Wait," she said. She stood and went into the back room returning with a full cup of aromatic hot coffee, this time no cream or milk. She sat down again. She brought nothing for him.

"Just what you searching for? Here in the boondocks," she said.

"I'm camping. On vacation."

"See there. You be straight. You just lied."

"No different than any human being. I've got things I can't tell. That's a necessity in life."

"Then why don't you just say, 'I can't say.' Don't lie."

"You've got things you can't tell people."

"You may be camping but you ain't on vacation."

He fumed. She was prodding him again. He wasn't used to responding to the will of others. He brought one of the chairs from around the table and sat in front of the desk.

"I've got people searching for me."

"The law?"

He hesitated. "Yes." *Was that wise?*

"Are you a murderer?" she asked.

"I can't answer that."

"Of course you can. No need to avoid the truth? Probably a lot of folks know, so what's wrong with being truthful with me?"

She'd slipped back into educated speech patterns, her farmyard-country accent faded.

"I'm falsely accused," he said.

"And convicted?"

"Yes."

She stared at him with blank eyes, unrevealing of her thought or emotion, as if in line for food stamps and waiting for her name to be called.

He couldn't help himself. He had this great need for her to know. *What's wrong with me?* There was real danger in telling all. But he had to tell her something. He felt an inner compulsion for truthful catharsis.

"I assisted in the death of my seriously injured, unresponsive grandson."

Her stare didn't falter, her eyes sharp now like a cat's eyes waiting for the close approach of a bird on the wing.

"Euthanasia?" she said.

"I was convicted of second degree murder."

"Oouu. That's not good."

"Friends and family turned against me."

The woman thought for a moment. "So what brings you to this bookstore?"

"I'm writing my memoir."

"Why would you do that with all you've got going on in your life?"

Crazy woman. "To tell the world the truth."

"Which is?"

"I'm innocent."

"You caused the death of your grandson? Convicted? And you say you're innocent?"

"I assisted in his demise. I didn't tell you he was a mass murderer of children and adults. And then tried to take his own life. That's a truth. And no judge or jury wanted to believe his self-inflicted wound was suicide, that he wanted to die."

"What do you think you'll find here to write in your memoir?"

"It's not about finding something to write. I want to create something for the world to read in my isolation. I've been without real human contact for months now."

She stood again, went in the back room, brewed more coffee, and returned with her coffee and a cup in the other hand for him. Hiram stood and looked at books on the shelf. *Nothing's current.* Pages were yellowed, covers frayed.

"How do you make a living in this place?" he asked.

"I don't sell many books. Most of them I value more than the pittance they might bring. I make fudge at home that I sell at the gas station store and the throw rugs my daughter weaves are popular at the craft store in Butte. They bring a good price." She was talking softer and more direct in her educated accent.

Hiram sat down again after the woman regained her seat.

"Will you call the authorities about me?"

She took a slow sip of coffee.

"I don't know you."

"What difference does that make?"

She shook her head. "Lord. Don't push me. I'd like to make my own decision on whether you need to go to the gas chamber."

"Just jail. And they do it by lethal injection now."

"You'll go sooner or later. I just got to decide whether I want it to be sooner."

I shouldn't have confided in her, he thought.

"Really nice talking to you," he said as he stood.

"Sit down," she said in a demanding tone.

I've got to leave.

"I mean it. I'm not going to have you back on the run because of me. So sit down."

He sat down.

"I know what you're looking for in books," she said. "You think you're a good person and you want to know why bad things happen to good people. But that's not in books. It's in the living. I've known many like you. They come through here every now and then."

Hiram stayed silent. She knew pretty damn well what constantly bothered him.

"Do you think God did this to you?" she asked.

"I'm not sure I know God. And I'm pretty sure if He's around, he doesn't think much about me."

"What else did you do? Can't just be your grandson. You're not a saint."

"There was a colleague who investigated my lab and found discrepancies. He made a big deal about it."

"But the discrepancies were accurate?"

"I wasn't the cause. I was head of the lab. Loose management resulted in improprieties. Bad things happened that I wasn't aware of."

"But you had the responsibility for accurate results?"

Hiram shrugged.

"What else?"

"I was accused of fundraising malfeasance. I was the founder of a philanthropic organization for care for the indigent in Nepal. It grew. Forty plus staff. Hundreds of millions of dollars raised. I was accused of mismanagement at the least, and fraud at worst. This television reporter seemed on a mission to destroy me."

"I don't understand."

"She found travel funds used but not related to the foundation's mission. I was implicated. I didn't really know anything about it."

"Did you always travel for the foundation's benefit?"

"They accused me of using foundation money for mountain climbing."

"Did you climb when you went to Nepal?"

"Two, sometimes three, times a year. But I was always primarily on foundation business. I built a hospital in Nepal for indigent natives. All on monies raised by the foundation."

"Did the foundation pay for any of the climbing expenses?"

"Only once. And it was a bookkeeping error. That was what the reporter kept harping on."

"But they paid for your travel there. Even when you climbed?"

"I was there for delivering care, and I climbed when my work was done."

"Were you paid by the foundation?"

"After it got started."

"How much?"

"$450,000 a year."

"And you had other income?"

"Academic salary. Surgical patient-care. Patents on instruments I've developed. Investments from family money." He'd gone too far but he felt pride in letting her know what he achieved.

"That's all?" she grinned.

"I inherited our family's race horse stable. We made money on breeding, occasionally on a big win."

"Seems to me with that much money you didn't need to charge for travel."

"It was standard practice for many foundations. This TV investigative reporter distorted the facts, made something not illegal sound like a crime. She and her cronies were ready to bury me with accusations when all the trouble came up about Jeremy."

She gave him a questioning look.

"My grandson," he explained.

"You seem to think a lot of people had it out for you."

"They did!"

"That can't feel good."

"I'm angry all the time. I can't get rid of it."

She drained her coffee cup, got up, and put it in the back room. She began turning off the lights. "Come along with me. I'll give you a solid meal."

"I've got to go," Hiram said, beginning to panic by how much he had revealed.

"I ain't going to be telling no one about you. It's only my husband and my daughter." She'd slipped back into her common accent.

Hiram hesitated. *I can't do this.* He was risking decades in jail, even with parole. But he felt better talking to this woman. She wasn't special but he now knew he needed human contact and that he couldn't live isolated forever, or even moderately long periods anymore. Jesus. He had to go with her. Chance it. See what she was all about. One thing was for sure, she wasn't as dumb as she tried to make herself out to be.

The sun was still above the horizon far enough to provide soft light and deep-gray shadows as they passed a copse of trees.

"What do people call you?" she asked as they walked on a worn dirt path through tall hay-colored grass toward a forest of evergreens.

"Tom. Tom Blakely."

"You lie."

"I can't give my real name."

"I guess that's a truth."

They walked for many minutes in silence.

"That's it," the woman said pointing to a house becoming visible in a clearing among a nest of hardwood trees. "Been in my husband's family over one hundred and twenty years."

The two-story house was all wood and painted white years ago but now with bare grey patches of surface wood rot. A portico had been built over the front single door, two four-by-fours holding up a scant peaked roof a few feet across that had only a few scattered roofing tiles remaining. On each side of the door was a double hung window with two glass panes. On the left window, duct tape crisscrossed over cracks in the glass. Two smaller windows were above on the second floor.

As they walked into a clearing with still grass glowing golden in the fading light, Hiram saw damage on the back of the house with open rooms exposed to the elements on both levels. The walls on the interior and exterior were blackened and exposed beams hung down at odd angles. More than half of the house appeared useless.

"Fire?" he asked the woman.

"Lightening. We got enough left to live comfortable."

Inside the living area was a large room with a wood-burning fireplace with a single glowing log on an iron grate amidst ash and embers. A kitchen was off to the rear in a room that looked like an add-on. There were doors on the left and right to what Hiram thought must be bedrooms. There was a lounge chair with stuffing oozing through a ten-inch slash in the plastic covering. Three straight-back chairs were positioned at a small, unpainted oak table. A fourth chair was against the wall near one of the doors. To the side was an antique hardwood weaving loom with foot pedals and a shuttle more than a foot and a half long, lying diagonally on the warp of a half finished throw rug.

Over the fire-hole in the back of the room, boards as big as a barn door had been nailed with insulation attached and held in place by plastic covering.

A bearded and partially bald man, dressed in blue coveralls and a buffalo-plaid shirt, came from the kitchen.

"He's my husband," the woman said. "We call him Pops."

Hiram greeted the man and shook his hand. The man left to return to the kitchen with only a nod and no words. Through the front door came a stocky girl who was three inches below Hiram's shoulder in height. She had brown hair gathered back in a ponytail. Her eyes were a darker brown than her hair and with a still-water stare.

"She is Selena," the woman said.

The girl gave an awkward curtsy, as if exiting from the stage at the end of a school play.

"She doesn't talk real good. But you'll get to understand her."

The girl dropped a log by the fire and retreated to the kitchen.

"This is where we live. The three of us. And you're welcome. You can sleep out here near the fire. We don't have a bed for you, but we have a pallet that will do since I imagine you haven't had a decent place to sleep for a longtime."

Hiram nodded his gratitude.

Pops cooked a dinner of fresh corn, spinach, mashed potatoes with gravy from a left-over leg of lamb and finished off the meal with half of a chocolate cake with white icing a couple of days old.

Hiram learned about the family. Selena was premature and with birth complications. She was mentally slow with slurred jerky speech that made her difficult to understand. She'd never had formal school but had been home-schooled by the woman whose name was "Maud."

Pops, Maud confided when he was outside and away from earshot, had been dismissed from a New Hampshire college where he taught chemistry. A female student had fallen in love with him and made advances that he rejected. The student claimed sexual harassment and sued the school. Pops was let go.

Suspicious, Hiram thought. He wondered at Pops's true involvement in such a scenario. Hiram had seen too many of these entanglements at a graduate level. Rarely was there any clear way to know in retrospect the emotions and attractions that arced between people. And to assess blame fairly was usually impossible.

Maud had taught French and English literature at the college and resigned when Pops was dismissed. Selena was an infant at the time. They fled here, to family land never able to be sold and began to rebuild their lives and raise Selena. Pops grew crops. In the barn he nurtured mushrooms that he sold to a restaurant and a market in Watertown. With the bookstore that had been bequeathed by a cousin of Pops, they had an income sufficient to live and pay taxes on the land.

Hiram spent the next day at the bookstore writing notes for his memoir at the wooden table. Only two customers came, friends of Maud's who had come mainly to chat and borrow books. Maud introduced "Tom" as a writer who'd come to get away from distractions and finish his book. Hiram said, "Hello" and went back to writing.

He continued eating meals with Maud and her family. He slept on the pallet near the hearth. He helped Pops make repairs that required two people. They made him feel like a family member. And he talked to Maud about her past and her dreams and aspirations. And he learned farming and repairs from Pops, but Pops never talked about his past. And Hiram's anger became less, and he began to think about how he could make a future he could bear. He needed to belong.

Chapter 43

New York
Maxine Rojas

Max Rojas had no official office for clients, and she asked Paige Sterling to meet her in a deli. Harmon Tressler, Editor in Chief of Rothschild publishing, had hired Max to find Hiram McDowell who had escaped from prison. Tressler had emphasized that McDowell was the subject of a biography anticipated to gross in the millions. The author was Paige Sterling, and Tressler thought she might be a key link in the investigation. At least two other publishers were planning books on McDowell. Tressler needed to be first to publish, and he wanted McDowell's input and an update on his activity after escape. Tressler offered Max a generous retainer.

Max was among the top skip tracers in the country. In an unused furniture warehouse in Brooklyn she had rooms for computers and files, a manager, an IT woman, and a male secretary who had a cubicle next to Max's office. Outsourced investigators came when they were in town to use four private workrooms where all sensitive electronic and paper documents were kept. She provided reports and updates to clients by phone or Internet. She maintained print copies of all activities on file, and taped almost all conversations for electronic storage. Two lawyers worked with her out of their private offices in Manhattan providing her with valuable clients. In her social life, her female partner of sixteen years, Teddy, was a city cop who was too busy to support Max's organization, although Teddy provided advice and access to information that might not be readily available through any other source.

Paige Sterling, as the celebrity who had talked to McDowell many times, interviewed him, and who had studied his career and downfall for two TV specials over the past three years, would be a key resource.

Max sat across from Paige, who was smaller than Max 's 5'11" and 167 pounds. Paige Sterling didn't look in person as she did on TV—she looked smaller and older off the screen. Still, Paige seemed composed and pleasant if not slightly distracted—a welcome change from the stressed out, near hysterical clients and witnesses Max usually worked with.

Max explained what she wanted.

"The guy that murdered his grandson?" Max said. "Nominated for the secretary of something?"

"Health. His defense was euthanasia."

"You knew him well?"

"I've done a number of TV spots on him, interviewed him and some of his family, covered his grandson's murder spree. I could get you tapes of my specials on McDowell, if that would help."

Max nodded. "And the family, friends, colleagues? Would they let me know if their father contacts them?"

"I think they'd like him to be found. For financial if not personal reasons. He wasn't the best father in the world."

"Do they support him still even when he's a fugitive?"

"Not enthusiastically, anyway. McDowell's wealth is tied up and he's no longer available to get to it as a fugitive. They did support ongoing appeals that progressed on huge retainers paid to lawyers."

"You think McDowell will ever talk to you? Ask for help?"

"Never. I'm sure Tressler told you *I'm* doing a biography on McDowell. I doubt that that will make McDowell happy. My reporting of his crimes has been truthful, but I don't think he wanted certain revelations to go public."

"Because?"

"He thinks I ruined his career. His life."

"Are you still doing TV?"

"Occasionally. But I'm officially on leave with reduced pay to write the biography."

"Do you like McDowell?"

"Not really. He's arrogant. Full of himself, at least before his life crumbled around him. And I think he's guilty too. I think he should be punished."

I like her. She's straightforward. Paige would be useful in the investigation, especially since the family wasn't cooperating with any enthusiasm.

"Why are you working for Tressler?" Paige asked.

"He's paying me well."

"Aren't police and FBI enough?"

"I have advantages. Better contacts and resources and less restrictions and oversight."

"And you do this often? It's a form of bounty hunting, isn't it?" Paige asked.

"It's my career. The various authorities aren't well coordinated in their searches. State and locals don't like feds and don't show much initiative in helping. It's an opportunity for me."

"What makes you special?"

"My approach is straight forward. I'll look for shelter, income, transportation, and social contact. I'll create a detailed profile. From you, I'd like written material, minutes, notes, published material you have on McDowell that I can't find on the Internet. I'll need anything you can remember about McDowell."

"He's smart. It won't be easy," Paige said.

"All the more reason that I need you and people who have been close to him."

Max began asking questions, writing in her notebook and taping the conversation while they ate.

After forty-five minutes, Paige seemed tired of the probing and got up to leave. She'd eaten little and left the food. Max wrapped the remainder of her half-eaten sandwich in a handful of paper napkins and left cash on the table.

"You seem uncomfortable with parts of our talk," Max said. "What did I say?"

"You were doing your job..."

"But you weren't pleased?"

"I'm beginning to wonder what role the press played in the many accusations against McDowell. Did the press influence public opinion in ways that weren't justified?"

"You can never be sure, can you? You do the best you can."

"I hope so," Paige said. "But as I look back, it bothers me."

Max wrote down contact information and walked with Paige until they flagged separate cabs. Max said a sincere goodbye. She wasn't sure about Paige. Paige was extremely confident, but cold and officious too. Now she had lost a little of that confidence as they talked and Max sensed loneliness. Max knew the loneliness of a loveless, single woman before she fell in love with Teddy. That's what she sensed in Paige; behind all the glamour and wealth, long hours without a friend. Teddy and Max hoped to legally marry soon. Max wondered if that wasn't exactly what Paige needed to do, relax a little, find someone to love who loved her. Man or woman, it probably wouldn't make any difference.

Chapter 44

✦

Montana
Hiram

Each day that Maud opened the bookstore, Hiram sat alone at the table in the center of the room writing notes for his memoir. Bookstore hours were never the same, and opening days still seemed random. The days Hiram couldn't write inside where he was comfortable and could use resources to stimulate memories and recall dates and locations, he helped Pops in the fields or to repair the back of the house to provide protection for upcoming winters.

He was almost satisfied with the four chapters that he persistently revised as he added new material. He couldn't tell when he had reached his maximum authorial accomplishment and he needed advice as to what to do next. *I'll ask Maud. She runs a bookstore, for Christ's sake. That ought to qualify her for some valuable ideas. And she's the only literary-educated intellect around. Pops has been away from academia and to maintain their existence, his thinking has petrified to physically punishing chores on the farm.*

He had to ask Maud three times before she responded to his requests to read. She never said no, just wouldn't agree to help. He became more desperate to escape from his fear of writer's block.

"I'll do it," Maud finally said with a frown, "but you got to type it out. I ain't going to fret over your scribbles."

"I don't type with all my fingers."

"Use as many as you can. You gotta learn. Use that computer." She pointed to the boxy old desktop on the central table.

Hiram took five full days to get his chapters into Maud-acceptable readability. On the day she printed out his chapters at the store next door and agreed to finish reading them, she closed the bookstore for absolute quiet and told him to get out, go help Pops in the field or help Selena carry her rugs for sale to the general store in town.

Hiram asked Maud at dinner that night if she'd finished.

"Still thinking," she said.

She didn't open the store the next day. Hiram waited till the evening. "Any ideas?" he asked.

"Need a couple more days," Maud said. "I need some distance."

"From what?"

"What you got on paper."

What does that mean? His anxiety mounted but he didn't push Maud. Her approval was becoming important to him.

Hiram left the house before Maud on Wednesday morning and waited at the door for the store until Maud arrived a few minutes later. She said she would talk. She kept the closed sign on the front door turned to the outside, made coffee for herself and him, and sat behind her desk. She told Hiram to pull up a chair. When Hiram sat, both feet on the floor, his hands clasped in his lap like a schoolboy, Maud stared at him, her gaze unwavering, saying nothing.

"Well," Hiram said, "what did you think?"

"You've worked hard."

"That's not what I meant. Did you like it?"

Maud took another sip of coffee, not looking at Hiram now.

"You can tell me," he said. "I know I've got things to correct. Did you get what's happened to me? I want it to be clear."

Maud put her mug on the desk, locked her hands behind her head, and leaned back in the tattered office chair.

"You said you'd read it."

"I read it, Tom. Many times."

"So what should I do?"

Maud paused again. "It needs more polish. Just keep writing. Do the beginning and the end of each section so it has some story to it. Insert a sense of time. Let it all come out. Then you can revise it. And you need to get an editor."

"Is it good?"

"There will be readers who will be interested in it."

"What is it those readers want from me?"

"What happened? They're voyeurs, mainly. They'll like to see your suffering. Add something salacious, outrageous. That'll solve their needs."

"Will they see the injustice of it all?"

"You got a lot of 'why me?' in there."

"What does that mean?"

"You're explaining all the things people did to you from your point of view."

"That's what a memoir's about. Is there anything wrong with that? It's what readers need to hear."

Maud poured hot coffee from a screw top thermos she used between pot brews in the back room.

"Well," he said with irritation, "why not tell them what went down?"

"There're many ways to do that."

"What's wrong with what I'm doing. I'm not an illiterate."

"You're a fatalist, Tom,"

"What does that mean?"

"That you take no responsibility for your life. That things are pre-determined... essentially unchangeable."

"I don't believe that at all."

"It's the way you write. Did you have any responsibility for the troubles you've been writing about?"

"I did what I could to provide healthcare for others. But I didn't cause disease or illness, or death, for that matter. I survived the politics of academic healthcare. Hundreds of thousands of lives changed for the better."

"But did you care about them?"

"Of course."

"You don't have a clue, Tom. We love you. And you're a joy to have around. But you don't have any insight into who or what you were. And it affects the writing. "

"I know exactly who I am. I was leader of the most influential group of surgeons in the world. I was chair of a department of surgery ranked among the top ten in the States. I founded the only hospital for complex care in Nepal, a third world country. I commanded respect of all those who worked for me or whom I trained. I came from a top family in Louisville. I'm related to President Polk, my uncle was a senator..."

"That's not the point..."

"And I've climbed all peaks in Nepal over 8,000 meters, some more than once," Hiram interrupted.

"That's not what I mean," Maud said, exasperated.

Hiram didn't like to be misunderstood. He prided himself on clarity. "Tell me what you mean then, damn it."

"I don't think I can explain it to you," Maud said.

"Well, at least try. I've been waiting."

"You don't listen."

"Damn it. I do listen."

"You hear. And it's not just about your memoir."

"It's okay then. Is it publishable?"

"I don't know. I guess there's always someone who will publish anything."

"Just tell me what you think, Maud. You don't need to rewrite it. I want to create something worthy. What would make it better?"

"I'm not an expert on publishing memoirs, Tom." Maud poured yet another cup of coffee, now lukewarm. "You keep working. Get it finished." Maud stood up. "That will be the time to find an editor."

"Goddamn it. What did you think?"

"I've told you."

"You haven't said a thing."

"If you're satisfied. Let it be." Maud said.

"Just tell me! I'm not sensitive."

Maud hesitated. "Okay. If that's what you want. I'm no expert but I felt you were trying too hard to expose those you feel have wronged you. You write to detail the victimization. Even if you are a victim, it seems too much. If you could be more objective, see all that's happened, and see what responsibility *you* had in what happened to you on so many fronts. Was there anything about you that contributed to this mess? Something you can discover about yourself that would be enlightening to a reader and difficult, if not impossible, to discover on their own. It would make the reading more interesting and add credibility and understanding as to who you really are. That's what I think the reader will want."

"I did all that. It's all in there."

"And if you're satisfied, keep at it. You asked me what I thought."

"I need a prose editor," Hiram said. "My writing is all from science education."

"You've missed the point. You need to think about who you are. What you wanted in life and what you want now. How your desires and dreams might have caused wrong decisions on your way to the top of your career. Take a direct approach to the storytelling. Don't let your emotions cloud truths."

"It's strange advice. Not what I wanted to hear."

Maud shrugged.

"I need more opinions," Hiram said, resenting Maud's thoughts.

"Can't disagree with that. Get as many as you can find. But look inside you too. If you're really going to be successful and satisfied, you've got to find someone who will provide you with a different perspective, at least some objectivity to the telling."

"Why not you," he said, exasperated.

"I don't have the experience or the ability to help."

"But you criticize..."

"Just giving what you asked for as best I can."

"And you don't believe what I put down?"

"I'm trying. You're just not the most unbiased of observers. It's hard to know what's true."

Hiram left and took a six-hour trek to think about what Maud had said. He was upset. She gave no praise. He didn't believe her reasoning. He felt as if he should start over. But what would he do differently? He arrived back at the house two hours after dinner had been served. Maud had left a plate for him on the table. The family had gone to bed.

Chapter 45

Montana
Hiram

On a summer evening after dinner, Selena had been in her bedroom. She came out in an ankle-length white nightgown, barefoot, carrying a hand-blown glass bowl partially filled with water. She sat on a three-legged stool. Maud closed her book and laid it on the floor by the chair. "Pops," she called to the kitchen. Pops came out and sat in a chair at the table.

Selena's freshly washed and dried long hair glowed with a youthful radiance. Her round face had a flat slightly upturned nose and a wide mouth with full pale lips that formed a persistent smile. Her teeth were noticeably uniform but had spaces in between. Her eyes were crystal brown and blunt tonight. They held a certain wonderment and lack of expectation, as if she might need myopic glasses to see the world's demands.

With slow deliberation, she dipped the fingers of her right hand in the water inside the transparent glass vessel on her lap and she began slowly circling the rim until a sound emerged, course and variable at first but with a quick adjustment it became even and constant with a strange ethereal quality. For many seconds she created the sound, her eyes closed, her face relaxed and peaceful. Then she sang. A single tone in perfect pitch with the sound from the glass vessel. Her voice was full without vibrato. There was no hint of the airy echo-like quality from the head and sinuses of her speaking voice. The sound seemed to emanate from within, rich and full... and uncontained. She held the note for many seconds and then, taking in a breath, moved the tone to a minor third above the tone from the glass container. She held it. The minor interval blended as a single tone. Faint overtones flowed like gentle breezes over still ponds. After many seconds, she raised the tone another minor third. Still the basic tone persisting from the vessel supporting her voice. The new interval produced new overtones, thinner with waves more urgent than the interval she had left. Then she went to the octave, still clear, but without overtones now. She created a feeling of energy at rest, not quite placid, yet still full of concentrated vibrancy. She lowered her tone to a major seventh. A sharp tone with energy as an atom's electrons heated to extreme. And she began to produce other intervals, a raised fifth, a flat seventh, and half tones. The transitions relaxed and measured, the new intervals sustained.

At first Hiram thought she was singing without regard to tempo, but as she progressed, he felt an acute sense of rhythm, slow without accents but with the changes in her breathing and pitch falling into a pleasurable feeling of progression, of heartbeats, and breathing, and sleep patterns, hunger, laughter, and of life itself, all contained in the richness and simplicity of her presentation. She continued for fifteen minutes. She unassumingly stood and went back to her room. No one spoke. Maud sat with her head back, eyes closed. Pops remained at the table, his head in his hands.

They didn't move for many minutes. Finally, Pops got up to take Maud's hand and lead her back to the bedroom. Hiram had experienced entrance into a consciousness beyond language, beyond description—a feeling of unencumbered joy. As if he had entered the life force of common awareness without knowing what it was, where it was, or whether it had ever existed in his world of experience.

He extinguished the oil lamp and the two candles on the table. He lay on his pallet, his backpack with all his possessions under his head as a pillow, and let his mind float like a dandelion seed in still air on a summer morn.

He dreamt without fear, needs, hates, or resentments. He felt a peace he never remembered before. And he hoped for Selena to give him the gift of her compassionate talent again soon.

The next day Hiram labored over his memoir notes at the bookstore taking breaks to read books from collections on the walls. There had been no clients in this morning and Maud was reading and drinking from her ever-present cup of coffee.

"That was beautiful singing... what Selena did last night," he said.

Maud said nothing.

"She should sing out in public. Make a recording to sell. It's really cheap to do."

"Really?"

"She's unique. I've never heard a voice like that. Her presentation was beautiful."

"You'd see her doing night clubs. A celebrity?"

"No. But she could entertain a lot of people and make money doing it."

"She used to sing at the church before it closed."

"She deserves more than that."

"What do you think she wants?" Maud asked.

"I don't think she knows her potential," he said.

"To do what?"

"Produce and enjoy a valuable profession with singing."

"And why would she do that?"

"To be successful."

"But what is this success? What do you think that means to her?"

Hiram tried to block his rising frustration at Maud's persistence in questioning the obvious. "I don't know. Admiration for her talent. She could make money."

Maud got up bringing her coffee cup and sat down at the table where Hiram was working.

"You were pleased with what she did for you. She made you feel good."

"I was awestruck."

"She did it for you, you know. She likes you. And she wanted to give you something of value. Something without strings attached. Uniquely hers, too. She doesn't think in terms of success and money. Her world is mostly void of subtle meanings, competition, and maneuvering."

"I don't see what's wrong with success and money."

"It's no good if people seek success and money only for their own satisfaction and self-worth. People content in themselves learn to give selflessly, without concern for personal gain, to learn the joy of being human. How many times a day do we do things for others that are really for our own pleasure and advancement?"

Hiram didn't respond. The bit about selflessness was semantic frosting over an argument about the nature of success not being materialism. *Well, wealth does make a lot of people happy*, he thought. *Maud couldn't appreciate that. She'd never had wealth, barely enough to exist, for that matter.* "Still no reason not to allow her success," he said.

Maud sighed. "I'm going to the store for more coffee," she said over her shoulder.

I still don't get it, Hiram thought. *I've never heard anything like it. Why not let her be admired for her talent?*

Chapter 46

Paige

Paige got a call six weeks after she met with Max Rojas.

"I got a lead," Max said. "Can you go?"

"Do you really need me?"

"I want you there to ask questions only you can ask. You know McDowell."

"Where do I go?" Paige asked.

"We'll fly into Butte, Montana. Rent a car there. Meet me at LaGuardia in two hours."

Eight hours later Paige sat in the right seat as Max parked the rental car to the side of the rough-hewn log store with gas pumps in front. The only other buildings visible were a bookstore fifty yards down the road and, a little farther away, a church that looked abandoned and Godless. Paige stood by the side of the car looking in her shoulder bag for a tissue as Max pumped gas. "Never ask questions without buying something first," Max said.

Inside a heavy set man with dark eyebrows, a receding hairline and a white rectangular plastic badge with "Errol" in black block letters above "Owner" in script. He leaned against the counter, his hands flat on the surface. "You need a receipt?" he asked.

"Please," Paige said.

He handed her the receipt.

"I'm looking for a man," Max said. "We heard about a stranger in these parts."

"Most the people come through are strangers."

"Are there many?" asked Paige.

"A few in the summer. Rare in the winter. We know most of the hunters."

Max showed her private-investigator card. She showed him a composite of photos of Hiram. "We're looking for this man."

Errol stared at the photos with excessive concentration, Paige thought.

"Never saw him," he said. *He's lying. He recognizes something familiar in the photo.*

"Someone like him?"

"All look about the same at that age."

"What did the men look like you did see?" Paige asked.

"Can't remember anyone directly. Been a long time."

The man's eyes shifted away looking toward a rack of motor oil. *No doubt he's seen McDowell.* Paige glanced at Max. Max nodded to let her know she was thinking he'd seen McDowell too.

"Is there some place we could stay around here?" Max asked.

"Might be someplace in Butte."

"No place nearer?"

"Can't think of any."

Max gave the owner her card. Asked for him to call her direct at anytime if he had anymore information. Paige wanted to ask the man about neighbors but Max grabbed her arm. They went out the door together.

"McDowell's around here. I'm sure. I want this meathead to contact McDowell. If we see movement, we can make a move."

"Why is he lying?" Paige asked.

"Protecting someone he knows. And I bet it's McDowell. These folk protect their own. And they don't like authorities," Max said. "Let's check the bookstore." They walked the few hundred feet to the bookstore.

The door was closed but unlocked. "Hello," Max called out.

A withered woman in her sixties came out of the back room holding a cup of coffee.

"Are you the owner?" Max asked.

The woman did not smile. She stopped behind a desk many feet from the door where Paige and Max stood.

Max said, "We'd like to ask some questions."

"Who are you?" the woman said.

Max introduced herself. Paige stepped forward, saying her name and offering her hand but the woman did not respond. "We mean no harm," Paige said.

"I ain't afraid," the woman said. She turned to go in the back room.

"We're looking for a man," Max said. "Have you seen any strangers?"

"I see strangers. Every few days."

"Look at this picture. Is he familiar?" Max asked.

The woman looked briefly and shrugged.

"That mean you have or you haven't?" Max asked.

"Can't say either way."

"Where do your neighbors live?" Max asked.

"Just Errol. At the store."

"You don't have any neighbors?"

"In town."

"That's twelve miles away."

"Not that far," the woman said.

Max handed the woman her card. The woman placed it directly on her desk. Paige had already opened the front door and waited for Max. They left together, pausing outside after they closed the door.

"Another liar," Max said.

"At least she avoided the truth. And she didn't like us being here."

Max turned and pointed to a boy running down a barely delineated path through the knee-high grass that led to a line of trees. The boy turned at the edge of the grass and ran to the store, disappearing through a back door.

"You think he might know something?" Paige asked.

"Strange timing. He's running full speed minutes after we talked to the owner."

"You think he's a messenger? He's told someone we're here?"

"I'd bet reward money on it."

They headed for the path. When they reached the woods, the path disappeared but they headed west, the early afternoon sun in a cloudless sky overhead. In a few minutes they saw a two-story framed house. Paige and Max went directly to the front door and knocked.

They heard sounds of activity inside but no one answered a knock on the front door. Max knocked again. Louder. Now silence inside. Paige took Max's side glance as a command to follow. They walked around to the back of the house. A fire had destroyed a portion of the rear. Near a door on a still intact portion of the house a woman, less than five feet tall wearing an off white cotton shift sat on the stoop, her forehead on her knees, her arms to her sides, her long brown hair held in back by a faded blue ribbon tie.

"Hello," Max said.

The woman moaned a pitiful inhuman sound and cupped her hands over her ears.

She's a child, Paige thought. *Sixteen at most. A sweet face. God, she's scared.*

"We want to ask you about a man," Max said.

The girl cried out as she jumped up and ran into the house. Paige and Max followed through a kitchen into a larger room with a wood-burning fireplace and an oak, wooden foot-treadle floor loom with a half finished rag rug in shades of green, red, white and cream. *A late nineteenth century loom in beautiful condition.* The girl had disappeared. The door to the side room was closed. *Probably the bedroom. She's in there.* Max was headed toward the door.

"No," said Paige.

Paige pointed to the back of the house.

"I need to talk to her," Max insisted.

The woman from the bookstore entered from the back. "Leave her alone," the woman said before Paige had a chance to speak. "She don't talk good. She got hurt in the birthing,"

"She your daughter?" Max asked.

"You're trespassing," the woman said.

"You got other people living here?" Paige asked.

"This here is private property."

Paige turned when a man in coveralls and a tattered green long sleeved shirt came into the room. *A farmer*, Paige thought. *Wiry and strong.* Not McDowell.

"Put them out, Pops, they're harassing Selena." *The old woman has dropped her country accent. She's had education, maybe beyond a college level.*

"We are not..." Max began. But Pops grabbed Max by the arm and pushed toward the front door. The old woman shoved Paige from the back. *She's strong!*. Paige stumbled as she tried to steady herself on the way out. "Don't come back," Pops said.

The door slammed shut. "He's here," Max said to Paige. "Did you see the backpack and the rolled up pallet in the main room?"

"What makes you think it's McDowell?"

"Well, that backpack didn't seem to fit in a home that's been lived in for a long time. Or the pallet. And I can feel he's around here somewhere. And they're all protecting him."

Paige followed Max into the forest out of sight of the house. Max stopped her. "Let's just wait here a while. See if something happens," Max said.

"What are we waiting for?"

"McDowell if we're lucky. But with no luck we might find someone who at least will confirm he's here."

"Will you arrest him?"

"We'll have to get the authorities."

"Should we call them now?"

"Soon as we see some sign," Max said.

They waited in the woods near the house for half an hour but nothing happened. Then Max led a trek around the settlement looking for neighbors' houses or other signs of life. They found nothing.

———◆———

Hiram

Errol's son had alerted Maud that people asked for Hiram. Maud sent Selena to tell Hiram who was helping Pops cull trees for cutting firewood. As Hiram confirmed it was Paige and another woman from a safe vantage point in the woods, he made mental plans to leave. They would alert authorities to their suspicions. A search at some level was inevitable.

Hiram began packing his backpack. "I've got to go," he said to Pops. "Would you check to see if they went east toward town?"

Maud walked into the room. "I'll fix you some supplies," she said.

Selena was working at her loom. "Wraa?" she said with concern.

"He can't stay, sweetie," Maud said.

"I don't want to go," Hiram said.

"Naw," Selena wailed, anguish in her tone. Hiram was never coming back.

"We'll miss you," Maud said to Hiram. "We like having you around."

Selena slid off the seat at the loom and ran to Hiram who was about to shoulder his backpack. Maud went to the kitchen to put bread, slices of beef, and what fresh fruit she had in a plastic grocery sac. She placed it near Hiram's gear and went to be sure the two women were not around.

Selena was weeping. She threw her arms around Hiram's neck and lodged her face on his chest.

Hiram hugged her, felt strength in her arms as if she would never let him go. And he didn't want to let her go and for more than the few minutes it took for Maud to return with the supplies, he held her as tightly as she held him and he felt the pain of her loss sweep over him.

Finally she backed away and ran to her room.

Maud returned. "I just heard on the phone the sheriff's deputy is asking questions of people who come to Errol's," she said.

Within minutes, using his GPS, Hiram tracked north away from any roads. He went from behind the house and avoided any possibility he could be seen from the convenience store. In minutes, he was deep into virgin forest.

——◆——

Max and Paige spent the next day around the bookstore and the convenience store, talking to people who came for books, gas, or supplies. But no one admitted to knowledge of a male stranger. Max called the sheriff. He came with a deputy and talked to people and looked around but found nothing suspicious. The following morning, Paige rode with Max to the airport. "I'm pretty sure McDowell was there. But he was well gone by the time the sheriff arrived."

"Shouldn't federal and state investigators start a search?" Paige asked Max.

"They won't budge on what we have."

"I'd hoped you'd find him," Paige said.

"I think we did. At least we narrowed the focus to the north part of the country. And we found the one place he's been, which helps narrow where he might be next. And we're sure he's on the move again. There's a good chance he'll make some mistake and be discovered. Keep in touch with his daughter. Sooner or later he'll have to contact the family, and I would think it would be her."

"Sophie actually lived with me for a few weeks," Paige said. "She didn't talk to McDowell."

"Are you sure?"

"I was with her a lot. I think I would have known."

Chapter 47

Hiram

Hiram spent three months in the Cascades before moving toward Seattle. He needed contact with city civilization for a while to break the monotony that pressed him when he'd been in the boondocks alone for many weeks. But he also needed documents, and it would take time to find the right forger to make the quality he needed. Seattle was a prime entrance point for illegal aliens needing papers, and far away from where he would eventually settle. He knew the city well. He'd always moved in the upper layers of wealthy society, but on arrival he oriented himself to the homeless underworld quickly to avoid recognition.

He planned with caution; undercover police and agents frequently canvassed homeless populations to find felons, aliens, and fugitives. He would be on alert, orient his days so possible exposure to those who might recognize him or find him suspicious would be minimal. For a few days he'd scout out the downtown, see what went down, spot the dangers, blend in to be invisible, and always have a plan to escape.

He traversed the waterfront and Pike's market looking for a homeless man he could follow or maybe befriend to help him find the shelters that the displaced and downtrodden frequented. The knowledge would allow him to find safe gatherings and establishments where he was less likely to be discovered. And he could also meet people to talk to. He missed Maud, Pops and Selena with an intensity that surprised him and he thought of them often with warm memories.

He hadn't seen a likely vagrant and he decided to work the crowds with a little harp music. He set up on the street on a low retaining wall on the wide stretches of a walk on Alaskan Way near pier 52, his backpack behind him, a hat out front for change that he primed with a few bills and coins. He stayed out of view from the street where he might be seen by authorities.

Tourists moved up and down the walk in groups mainly, with the regularity of tides. But there were individuals, and more frequently couples too; those were the most likely to donate to his cause. He was playing sea-shanty songs, folk songs from nineteenth and early twentieth century. He liked the way the familiarity of the melodies attracted people. He'd become more attentive to pleasing people with his music. And he never ignored that his enjoyment in entertaining them fueled money into the hat. He made forty-three dollars in four hours, not bad but he could do better if he found the right place for the generous givers. He'd move closer to the market.

A cop on patrol passed by seemingly uninterested in Hiram. Hiram made contact, asked where he could and couldn't play, said he'd look forward to seeing the cop again. He wanted to be a familiar figure in the landscape, not a stranger who evoked suspicion.

There was a lull in the tourist pedestrian flow and he took a break, taking a sip from a bottle of water. A guy approached with tennis shoes and no laces, baggy black flannel pants too hot looking for the day, a faded red sweatshirt and a tan herringbone two-button wool sports jacket two sizes too big for him. He was carrying a duffle bag strapped to his back with a cane and a tennis racket with broken strings tied on. In his right hand he gripped the handle of a black cardboard guitar case. A baseball cap with a Miami Dolphin logo on the front sat backward on his mostly bald skull. He plodded along laboriously while looking at the palm of his empty left hand and talking to his lifeline in an incoherent but mellifluous tone.

That night the guy went to a vet shelter but they turned him down and he slept on a heat vent near Pike Street for the night. Hiram followed at a short distance. The next day the guy walked the waterfront, panhandled a little, and ate food someone handed to him out the back door of a fast-food place. Hiram left, irritated he'd picked a guy too insane to be of help.

Hiram went to the Recovery Cafe and saw a scruffy man who was fairly well put together but still had the branded look of homelessness, and followed him. He was perfect. Over a three-day period, Hiram found places for free food, sites where homeless gathered to sit and talk and nod off, and the best spots to panhandle. He found out where drugs were sold, where you could trade a stolen bracelet or credit cards for food or cash, where you could find in-store bathrooms for paper towels, liquid soap, toilet paper, and plastic bags from trash barrels. The guy even slept in a fleabag hotel one night where there were no identity checks and you could share a room with a stranger, placing cash on the counter before you got a room number. There were no keys needed... there were no locks on the doors.

Once comfortable in his daily existence, Hiram found the public library, which held the best nooks and crannies to seek some isolation to do what he needed. Lots of homeless people spent the day in the library. And soon, Hiram did too—using the computers, reading, studying news about health, keeping up with new advancements in surgery, catching up on world news, and putting together thoughts for his future travels. He became a regular visitor, always as inconspicuous as possible to lower the danger of someone suspecting or accidently discovering his identity. He slept near the waterfront where other derelicts slept and there was little worry of police harassment.

Soon he began to identify the drug crowd. He thought a supplier might give him tips on where to obtain new documents without revealing himself. It would take time to build trust, but Hiram had time. It would also be risky; all successful drug dealers would most likely be under surveillance at least some of the time and he couldn't afford to be caught through association.

With persistence, Hiram found a contact with ties to those who could create identity documents without his ever seeing the artist. With time, he got to know Seattle even better than he had before. He found relatively safe niches to exist in the Seattle underground. He made friends with a lawyer half crazed and disgraced for reasons Hiram never knew, and a woman high school teacher whose husband left her with nothing and whose school dismissed her for some infraction that she would not reveal. She'd been drifting up and down the west coast for more than three years and gave resources on the treks to San Francisco and Los Angeles.

He checked weekly for word of his documents and made friends. His days became tolerable as he worked on his memoir and played music for tips.

Chapter 48

Seattle
Maxine Rojas

Max Rojas sat in the waiting room at Seattle police headquarters until her name was called.

She entered a large room filled with desks in rectangular cubicles separated by white composition board perforated with round holes evenly spaced. Each cubicle had a number in blue print pasted on a metal pole that jutted seven feet into the air. She went to number five and introduced herself to the detective who had agreed to see her.

"Who saw him?" she asked after introductions.

"We've got people undercover in the homeless crowd. One of the guys had been in for maybe two months looking at five transits he thought suspicious. He knew all the local permanents from a previous trip into the pit."

"The pit? Undercover in Seattle that bad?" asked Max.

"I'd never volunteer to do it," the detective said. "But this guy, our man, saw a guy looking in good health, agile, and quick with the mind that he thought matched an FBI flyer when he was going through wanted posters. When he showed me the flyer, it looked a little like the guy in the photo you circulated a few months ago."

"Did he ask the guy's name?"

"No. But he asked for identification one time and he bolted. Sightings since have been questionable and always from a distance."

"He couldn't arrest him?"

"He had no cause. And he wouldn't break his cover by an arrest in public."

"Can I talk to your man?"

"Still undercover. But your guy panhandled near Pike's market. He taps out rhythms with sticks on a metal trashcan to back some guy playing fiddle."

"Not harmonica?"

"Never heard that about him."

"You got photos of him as he is now?"

The detective reached into a drawer. "You can have this. Taken about a month ago."

It was a distant shot with many figures.

"Which one is the suspect?"

He pointed to the one he suspected, a man with a beard and a broad brimmed hat... no facial features visible. She doubted enhancement would give any clues. McDowell would not be caught because he was careless. "Thanks," she said with a lack of sincerity for what she knew was probably a false lead. "Do you think he's still here?"

"I do. He's hunkered down somewhere."

"We'll take a look," Max said. "I'll call someone who knew him pretty well."

"Keep us involved," the detective said.

Max called Paige in New York to join her in Seattle.

With his usual intensity about everything, Hiram had learned to drum. He worried that a harmonica in public might be a consistent clue to his identity. And he could carry sticks and brushes and make rhythm on most anything. He sought out drummers he met in the underground homeless crowd, most on the dole and all living hand to mouth but many were good musicians with all sorts of backgrounds in Cuban, Brazilian, African, Asian, jazz, and Native American beats. Making rhythms pleased him and he actually made money on the streets alone and backing other musicians.

Chapter 49

A few days after Max left Seattle on a busy Saturday, Hiram drummed on a metal trash can for tips on the corner of Pike Street and First Avenue when he saw the crazy guy with the guitar case and baseball cap he saw when he'd first arrived months ago. He looked the same as when Hiram first arrived. This was the third time Hiram had seen the guy that day. The man hunkered down before sitting in the wedge where the building wall met the sidewalk. He took sunglasses from his pocket and slipped them crooked on his face. The right temple was cracked and barely reached the ear. With deliberation, he loosened his battered white cane from his pack and held it out in front, touching his coffee can for donations. Hiram decided to go up to him. He sat down and said nothing. The man mumbled something to himself over and over again, sounding like flow from a cornucopia, rocking slightly back and forth against the wall now, his legs bent at the knees in front of him. There was something not true about the guy. When no pedestrians were in sight, Hiram spoke. "How much you think about making today?" Hiram asked.

"Not much," the man said with clear speech different from his babble.

"What are you doing here then?"

"Same as you. And I'm thinking you'd better go somewhere else."

The guy scratched his side then he made a sign and pulled out a pen from his coat. He wrote, "Please Help. Blind and Hungry," on a piece of cardboard with Magic Marker. "What's up?" the guy said as he was settling back against the wall.

Hiram didn't respond.

"Move on," the man said, his voice aggressive and harsh.

Hiram smiled without humor. "I've seen you before. Long time back."

The guy propped up his sign on his chest, his legs outstretched.

"That a guitar?" Hiram asked, pointing to the case.

"What's it look like?" the guy mimicked, sinking back into his no sanity mode.

"Sing me a song," Hiram said. *This guy is all fake. Not homeless. Like an undercover cop!* The guy didn't move.

Hiram undid the one latch remaining of four. The case held dirty cloths and gloves and scarves, a half-eaten sandwich, peanut butter cup wrappers, a length of tattered rope, two empty plastic Coke bottles, an almost used up roll of toilet paper, the black top from an ink pen.

"No guitar," Hiram said. "Good for carrying stuff?"

The guy stared. "Someone stole it," he said.

"You play?" Hiram said.

"Used to."

"I do rhythm. Back you up?"

"Don't con me, dude."

"Just making talk," Hiram said.

The guy's face turned intense. "You got some identification?" the guy said, standing up and reaching out to grab Hiram's coat. Hiram pushed him hard enough that he fell to one knee. He was reaching inside his jacket, taking out a photo, holding it up to compare to Hiram. "I want some identity," the guy said.

Hiram shoved him again. "I don't think so." Hiram turned and walked briskly toward the market where he could not be easily followed in the maze of stairs and multilayered corridors filled with tourists.

"Hey," the man called after him, leaving his junk on the sidewalk and following. "Stop!"

Hiram broke into a run inside the market and exited a few seconds later. He entered a department store. He saw three exits by way of women's lingerie to the west. In twelve minutes he was on the waterfront. The crowd was heavy. He spent two hours on the move through and around the crowd, and when he was sure he was not being followed, he went to a used clothing store for a complete change of clothes. Another hat. He trimmed his beard to change the shape without cutting off so much to lose the shielding it provided. He darkened his beard shade while keeping it brownish.

He checked that he could pick up his new documents in two days. He would leave Seattle. He was sure the intensity to find him would escalate after this encounter. That would be okay, as long as he was elsewhere. It was wise to leave a deceptive trail to focus those who were following him away from his true location.

He got his papers, and when he was sure no one was following, he headed south—walking, avoiding major thoroughfares, leaving no traces. Even along the coast road, he avoided any possible sightings. He was heading for Mount Hood in Oregon where he'd climbed often with Peak Waring and where he knew the surroundings. He could easily avoid most human contact for weeks or months. He walked with little sleep for five days, then sought the obscurity of unpopulated areas.

Chapter 50

Winter closed in when Hiram was around Mt. Hood. He'd kept to himself, camping often, only occasionally sleeping in a motel paying cash and testing his new identity papers from Seattle. But any tolerance he had of being alone was fading. He always believed he was a loner. He had loved excursions where he needed no one. But now he needed human contact more than he ever would have imagined. He figured out an untraceable way to talk to Sophie. At times she had seemed more distant than he had hoped, but talking to her gave him satisfaction and she seemed to no longer just tolerate his calls; he believed she liked to hear from him.

In the spring, he headed south toward milder climates where snow ground cover never lasted long. Oregon, northern California. He had to try civilization again, as long as it wasn't dense and without too much sophistication. He admired coyotes that, through quick wit and intelligence, could exist undetected in densely populated areas. Hiram would seek to belong. He vowed to sense when danger of detection mounted and move on. He wanted to be part of society again for at least two years as he began to establish identity in a place of permanency.

By May, he had cautiously progressed to the upper California coastline near Eureka. He traveled with a half-crazed lay preacher and former CPA, Eric Paget, who spent time in a state penitentiary for fraud. He'd taken on religious preaching on the streets and traveling from city to city. His family rejected him and he couldn't find work. But he had a love of reading, and he was together enough to talk about literature and the Bible without a pause. He carried a radio and listened to NPR so that he was always adjusting his opinions on people and things, usually contrary. Hiram talked to him about his memoir for hours on end on walks and at night before they headed off to sleep on their own so as not to risk attention. Hiram discovered new and useful ways that memoir could be written. But they split up when Eric missed his wife so bad he decided to bus back to New Jersey and seek reconciliation. In the days before they parted Eric turned serious.

"I'll miss you, my friend. Think about God," Eric said.

"Why?"

"For your memoir."

"How will God fit into my memoir?" Hiram asked.

"What could God have done for you that would have protected you from your consequences."

"I'm not sure I believe in God."

"Ask what does religion do for people then?"

"It gives them a sense of superiority. They think faith makes them special."

"Given the exact circumstances you faced, would a religious person have had a different outcome?"

Hiram was irritated by the question. "That's shit."

"Might help you find what you could have done differently."

"I can't prevent evil people falsely accusing me of research misconduct. God wasn't around to prevent that."

"Where did you miss out in the prevention of such charges?"

"Jesus, Eric. You're not making sense."

"You made people angry. You made them feel belittled, inferior. You lied to them and they felt cheated... demeaned."

"If I did, it was their problem."

"And you didn't care?"

"What's caring? I don't care what you believe. And I treated them fairly with truth."

"But you never really cared how you made them feel. Never wanted them to feel better about themselves rather than worse."

"You could waste a lifetime doing that."

"But if you could find out where it might have made a difference, it might make a hell of a memoir. It's the stuff that pierces a reader with truths about life."

"What's it got to do with religion?"

"Religions show some people a way to live. Christianity teaches selflessness in the main. Charity, forgiveness, love."

"I don't think I need religion," Hiram said.

"But maybe you need a different way to live your life."

"And religion did that for you?"

Eric stared with a frown. "You know what I learned from religion? And it got me out of the church... away from the fire and brimstone. I learned how selfish it was to live your life in some self-perceived goodness to be sure you got into heaven. What the shit was that? I came to know the message was: 'Do unto others as you would have them do unto you.' Matthew 7:12. That's the marrow."

"I don't get your point," Hiram said.

"We gotta treat people fairly."

"And you think I don't do that?"

"Know it. You wouldn't be walking in the rain with a dude like me."

"You say you're a man of God. That doesn't impress me," Hiram said.

"I like the preaching. But I don't think God's got his hearing aid tuned into me one way or the other," Eric said.

Hiram laughed derisively. "You don't believe in God and you preach the Gospel on the corner in cities brimming with evil. That's a con."

"Nothing wrong with that. And I make survival money."

"That's hypocritical."

"See there. You ain't thinking right. I make people see different. And I don't do no harm."

"You're scamming people. You make people believe a donation is like buying a prepaid ticket to the afterlife."

"I'm giving them advice about how to live. Donations optional."

"It's thievery." Hiram wouldn't let Eric think his words were effective. Yet under crazy Eric's logic a truth seemed to be buried.

"Just think about it for a while," Eric said. "Make your memoir better."

He thinks my memoir is shit. Even though Eric read only a few chapters carefully selected by Hiram to reveal as little as possible of his previous life, it still hurt Hiram that Eric wasn't impressed. After they parted, Hiram jotted the conversation in his notebook to contemplate as he traveled down the coast.

Chapter 51

Northern California Coast
Hulga Steinweg *meets Hiram*

From her mortgage-free Alba Inn with six bed-and-breakfast cottages, all savoring Pacific-ocean views, Hulga Steinweg walks down the serpentine drive to the road. Topiaries line each side of the drive to the end where two boxwoods mark the entrance that opens onto the two-lane coast highway just a walkable distance south from the town of Elk in Northern California.

She carries a handwritten sign in black-ink marker on a rectangular piece of brown cardboard, cut from a box and stapled onto a stick that she plunges into the soft earth, wet from an early morning storm. "Help Wanted," the sign says. She's decided to be non-specific. She needs maid service for the rooms and a handyman for the inn and grounds and an assistant to staff the desk, answer the phones, greet the guests... and talk to her. She has had no staff now for more than a month, all leaving about the same time saying she paid too little and was too demanding. She is an adequate host, strict on the rules of not smoking, no loud noise, and no parking except in designated spaces. She serves a glass of wine and a selection of cheeses from four to six each day, her "happy hour." She smiles and chats with an unmeant standoffish restraint to her guests—not offensive but definitely lacking in warmth; although she wants more, her guests are never friends, only pass-through acquaintances. She feels trapped and alone.

She is divorced fifteen years from a piano-player husband, popular but underpaid, who still performs late nights and carouses in the environs of San Francisco. She has two estranged children, an older son in the Navy and a younger daughter in and out of school, who has significant addictions to a variety of substances and practices. Although in America now twenty-two years from her native Stuttgart, she knows her manner is harsh and stolid to the whimsical, carefree Americans. She can't seem to engage people, although she tries to be kind and generous. Above all, she values honesty and integrity. She does not tolerate deviousness.

When she records herself and listens, her accent in English is guttural and harsh even to her. She's concluded her opinions lack pliability to be considered and pondered by others, and her ideas, structured with precision are in bulk like highway overpasses and make her more masculine than the feminine she wants to be. She dedicates to shaving her legs twice a week and using conditioner to soften the straw-like consistency of her still naturally blonde, short-cut hair. Her blue eyes, she's convinced, should be the bait of her attraction, the color of sky when the sun is high.

She walks back to the inn to service the rooms and clean up from the breakfast served in the dining room from 7:00-9:00 AM, with coffee available from 6:00 AM—all included in the room price. She tries to go to bed by nine o'clock PM, but is on call for guests twenty-four hours a day and often gets only a few hours of restless sleep a night.

Her makeshift sign—her call for help—is successful. After lunch a domestic from Mendocino, released when her employer sold his house, comes and accepts a job at twenty percent below what Hulga paid the previous girl. The new housekeeper is unattractive, overweight, and silent—all characteristics Hulga does not embrace—but the woman is a Godsend in every other way. She works hard, never complains, takes life with serious attention to what she feels is right or wrong.

The next morning a man applies for the handyman position— bearded face with sharp eyes, good teeth, wiry but strong, and dressed like the homeless that drift up and down the coast seeking sympathetic weather. But he is clean, the skin on his hands is toughened but without cuts or sores. He is a vagabond, he says, in grammatical English. She likes this, with its promise of education and at least some thoughts toward the value of beauty and appreciation of art.

He says his name is Bill Mason. She does not believe him, but it makes no difference. She assumes he has his reasons for an opaque past and a false name, and she will not pry. But he is not common. He has an aristocratic walk and the quick, sure movements of an athlete. No, he doesn't have an address, or a post office box, or references, or even a phone. But he says he is a good worker, ready to pause for a while from his journeys. Here and there, he says, when she asks where he's been. She now is sure he is homeless and wonders if he has committed crimes that make him shun society and humanity—and authorities. But she is desperate and confident she can quickly detect dishonesty or idleness in his character. But is he violent, a thief? So far, she detects nothing to even suggest it.

For the next week, Bill Mason comes every day at 8:00 AM and leaves at 5:00 PM. He trims the grounds, repairs the cottages, strengthens a spot of eventual erosion on the cliff edge and constructs an attractive restraining fence to protect guests from a two hundred foot drop to a rocky beach. After two days, he comes into the inn to help clean up after the breakfast crowd. And he begins staying later in the day without a request from Hulga, taking luggage from cars to cottages at check in and the reverse on checkout. He is off on the weekends, leaving Friday afternoon after requesting, respectfully, his week's pay in cash. As a vagabond, she would expect him to drink but she never sees him with alcohol, nor does he smoke. She doesn't know where he takes his meals—or where he spends nights. And he brings his own lunch in a white paper bag she knows is from the deli at the convenience store in town three quarters of a mile to the north.

Soon, when Bill is working and Hulga takes a break from her duties, she talks to him. He works on, responding to her with pleasing questions and almost always agreements. He is very smart and he knows a lot. He's been to Germany and many parts of the world. He speaks a few German words and knows French well. He is copacetic with her views on health, conditioning, and diets. He compliments her reduced fat, low calorie, leafy and colorful fruit-and-veggie breakfasts for guests. He agrees with the changes she proposed for improvements in the inn and even makes suggestions. She tells him about her dreams of working for conservation when she retires. And she will retire soon, she's quick to inform, and sell the place—it is hers, worth more than 2.5 million on pristine coastal cliff property, and that is a low estimate since it was appraised four years ago. There are forests to be saved and species to be preserved. Save the cone-billed brown tanager too, unique to the region. She wants to prosecute those lumbermen illegally logging redwoods, cedars, and sequoias.

Now, each day, she awakens to thoughts of her desirability as a woman. She starts wearing shoes, not sneakers. Her clothes have always been fresh and clean everyday, but she starts to press out wrinkles for a smooth, more elegant look. She becomes acutely aware of color, and stands before the full-length mirror on the back of the bathroom door, matching shades of primary and complementary colors to her hair, skin and eyes. She makes a trip to San Francisco to buy new clothes. But she never knows if Bill appreciates her efforts.

She believes she has physical characteristics that attract men, but they are rarely uncovered. She must adapt. She is health and exercise conscious. She is heavyset but without excess fat, although she carries some middle aged inherited thickness to her thighs, glutes, and upper arms. Her breasts are a strong point, admirably firm for her age and without skin blemishes. She has a pink areola with well-proportioned nipples, succulent in appearance, she thinks, with a flush of embarrassment when the idea pleases her. Her nipples respond to give pleasure to men when stroked. She has seen that on occasion, although she is usually only excited by self-stimulation. She is careful to avoid sun tanning on her skin, so she has no bra or halter lines. She wants to display cleavage. She experiments with as-modest-as-possible over-abundance… and revealing at the same time. She adjusts buttons downward on one of her favorite dresses. She buys a sweater. Usually she wears Irish wool knits, but she buys thinner and more alluring fabrics of cotton and polyester mixes. In the new sweater, she is proud of her feminine, unenhanced fullness and the way her graceful, paired glands sway when she leans over or turns to one side. *Sehr gut.* She begins to look for a sign that Bill appreciates her efforts, but she is never able to tell.

On a day she knows he will come to clean the breakfast dishes from tables in the dining room, she plans her seduction. Her bedroom is in the back of the house with a door that opens onto the kitchen, installed for convenience to quickly prepare for guests. She awakens early, does her routine chores, and at the time Bill comes to help stack the breakfast dishes, she showers and dries her hair. She leaves the door to the kitchen open, as if accidently, and she positions herself in the bathroom so the full-length mirror reflection is unavoidably visible to anyone looking through the open door from the kitchen. She waits, her fresh unclothed image fully captured in the mirror. She poses with one foot up on the toilet and dries herself repeatedly, waiting for the sound of Bill entering. But he does not come into the house until after 9:00, well after she has dressed and awash with shame and humiliation at her inane impulses. But the next day she does the same thing, and feels she's beginning to make her position in the mirror feel more natural, casual and appealing for Bill's discovery of her strongest, most attractive features. But two more tries result in no success. Bill doesn't arrive when she expects him.

The weekend comes and she doesn't expect Bill, but on Monday she tries again, now determined. And her timing is *perfect*! Bill enters the kitchen with dishes. The door to the bedroom is open with a full view of the mirror that she has filled again with her nude side view. She knows Bill sees her, but she will never see his reaction because she keeps her head down so it wouldn't look like she was aware of his glimpse. He leaves the kitchen and she rushes to close the door. She's not satisfied. He left so fast. But did he see her?

At first, she reassures herself his glimpse can only accentuate his appreciation of her as a woman, but then she sees no change in him throughout the day, not the slightest indication he saw or was moved by her body, and she feels shame and foolishness again.

Weeks go by. Hulga still yearns to spend time alone with Bill, share leisure time to get to know each other better. He's a loner, so much like her. Even after her debacle, she has convinced herself he must like her at least a little. After all, he's still around. He must need someone and she concentrates on making that someone her. She thinks she's in love. She imagines the joys of a love affair she's known only in books and the movies. She wants to meld the souls of a man and woman into one joyous union. Of course, she knows nothing is ever pristine, but it doesn't stop her from seeking Bill's interest. She has never seen a man so polite, considerate, industrious, strong, dependable, even with his ragged dress and unkempt beard. She ignores that he's still never said an impassioned word or made an ardent gesture, but she is convinced he is amorous in ways that, because of his life's burdens, he's learned to cloak. But even with his reticence, she is certain he is vulnerable with need that he does not recognize, vulnerable to discover the attraction of his life that will bring him the fulfillment he must have always wanted.

Since she has new help, Hulga hikes four or five times a week in the foothills and up and down the coast. On the Friday of his ninth week of work, she asks Bill if he would like to trek Sunday afternoon into the hills for miles along vistas of the coast. He could stay at the inn for the weekend, sleep in the still unfinished cabin near the road if he liked. They could start in the national park then walk through a pigmy forest and then onto private land that has a private trail she has discovered and has told no one else about—her own private sanctuary.

Bill hesitates before thoughtfully agreeing.

"It will be fun," she says.

Bill nods slowly and she fears he's not enthusiastic. But he did agree. And she must remember his nature is shy-restraint. It makes her love him in the way a mother loves her firstborn... and the way a maiden craves her Adam.

On the trail, he is surefooted and determined to a brisk pace. After two hours or so she falls behind by twenty yards, her pulse up and her breathing quickened.

"Wait," she calls to him and stops to recover. He turns, waves, and comes to her.

She takes out a container of face powder, dabs her cheeks and neck with a small puff.

"You okay?" he asks.

She smiles and blurts out more than she wants to reveal. "My face gets this horrible blood red when I'm active. I can't stop it. My Deutsche origins, I think." She smiles apologetically, thinking she has spoiled some sweet image she hopes he holds of her when he is not with her. Her yearning to please him as a woman has become her only preoccupation. She needs to please him to turn his heart receptive to all she has to offer.

"Should we turn back?" Bill asks.

Don't you like it here? she thinks. Like to be with me, she almost says. She fears her accent is too strong; it gets that way when she's stressed.

"It's not that. Shouldn't we be there when the guests start to arrive?" She imagines concern in his voice and feels a measure of comfort that he seems to care.

"Oh, no," she says. "Antoinette will take care of it. I have a surprise." He smiles, but it's more subdued than she would have liked.

"Really, just a half mile or so," she says. "We have plenty of time."

Early that morning in the light of dawn, leaving the morning duties to her newly hired assistant, Hulga had trekked to a favorite clearing in a dense forest, a naturally reforested clearing near a stream trickling down from the surrounding foothills. There she stashed a luncheon in thermal containers and protective wraps.

"Let's go when you're ready," he says.

"Is my face..." she says, looking to him earnestly.

"You look just fine," he says. "It doesn't look bad, really," he adds. Her heart soars. Because the trail is narrow, they must walk in single file, but he keeps a slower pace so she can stay close to him. In less than twenty minutes, she touches his arm and leads him off the trail through a dense patch of evergreens to an open circular clearing, no more than sixty feet across with tall, ripe, wheat-colored grass and two fallen logs, one almost hollow from decay... a spot cleared by loggers for camp more than a century ago. Hulga loves the light here, warm and yellow, the trees casting blue-green shadows. She looks to see if Bill's feelings are her own. She is not sure, but he seems content. She is exhilarated by their arrival at her chosen hideaway and by their being together. She directs him, both hands on his arm, to sit on the log more freshly felled.

From the hollow log she removes her surprise luncheon and a linen tablecloth that she drapes over the log between them. She places her stash piece by piece on the crest of the log—Brie cheese, cheddar wedges, Belgian crackers, seedless red grapes, Rainier cherries, chocolate truffles. She opens a split of Veuve Cliquot. She uses two plastic cups, afraid to bring her costly flutes from the inn.

"Beautiful," Bill says. He seems to like the cherries best.

"Do you like the food?" Hulga asks.

"This is very good," he says.

"Do you cook? Buy special cuts, fresh produce, enjoy food when the preparation is done to perfection?"

"I've had the most expensive of cuisine," Bill says. "But I never paid attention to what I thought was best, or why it was considered special. But you've shown me something I'll not forget today." *He is so polite!*

"Do you like the champagne?" she asks.

"Yes. Yes, I do. I don't drink normally. But this is special."

"Is it because of religion, this not drinking?"

"My line of work."

"What do you do?"

"Whatever's available," he says.

She refreshes her glass of champagne; his is barely touched. She raises her glass in a toast. "Prost," she says and smiles. He matches her gesture.

They sit silent among the rustle of sparrows in leaves and the call of a lone warbler high in a giant cedar. The air is still around them but a gentle breeze rustles the forest canopy above them. After some time Hulga says, "Would you like to lay down on the grass? It's dry here. A perfect place to rest."

He smiles and begins to pick up. She worries about her suggestion of lying on the grass together. She wonders if he's offended.

"Did you like my lunch?" she asks hesitantly.

"I did."

"Really?"

"Really."

And she believes him but she worries because she wants it to be true so bad.

That night she is in bed. The only light seeping through shuttered windows on the ocean side is a half moon hovering among a bed of protective stars. She thinks of nothing but her humiliation. Asking him to lie down! God will punish her for her false pride; she has no doubt. She has never been attractive. Never! Not in her fervid days of youth, or the wretched days of her marriage, or now in her declining years. God. What was she thinking? And she cries for herself, cries for her lonely unfulfilled existence. And then, God forgive her, she nurses the injustice of who and what she is. She is racked with hunger now, but her stomach is too nauseous to hold food. Her mind is trapped in self-pity so that she can think of nothing but the empty painful void inside her.

There is a knock on the door. A man slips into the room. She can tell by the ease of his movements it is Bill. She throws back the cover, pulls her nightgown back down over her knees, and prepares to get out of bed.

"Stay there," Bill says, sliding a wicker armchair from near the door closer to her bed. He sits.

She wants to know why he is here but is afraid her voice will reveal her anguish. She lies back and pulls the cover to her chin.

"Mrs. Steinweg..." he begins.

"Don't you remember? That is my maiden name!" She is irritated that he forgot. "My former husband was Mancusi." She knows her voice is laden with her sadness.

"Miss Steinweg, " he says. His hand finds hers under the quilted cover.

She wants him to call her Hulga, or honey bear, or sweetie pie... anything that hints of endearment but she says nothing until the silence separates them, like a meat cleaver through a hambone.

"I must leave..." he starts.

She loses all her confidence, her will to go on. "Now? Tonight?"

"Soon..."

She moans softly. "Stay a little longer..."

"I have to move on," he says.

My God! She never allowed herself to think he would leave. "Is it...?"

"It's nothing you've done, Hulga." It's the first time he calls her Hulga, and she hears compassion that may hold a touch of desire.

There is the sound of a squirrel on the roof of the kitchen, the toilet constantly refilling to the cut off because of the slow leak in the rubber stopper in the tank.

"I've come to really like having you around," she says. She hesitates. "I would miss you," she says. She wants to cry; why can't he see her need, share her attraction? But she holds back tears. She is strong. She'll face this rejection head on. After all, he's a vagrant.

"You are an amazing woman, Hulga," he says.

Her mind jerks with surprise. "What?" *He is mocking me! Maybe not. He sounds sincere.*

"You're attractive. Intelligent. And most of all, you're kind. I thank you for all you've done for me."

She cannot hold back the tears. He moves the chair closer to the bed, reaches under the cover to find her hand. He turns to rest his elbow on the bed where he can be comfortable. His touch is soft and relaxed. She matches her tension as best she can. My God, do her calluses repulse him? She resists pulling her hand away. Not to worry. He is no stranger to the calluses of hard work.

"Would you miss me?" she asks softly.

"Very much," he says. "You've filled the loneliness that haunts me when I travel."

Is there a chance he might like me. Do I dare ask? She holds her breath for a few seconds, dreading humiliation. *He seems like a gentleman.* "Do you find me attractive?" she says.

He doesn't answer as quickly as she would have hoped. "You are attractive, Hulga. In body and soul."

My goodness. She is emboldened by his kindness. Even if not completely truthful, he liked her enough to say it.

She feels the warmth of a smile although her face barely moves. It is too dark for him to see. Then she feels a touch of unwanted shame at how much she wants him to like her. To love her. He must not see her need; she pulls the coverlet up to her nose. She wouldn't survive the mortification if he laughed at her. She'd reveal how desperately she needs him. Silly. It's too dark to see details now; a cloud layer has blotted out the faint, new-moon light that had filtered through the small skylight above the bed. Her heart wouldn't slow down.

"Am I attractive enough? Do you want to make love to me?" she asks, her voice muffled by the covers. She almost hopes he would not hear. He might spurn her for a ridiculous question. *What does he think?* His hand still covers hers beneath the sheets. She waits for a squeeze, a stroke, a sign of affection to relieve her tension. She imagines his conquering his struggles to not reveal the depth of his feelings, and once released, he would reach out and emerge into her with the joy of union. But he does not move or say anything for many seconds. Then he lets go of her hand.

"Don't go," she says desperately. *In the name of God, don't go.*

"I'm not leaving," he says. He stands and undresses, placing his clothes on the chair. He walks to the other side of the bed and slips under the covers to take her in his arms from behind.

Now she is terrified. It's been years since she's had a man. And in her marriage and the years after, she never felt she satisfied a man the way other women boasted. *My God*, she thinks, *what must I do? What does he want? Should I take him in my mouth to stimulate him?* She's never done that. The thought repulses her. But she'd do it to please him. She'd do it if it would hold him to her.

"Relax," he says and she obeys. He holds her still gently but tighter.

It is minutes before he touches her softly...tenderly in tender places. *He does care! How gentle he is. How considerate.* She feels his arousal. He kisses her. She savors the devotion he offers. Her heart slows a little as he lifts her soul into the warmth of a summer sky. Then, as he continues his exploration, her heart races again. She does not think, she feels. And she refuses to admit a fear of loss if it never happens again, a fear that hides in her heart that is filling with escalating joy. She surrenders, willingly, with thankfulness, and with bliss at being alive.

He is exhausted beside her, his arm still encircling her waist, her nightgown in a snarl. She knows her face is flushed from the exertion. But she does not turn away. She smiles at him. She feels worthy. She cannot allow herself to believe he wants to marry her, to be together for the rest of their lives. But the thought will not leave. And she marvels that she does not feel violated as she always had before, and she is not sore from the tension and resistance she had always faced after penetration.

"Was it good?" she asks.

He kisses her.

"Are you going to leave?"

He kisses her again. She fears a "yes." He says nothing, but will he at least stay until sunrise? She prays to God it will be longer.

The next day, Hiram works after breakfast in the dining room for all the guests. In the kitchen, the sink is leaking. Hiram works to upgrade the poorly functioning S-trap with a P-trap.

He felt very comfortable with Hulga last night. He admired her toned body and her stolid, if not attractive, features. And he knew her loneliness, which was not her fault. She still carries her old world upbringing, a more than modest guttural accent, yet she is not unreasonable or opinionated. She loves nature. She works hard at precision and cleanliness and to please her guests. Hiram is determined to stay.

The Inn guests come to the dining room for breakfast. Hulga gathers fresh vegetables and fruit from her small garden near the edge of the property. He hears four of the six guests clearly.

"It was mysterious. Two men came at breakfast to question the guests," a woman guest says.

"Here?" another asks.

"No. In Eureka. Days ago. They were looking for an escaped murderer. I forgot his name. They had pictures. Asked if anyone had seen him. They thought he might stay in bed and breakfasts or motels. Last he'd been seen was in Seattle."

"Had anyone seen him?"

"No. But they handed out cards and pictures. Have you seen anyone suspicious?"

She must have included everyone in the room in the question. There were a number of "no's."

"Were you scared?" a new voice asked.

"Not of the men," the original voice said. "But there is a murderer on the coast. And there are not that many places to stay."

After he knows investigators are near, Bill stays only three more days, working until dinner and eating with Hulga in the kitchen and then taking her to bed when the front door of the inn is locked for the night. In the morning Hulga asks, "Will you stay?" She pauses. "Please stay, Bill."

"Eventually, I must go," he says the next morning. He adds, "I don't want to leave, Hulga."

"Then why?"

"It's not you. It's the life I've been dealt. I'm wanted." *Is he a criminal?* But it makes no difference to Hulga in the face of her love for him. And she will always believe his attraction for her.

On the third day, she doesn't ask about his leaving. She doesn't have time. He is up and dressed while she still holds onto a feigned dreamless sleep. He kisses her closed eyelids. She acts as if just awakening, slowly recovering, but she's been thinking about Bill all night, dreading his departure.

"Goodbye, sweet Hulga," he says. "I'll miss you." And it's true. He sees the goodness and caring in the hard exterior of a woman matured through a foreign society who shunned her as a friend and never respected her honesty and work ethic.

She gasps and weeps softly. "I'll never forget," she says.

He leaves out of the front door of the inn, past guests who prepare morning coffee from a silver urn on a side table with a framed mirror against the hall wall. Hulga follows him to the door, her bare feet denting the pile on the oriental runner, unconcerned that her guests might see through her sheer nightgown. She watches, her shoulder sagging against the doorjamb, as Bill walks down the drive carrying his backpack in his right hand. Where the drive meets the road, he stops, shoulders his pack, and then disappears to the south.

The same morning, in a mixed state of sorrow and spirit-lifting ambition, and after the guests have departed and she has checked the maid's work in the guestrooms, Hulga makes a sign like the sign that brought her Bill—a cardboard rectangle on a wooden stick: "For Sale / by owner."

She dresses in a colorful attractive frock, wears a bracelet and two rings, pulls on hose and squeezes into low heel red pumps. She combs her hair, and pulls back strands from each side of her face with bobby pins. She begins to dream about her campaign to save the environment,

sad that she has no photos of Bill Mason except a cell-phone shot as
he carried baggage for a guest that didn't show his face.

*Hiram went south to Los Angeles, but living there wasn't as friendly as
places he'd been. Many of the homeless were criminals as opposed to mentally
ill or financially strapped and you spent time protecting your possessions
and your life. He moved on to Phoenix, where he stayed for two months. He
saw no evidence that local or federal authorities were looking for him. He
continued to Santa Fe and began to feel that he was in no immediate danger,
that the focus of the search was still on the west coast and the intensity of the
pursuit was decreasing.*

Chapter 52

New York
Paige

Paige interviewed both Billie in Denver and Ann in Louisville for the biography. Billie had done well in the music store where he was now half owner and was proud of the success of his drumstick-making business, which turned a profit. He smiled and said, "I'm my only employee and my only overhead is buying small amounts of wood." Tasha was pregnant with their third child. They lived in a modest house in the suburbs. Billie had had no contact with his father, he said. Paige wasn't sure she believed him, but knew he would never tell her. He seemed to blame the media and Hiram's colleagues more than Hiram for Hiram's troubles.

Paige made an appointment to see Ann at her home. Robert was working, Ann said. Robert was still on probation after his conviction for securities fraud, but had been hired as a low level analyst in a securities firm headed by a college roommate.

Ann had memory loss from her injuries and was not the woman Paige remembered. She wouldn't discuss Jeremy and became agitated when Paige asked even a tangential question about him. She was obviously depressed, her speech hesitant, her mind drifting from the topic under discussion, her movements slow and often without a clear purpose. She was void of anger, it seemed, and consumed with pity and self-recrimination for her plight. Her anxiety seemed pervasive, as if she feared any attempt to act in any circumstance that might result in pain and disaster. Paige wondered if she'd survive. She thought Ann was religious now and probably too afraid to take her own life, but she might just fade away like a muddy puddle in the sun.

In New York, Paige continued to see Sophie regularly. She still enjoyed being with Sophie, and admired her intelligence and drive. She found Sophie thoughtful and compassionate but lonely. Her creative drive was overshadowed by her portrait photography, which had few artistic opportunities. Sophie had lost the passion for discovery and catching the unique images that she'd so successfully captured in her series on the plight of women in Chicago and Asia. She needed to move on. Paige thought photographic journalism would be perfect and she planned to suggest it carefully without seeming pushy.

Max Rojas insisted Paige find out how Hiram was contacting Sophie; Max had no doubts he did it regularly.

On a weeknight, Paige met Sophie in a sushi restaurant they had enjoyed twice before. They sipped Sauvignon Blanc by the glass after they ordered.

"How's the biography coming?" Sophie asked. She held up her glass to the light to appreciate the color.

"I'm discouraged a little. I have huge gaps still. And I'd love to know the details of your father's activity over these two years."

"He would never reveal that. It would mean his capture."

"Not necessarily. Max Rojas knows he's on the move but has no idea where he might be to even search for him."

They sat in silence for many seconds, neither looking at the other.

"Have you heard from your father?" Paige asked.

"Of course not," Sophie replied curtly. "Why do you keep asking?"

"If I could just talk to him."

"For your friend the skip tracer?" Sophie asked.

"That's not fair!"

"She's constantly contacting me. She says she's calling on your behalf."

"I meet with her for consulting. She's not really a friend," Paige said.

"You still want him caught, don't you? You believe he's guilty on all charges. Illegal and improper," Sophie said.

"I'm not sure anymore," Paige said. "The more I write, the more I'm beginning to think your father made mistakes, but that he's not a criminal."

"You believe he's guilty of Jeremy's demise," Sophie said. "You've said you could never forgive him many times."

"You've said that too," Paige said.

"That doesn't mean I don't care for him," Sophie said. "And I'm not sure anymore. After I've seen what Jeremy did to people over time. The news continues to detail the pain of the families. It haunts me. And Ann is destroyed."

"But you still think your father should be punished?" Paige asked.

Sophie stared directly into Paige's eyes. "I don't want you to be the reason he's caught."

"You've been against taking any life!" Paige said. "What's made you change?"

"I still am against capital punishment and abortion... war. But Dad had special circumstances. The murders. Jeremy's suicide attempt. Jeremy's living hell if he became conscious."

"And you believe that makes him innocent?"

"I don't know. But I don't think what he did was evil. That's all."

"But you didn't believe that in the trial."

"I told the truth of what I knew. Nothing more," Sophie said. "I didn't make judgments."

"You said that Hiram said Jeremy should be put out of his misery."

"I don't remember the words exactly."

"That's in the trial transcript. It's public."

"Well, there were circumstances," Sophie said, her voice hesitant.

Paige reached across the table and touched Sophie's hand that was gripping a knife handle. "I'm not accusing, Sophie. I'm trying to understand what's changed you," Paige said.

Sophie released the knife from her clenched hand.

"Really, I didn't mean anything by it," Paige said.

"What has it got to do with the biography?" Sophie asked.

"You're the only one I depend on for a judgment of your father's purpose. Especially if I can't talk to him. You don't think it was premeditated now, do you?"

"It was not premeditated!" Sophie said loudly, and she looked left to right to see if patrons at other tables had heard. She was vacillating between her suspicion of her father's guilt and her growing need for him to be innocent. "I think he was devastated by our talk about Ann on that day," she said.

"His action was justified then because of what Jeremy did to his family and himself?" Paige asked. "Is that what you believe now?"

"I told you. I don't know," Sophie replied more softly.

"Was it revenge?"

"I just don't think he was evil!"

Paige saw change in Sophie. "You've talked to him a lot, haven't you? He's changed your mind."

"Don't accuse me."

"I'm not accusing, Sophie."

"What is it you want, Paige?"

"I want to know how he's changed. After his escape. And I've always wanted justice. And I've come to think he doesn't deserve to rot in jail." Paige looked away. She'd never expressed her doubt out loud this strongly.

Sophie seemed deflated, her anger mostly withdrawn, and she stared at Paige. "I can't believe you. He can't risk contacts with you."

"You mean a lot to me, Sophie," Paige said. "I don't want to upset you."

Sophie drained her wine glass and set it back on the table.

"But you *have* talked to him, haven't you?" Paige said.

Sophie sighed. "All right. Yes. I talked to him."

"Is he all right?"

"I think so. I don't know where he is. And don't think you can find him with phone records. His calls are untraceable. He told me not to try."

"More than once, then?"

Sophie didn't respond, but when Sophie avoided looking at her, Paige was sure. She talked to him regularly. "He uses some prepaid no-contract disposable phones," Sophie said. "I do the same now."

"Billie and Ann too?"

Sophie's silence again made Paige sure that Hiram had contacted them all.

"Look," Sophie began. "We talked for a long time. He wants his side known by the world. He's been working on a memoir. I'm the only person he thinks can help and that he's willing to trust. He wants it published. I said I'd help. I believe he has done a lot of wrong, but I don't think he's guilty of murder."

"Who can you contact?" Paige asked Sophie.

"I've asked the agent who published my books."

"I could make his memoir part of the biography," Paige said. She wasn't exactly sure how that would work, but she knew it could make more than a few editors in different houses envious.

"You wouldn't let it be his own. You've hated him," Sophie said.

"Never hated," Paige said quickly.

"You have. You never gave Dad chances to defend himself. You're always aggressive."

"He deserved better," Paige agreed. "Let me make amends."

"He's talked to me about it. About quality of existence. About dying with dignity, not like some rotting tomato. And he talked about punishment too. He said he believed the living have the right to revenge the killing of innocent people."

"Did he mean assisting in Jeremy's death? Isn't that against your principles?" Paige persisted.

"I told you, I'm not sure now. I think he'd thought it out and made a decision. And I don't think it was all revenge. I think he thought about Jeremy's condition if Jeremy was conscious; Jeremy must have been terrified."

"I'd like to talk to Hiram," Paige said.

"I told you, he will never talk to you or anyone he doesn't trust. That's why he wants me to find a publisher for his memoir. He's determined to build a new life without anyone knowing where he is, even family."

"If I could handle his memoir, I could help him get his points out."

"With the biography?"

"I think so. I've thought a lot about it as I learned more for the biography. I think the public reaction was unfairly harsh, and I think much of what he was accused of in his career was often judged without just consideration by unbiased minds. And people embraced rumor and speculation to vilify him. It affected his euthanasia trial too. He was targeted by activists and any truth was distorted to their wants."

"I don't think he was ever evil," Sophie said again, as if convincing herself.

"I'm beginning to think so too," Paige said. "He lacked caring, sometimes. Lacked consideration of the views and feelings of others. I do believe that. But I don't think he intentionally did harm to Jeremy for selfish reasons."

"He wants money, Paige. For family. We can't free up what's been frozen by the courts. He wants outright sale. Not an advance on royalties."

"If I can't get money from the publisher, I'll pay," Paige said.

"As much as a traditional publisher?"

"As much as I can get. Please call him."

"Not possible... he calls me."

"Then let me know what he thinks."

The next morning, Paige contacted Max Rojas.

"You were right," Paige said. "He's talking to Sophie. And I think probably the other children, too."

"Great!"

"But they won't help. He's careful. Sophie has no idea where he is. And you can't trace his calls."

"I'll work on it. We'll get him. At least he's probably in the States. And with Sophie's contact with him, we've got something to go on."

——◆——

For months Sophie continued to try to find a new publisher. There was no interest—just flat dismissals, unreturned phone calls, and un-answered query letters. With time, the interest in Hiram was waning. She considered Paige again.

But Hiram wasn't interested in Paige. "She doesn't have the smarts. And writing is not her career," he said. "I'd rather you self-publish it."

"I can't do that," Sophie said. "Paige said she would use a number of editors to remain objective. She said she'd make it right."

Hiram was not convinced.

Finally, frustrated and impatient, Sophie told her father by phone on his next call, "I'm sick of dealing with this. Tell Paige what you want. Give her the manuscript."

Hiram told Sophie to keep trying to publish. He'd think about Paige and her biography.

Chapter 53

From Phoenix, Hiram went briefly to Santa Fe, then angled northeast to travel up the east coast, briefly scouting out the coast of South Carolina and North Carolina. But something about the southern culture made him doubt the security of a false identity. He felt an inherent gossip sentiment, everybody wanting to know everything about everyone and with an annoying prying mentality. And it's not always friendly or genuine but more that knowledge will diminish you as a person, especially if you're not from the families immersed in the culture for a few generations. There is a definite need to destroy if you're suspected to be from the Northeast. Sociologists would probably deny it, Hiram thought, but it was true. This dislike of the unknown could eventually bring about scrutiny and reveal him.

He moved through the populated states of New York, Massachusetts, and Connecticut. He briefly looked at New Hampshire and Vermont, but felt both too insular and rustic. He felt paranoid about how others might feel about his inherent standoffishness. He traveled into Maine, along the coast, which was dependent on summer tourism for its economy. He found many people from away who commonly spent only a few months, or even only a few weeks a year in the area. People from away they were, PFAs. And PFAs were treated with a friendly attitude but a certain disinterest that seemed to supersede suspicion. PFAs bought property. Property needed to be maintained in PFAs' absence. And they often bought boats and arts and crafts, and had parties with other people from away. All adding to the economy that would propel locals through what could be long, icy winters... and lives.

Hiram decided on Russell's Point, a historic town where folks from away owned much of the property . The town was heavily dependent on tourists and a renowned ship building industry that produced hand-crafted ocean sailing yachts for competition. He rented a cottage on the harbor. He paid cash until he could open two bank accounts with his new identity. He bought and registered a used car, obtained a driver's license, and tested his passport at the Canadian border on a drive to Quebec City. He stayed weeks before moving on. He joined the Y and used the health club. He studied local history and lore at the college in Brunswick. He invited the attractive widowed professor of history, a native of Portland, to a concert and dinner. He toured the area on local water tours, examined surrounding cities of Camden, Boothbay Harbor, and Wiscasset, went whale watching, spent weekends in Rockland and Damariscotta. He met people at church and introduced himself to neighbors. He opened a mailbox. He made it clear he was looking for a place to retire in a few years, and wanted this to be his permanent residence someday. He would be spending free time here when he could. Then he drifted on, closing up the cottage and hiring a maintenance man recommended by a neighbor. He talked to the sheriff about security for his new place, but really worked to make a friend with a generous donation to the department retirement fund. He left only information about his new identity. Nothing to relate him to his past. He'd grown a full beard again while traveling. He flew or took trains now, and frequently stayed in motels and hotels, using his Seattle identity and paying with credit cards. He wanted to continue his movement and let his new identity in Maine settle to test any potential exposure. He would circle back in a few months at least twice to become a familiar part-time resident, friendly and above suspicion.

In Maine, he always remained clean-shaven, establishing his new appearance that was barely reminiscent of his former self and younger than his actual age. He would never relax, but was feeling more comfortable. He was ready to try to establish a normal existence with an identity as permanent as he could make it.

At the end of the summer in the North East, he headed for New Orleans. He planned to let his new identity in Maine continue to mature until it was as safe as he could make it. He'd settle down in a year or two; he aimed for winter when the native populace was pretty much inside for a number of months and he could make his permanent presence gradually noticed.

Chapter 54

New York
Max Rojas

Almost two months before Hiram arrived in New Orleans, Max delivered a copy of her official report on McDowell for her clients, Paige Sterling and Harmon Tressler, in person at Tressler's office.

"Honestly, we don't know where he is," Max said. "We can't find a trace of him on the West coast. We know he made three short trips to New Orleans over the years on medical business. I don't think he'll risk being around medical personnel. It's a long shot, but he's played the harmonica for a long-time and probably still does. He's a pro-level musician. He had a riff on his answering machine for a number of months a few years ago and you can hear the quality. And we know he sat in New York once with Swamp Water Hopkins. He might be playing in New Orleans and we're going to spend a week looking for him. We're going to contact most of the musicians on the streets and in the clubs. I'm going down personally."

Tressler's gaze to Paige said he doubted Max's competency.

———◆———

New Orleans

Max had a composite list of New Orleans' musicians from the musician's union, ads, and newspapers. She knew her skills to be better than most and thought New Orleans music contacts were the most reasonable way to nab McDowell if he was there. Meticulously she contacted those musicians on the list she could find and asked about McDowell.

Number thirty-eight on the list was singer Maria Petulant. Maria remembered Hiram well, but hadn't seen him since the night she had become enraged and he scared the shit out of her at a plantation up river. "More than a couple of years," she said.

Max gave Maria a card with a number to call. She'd pay for valuable information, Max told Maria, and she gave Maria fifty dollars to entice Maria to get in touch if she saw or heard anything about McDowell.

———◆———

Three weeks later Maria was in the quarter for the gay parade. She and her girlfriend had caught a bite at the Camellia Grill and had walked up to the Cathedral to avoid the crowds already gathering along the parade route before turning left to go to Armstrong Park. She liked her drummer friend and she laughed out loud when he waved from a float, swaying a two-foot long erect papier-mâché penis on a four-foot broomstick from side to side over his head; she pointed him out with pride to her friend.

In the lull between floats, she heard a harmonica toward the river, away from the parade. *Wait!. Is that the shitty doctor dude?* She stopped her friend to listen. For her, a musician's sound was unmistakable, more memorable than a face. The weird bastard freaked her out up river in that plantation hotel. "He was really creepy," she said. But he played a sweet harp with a lot of soul he didn't seem to really have.

With her friend in tow, she followed the sound back toward the old JAX brewery, across the tracks. But the sound was gone and she found no one. As soon as she was home, she called Max Rojas.

"I heard him," she said to Max on the phone in New York.

"Where?"

"Riverside of Jackson Square."

"Did he recognize you?"

"I didn't see him. I just heard him. I looked but he was not playing where I heard him."

"Okay," Max said hesitantly.

"Do I get the $500.00?" Maria asked.

"If the tip turns out to be good," Max said.

Max called the Feds.

Chapter 55

New York
Paige

Paige met Rosenthal at "The Tasty Grape" in SoHo. He looked the same as he had when she last saw him six months ago. He'd been solicitous on the phone. As lonely as she had been while working on the biography and with almost no social life, she was pleased to hear his voice and anticipated being with him for the first time ever. They sipped manhattans before ordering. Rosenthal asked how she was doing.

"I've missed production, presenting on TV," Paige said.

He paused too long for her comfort. He was choosing his words carefully, causing an uncharacteristic delay. "Are you close to getting to McDowell?"

"No real leads yet. Is that why I'm here? McDowell."

"He's still big news."

"That's what I don't like about you, Perry. You're dishonest."

"McDowell's not the reason I asked you. Jesus, I'm making conversation." Rosenthal closed his eyes and thought for a moment. Then he leaned slightly forward. "I've missed you, Paige," he said.

Paige couldn't think of a response. She wanted someone to miss her. Even Perry Rosenthal.

Perry's face intensified. "I mean it Paige. I think about you a lot."

"What exactly does that mean. You missed me?"

"Having you around."

Paige became more flustered. "What did you like about me that made it nice having me around?"

"I've always admired you," he said.

Paige laughed. She was nervous now.

"I'm attracted to you," he said.

Paige was still skeptical. "Amara still with you?"

"It's different now Paige. She's on staff. But I don't see her much anymore. Always accidental."

Is he being straight with me? She was beginning to hope so, more than she thought was wise. Yet, she yearned for more sincerity than she believed Perry was capable of.

They ordered food and talked about their lives alone and with each other. Paige was awed at the intimacy of the moment. Nothing confrontational. No suspicions. No external-world explorations. They just talked about themselves and each other.

After they ordered dessert, Rosenthal turned serious. "Paige," he said, "let's start on a special. Do you have enough on McDowell for an hour special?"

She was immediately suspicious again. What was his real purpose? But she was thrilled by the prospect. "About life on the run?" she said.

"How he disappeared. Remained obscure for so long. How he's avoided state and federal agents."

"We'd fill in with images of where he might be, people he would depend on for help and silence."

"You could interview those who might be involved, if not for facts, for opinions."

"I have enough for more than one special. Will Victor and Condoleezza be available?"

"Of course," Rosenthal said.

She didn't hesitate. "I'll make it good, Perry. I've missed work."

They ordered after-dinner drinks, and Perry turned serious. "I didn't ask you out just to talk about a special," he said. "Trust me. I wanted to be with you again."

Against her will she welcomed his interest in her, even with the risk that insincerity might humiliate her and make her the fool. She was unappreciated as a woman these days, and she wasn't sure, with her feelings muddled, if she was handling this right. Deep down she still didn't like him.

"Do you believe me?" he asked.

She smiled faintly.

Chapter 56

Paige sent her latest draft of the biography to Harmon Tressler. He scheduled a meeting.

"What do you think?" Paige asked.

"Good work," Tressler said.

"I need to have more about after the escape, don't I?"

"It's not all that. I don't like the narrative tone. It has to be less slanted."

"It's not slanted," Paige said.

"It is, Paige. And there's a lot of narrator attitude in it. It's not consistent."

"I report his history."

"It's judgmental. And it changes. Guilty, not guilty. Not good. And you need to talk to him and learn about his life as a fugitive. It's been more than a year now."

"Almost three."

"How has he done that? It's what people are focused on. We'll need it."

"We know he was in Montana. I'll try to get people to talk. But I'm not hopeful."

"Good. And I want to assign one of my best senior editors to help with the writing. Charles Gibson."

"This is my book, Harmon."

"He's not taking over. I just want the editing process active now, while there is still much formative writing to be done."

"It's hard to be enthusiastic," Paige said. "It's a damn good book."

"And you need to get started on illustrations."

"Photographs?"

"Historical, of course. But get contemporary updates. I think we need four sections of photographs at least to support the different phases of his life.

"Coming of age. Schooling. Career. Nemesis. That sort of emphasis?"

"I'd emphasize Nepal too. I'd get photos of that woman he lived with over there."

"His daughter is a professional photographer. She has thousands of shots on life in Nepal."

"Bring her to the production meeting tomorrow, nine AM."

"Would you hire her?"

"If I like her."

———◆———

Sophie rescheduled portrait sessions at the studio and the next morning met Paige in front of her publisher's office on Avenue of the Americas.

"You nervous?" Paige asked.

Sophie shrugged. But she could feel her heart beat. She wanted more than what she was doing in her career now.

They sat around a large, oval, darkly stained mahogany conference table, Tressler at one end, Paige and Sophie to his right, and Charles Gibson to his left. A secretary sat behind Tressler in a straight back chair to take notes.

Tressler outlined what he wanted to accomplish in the meeting. Sophie glanced at Charles Gibson when she could without being rude. Late thirties, sandy-colored hair parted on the right, professionally cut but with a front lock that seemed to stubbornly flop down on his forehead. She disliked his privileged look—old New York with deep family wealth and the heritage of stellar political careers. He dressed in a charcoal English wool pin stripe three-button suit with a pale lavender button-down shirt and an odd plum colored tie with a Mondrian-like design. He sat straight in the chair, his hands clasped in his lap. He looked athletic, in control, yet in no way tense. Sophie had to discipline herself not to stare at his hazel eyes, which were intent but quizzical. She didn't like the touch of arrogance in his demeanor and his speech and she didn't envy Paige for having to work with him.

"You don't have to see the daily drafts, do you?" Paige was saying to Charles.

"Weekly drafts with copies to me," Tressler said.

Sophie felt Paige's pain from the sound of her voice. Tressler and Charles were taking control.

Tressler asked Sophie questions about her photography. Sophie showed him examples of her work in Chicago and Nepal. Tressler wanted to start composing the photographic sections. "And start taking photos of workplace, family, properties, favorite recreational spots." He emphasized that in the biography they would be supplementing contemporary shots with all the historical photos they could find.

"Isn't it too early to choose? It will depend on text emphasis," Paige said. "We're not that definitive yet."

"I want excessive redundancy. Can you begin?" Tressler asked Sophie.

Sophie was pleased she'd been chosen. She nodded.

"Paige, you get with Charles to suggest shots needed and to research historical shots," Tressler said. "Sophie, you can work with our illustration department."

"Could I work alone on this?" Sophie asked.

Tressler looked at Charles. "Does that work?" he asked.

Charles nodded.

"Work with Charles in editing existing photos and with composition of the photos still needed," Tressler said.

Tressler closed the meeting. Other staff members entered the room as Sophie and Paige left.

"That was short," Sophie said.

"We're not important in their schemes of success," Paige said.

Chapter 57

Sophie and Paige went to meet Charles at his office. He led them to a room with projection equipment in the art department on the sixteenth floor.

Paige had brought copies of the current manuscript draft. Sophie had photos on her computer that she could Bluetooth project onto a screen. All had computers with internet connections and direct access to a color printer.

Paige had highlighted in the manuscript a number of sections she wanted to discuss for illustration.

"I think the foundation gala would be a good source," she said.

"When was that?" Charles asked.

"A couple years ago."

"Do you have photos?"

"There were many photographers there. And many celebrities," Paige said.

"We'll contact the foundation. I'll assign an investigator to track down resources. You'll need to find what we might need. I'll look for sources we might use," Charles smiled. "Is there a page size you prefer for formatting?" he added, looking at Sophie.

"I can work with what you suggest," Sophie said.

"We'll have to credit all photos from other photographers," Charles said. "And if we Photoshop any changes, even collages or montages, we'll have to have written permission to publish the change."

"I'll need legal advice for the permissions," Sophie said.

"I'll send legal with you when you make arrangements. Do everything right up front so that we don't have to backtrack when we're in production."

The following week, Paige called Sophie. "Hi. Free tonight for dinner?" Paige asked.

"Can't tonight," Sophie said. It was the first time she had ever turned down an invitation from Paige.

"Saturday then?"

"I can't."

"Do you have a boyfriend?" Paige laughed.

Sophie felt bad. She had no friends really. Paige was her only social contact these days. "I'm rowing in New Jersey."

"You? With a crew?"

Sophie resented the belittling tone. "I'm competing next month for the first time. I'll get back in touch," Sophie said.

Two weeks later, Paige called again and asked Sophie to go with her to Lincoln Center.

"I can't, Paige, I'm going sailing with a friend."

"Where?"

"Long Island."

"With a friend?" Paige sounded as if she didn't believe Sophie could have a friend. Sophie got angry. She didn't like Paige's new imperious tone.

"She's a good athlete. Works in ticket sales at Radio City Music Hall."

Sophie was making friends now. She was busy getting healthy. She'd submitted some of her photographs to national competitions. And she was feeling good about herself. God, it felt like breathing in spring air at sunrise.

"What does your father have to say?" Paige asked.

"Really, Paige. I've told you..."

"I still need to talk to him about the biography."

Sophie hung up.

Sophie talked to Hiram the next day.

"She still wants to talk to you about her biography about you. And I think she wants your approval."

"I've thought about it," Hiram said. "I can't turn it over to Paige Sterling. She's not exactly a friend."

"She has her faults, but I think she's changed her ideas about you and Jeremy."

"Changed?"

"I don't think she thinks of it as murder anymore."

"What do you think?"

"It's complex. The reasons. But I don't think it was criminal."

"Even I'm never exactly sure what it was," Hiram said. "But it wasn't all revenge and punishment. Jeremy really had no life. And after what he did, he didn't have any rights to ruin Ann's life any more than he had already."

"Well, neither Paige or I think it was murder."

"You like Paige now?"

"She irritates me at times. But I do like her. She's certainly dedicated and I think tries to be an honest journalist in a pit full of dishonest vipers."

"I can't forget she came down hard on me about the foundation and the research. And the book on Nepal errors."

Sophie held her response. She wasn't sure she knew the truth.

"Any word from a publisher?" Hiram asked.

"I can't charm them now that they've put my book on the shelf. I checked with my publisher again for the Asia series."

"What happened?"

"They said my photos were great for a mostly female readership of coffee table books ten to fifteen years ago. And times have changed. Photos now need an edge, need the tension of fear and pain of victims in slavery, not finding beauty in the ugliness of their world. That beauty is only in the lens of the photographer, not in the reality of their existence. I didn't agree. I said I gave them the cultures that isolated and imprisoned women. They said they didn't need the haughtily beautiful vapid stares of illiterate mothers of ten children surrounded by natural wonders. They needed the sense of a holocaust survivor, or a rape victim, or a mother grieving the loss of her only son on a purposeless battle mission."

"They couldn't make money with photographic displays on any subject anymore," Hiram said. "Publishing is not concerned with work of quality, only a profitable sales potential for the outrageous and provocative. Don't be discouraged. Keep pushing them."

"I'm sure they're not going to change their minds about your memoir either."

"Did you look for other possibilities?" he asked.

"No one is interested. Paige may be your last resort."

Chapter 58

Weeks later, Max Rojas listened to a recording in her office of Sophie and Paige having a conversation in Central Park near the Metropolitan Museum of Art the day before. An agent trailing Sophie easily captured all that was said with advanced technology effective at recording from distances of up to two hundred yards.

"He still wants a commercial mainstream publisher," Sophie said. "I've given up."

"A publisher you can't find," Paige said. "Did you tell him again that I want to work with him on a biography?"

"He doesn't trust you and he's so proud of his memoir."

"Did you tell him you trust me?"

There was a pause in the recording where only the rustling of the wind in the trees could be heard.

"I'm not sure I do trust you, Paige."

"We're friends, Sophie."

"Really? You're still working with independent investigators with direct contact to federal agencies. You know more about my father than the family does."

Paige didn't respond right away. Max smiled to herself listening to the taped conversation that was a fraction of all of Sophie's conversations investigators had recorded, analyzed, and were on file. But this interchange between Paige and Sophie might pry loose special information.

"You can't convince me you won't betray him." Sophie said. "You haven't changed. You're using me, just as you used my father for your own personal gain."

After another long pause, Paige said: "I am not working with anyone now to help in his apprehension," she said.

"I don't believe you," Sophie said. "And I'll warn Father whenever I can."

Not good, Paige, Max thought, marking the recording for further use when next talking to Paige. *Don't reveal sensitive data. Just be her friend.*

"You are my friend, Sophie," Paige said. "I love being with you. And I love what you do and how successful you've been," Paige said.

"You're using me!"

"I don't know how to convince you, but it's not true."

Oh, my, Max thought. *Paige Sterling hasn't been straight with me.*

"Don't send him back to prison," Sophie said.

"I will never do that," Paige said.

That's a lie, Max thought. She grinned to herself at Paige's lie, at knowing everything that was going down. Paige would reveal McDowell, whether she meant to or not.

"That can't be true," Sophie said.

There was again silence on the recording except for an approaching group with hysterical laughs and frequent swear words. When the group had passed, only the breeze in the trees was heard again. Finally Paige spoke, her voice cracked with emotion. "It's not true, Sophie. My boss does want the interview but now I only want to help your father get his word out."

Okay, Max thought. *Tell her what you want, as long as you let us catch the creep.*

Sophie seemed to be crying. "I can't believe you. What about the TV special? You'll make a bundle if he's caught," she said.

"I don't think I'll ever finish that," Paige said. "I'm not sure we won't present bias as truth. I'm not going to do that anymore."

That's going a little too far, Max thought, unsure of Paige's value now. But Max was pleased with the performance of her new spy technology.

Chapter 59

By late summer in New Orleans, Hiram plays rhythm harmonica and drums mostly on the street as backup. He doesn't think the interest in finding him is intent now and he feels comfortable playing solo again. He stakes out at Jackson Square.

How **Gatemouth Willie Brown** met Hiram McDowell

Gatemouth Willie Brown coughed into the microphone on a boom from a chrome stand with a black painted metal base and exhaled smoke he'd inhaled from the lit cigarette in his left hand. His right hand gripped his battered Gibson electric guitar by the neck to keep it steady. A small portable speaker amplified an eerie inhuman sound. He sat alone on a city bench in Jackson Square, on the Cabildo side. The grey sky blocked the sun and trickled a light misty drizzle, more relief from the heat than a bother. Tourists were sparse. He quit playing until he might gather a crowd, make a few music lovers put a little something in his Cafe du Monde coffee can for playing something they thought was New Orleans—special for them. But it wasn't much New Orleans jazz that he played. It was mostly Delta, some folk tunes, and a lotta just strumming what he felt like at the moment. White tourists weren't special to him and he didn't really care what they thought about his music except whether they might give up a little change, mostly ones, but maybe even a five or a ten. But big bills like fifties was like charity, and he didn't cotton to white folks treating him like charity. But he was low on cash. He'd take anything today. His wife was bad sick and needed a doctor.

Blacks rarely roamed around in the French Quarter where the

tourists clumped, except the punks, and it didn't make no difference 'bout the punks not helpin' a brother 'cause even Black got-the-stash almost never would put out even a dime. Besides the punks didn't have nothing to give that wasn't stolen. No, sir. Willie's life was tied to the whites when it came to money. Pissed him off too... ever since he first learned about whites when he stood about hound-dog high sixty-three years ago. But this day a white dude came into his life. Arrogant, too, like he was superior.

This white guy all beard and bushy-headed come toward Willie out of Pirate's Alley wearing pants with holes in the knees and a plaid shirt with buttons missing —like he crawl out of a Dumpster—and a wrinkled Panama hat with the brim down in the front so you only see his eyes when his head tilt back. He'd been in the alley for a while leaning against the cathedral-wall fence just staring. With all that hair on his face you couldn't tell what he was feeling, but he had these piercing eyes, cold like he don't be liking black folk. He don't say nothing, just hold up a harp, a "Big River."

"Split the take?" the man say. He don't talk like a crazy or even a down and out. He got some schoolin'. Probably he run from the law.

"Don't need no sidemen," Willie say.

The man sat down on the bench no more than a couple feet away.

"Said I don't need no help," Willie said strong.

"No law against me sitting here."

"You on my spot, my man. This my spot for a long time."

"Not on your 'spot.' I'm on my spot next to your spot. And I'll put my hat out for change in front of me if you don't want to work together."

"Look, my man. No playing. This is all I got."

"Don't bullshit me," the man said.

"I'm straight with you."

"You're on welfare. Probably got social security. Maybe a pension. Maybe got a woman turning tricks. Living in the Treme and liking life just fine."

"I don't like you," Willie said. "I be's young, I whoop you ass."

"Don't think so," the man said.

A tour group was walking down from the corner of Charters and St. Ann. Willie turn the knob to up on his amp and begin playing, kicking his money can out into the path. The white dude next to him put down his Panama a little farther out in front but a few feet from Willie's can, turning it top down to take money. Then the dude puts on shades he takes out of his shirt pocket; they sit crooked on his face cause they bent and cracked, like he sat on them.

Fucking honkie, Willie think.

So Willie's got the thumb on the downbeat on the low string in open tuning, and he's using his first and second fingers to carry an upbeat for rhythm, changed in with a little melody and a slap on the heel of his hand that with the amplifier sound like a gunshot. He ignore the white guy best he can but he see's him out the side of the eye sucking in on a note here and there on his harp, getting the pitch. He change his harp then, taking another—a Horner Blues—out of his jacket pocket. Willie start playing quick. The tourists getting close. The crowd slow to a stop like black birds swooping in for a roost, all gathered round looking at Willie, so Willie up his energy a little. But the tourist be looking through Willie after one chorus, eyes jerking around like they lost where Willie was. So Willie sing a song, and for a moment the group look back to him... but not for long. A few people in the back of the bunch of music lovers already start leaving with nothing in Willie's can.

Shit, the white dude going be blowing over Willie's guitar and the white dude start tapping his foot hard so his beat crush out Willie's faint slow pulse and the dude start wailing, sounding like a fast train's wheels clacking at a spur crossing. Then he's puttin' in fill, bending notes easy as a willow branch. Damn if them tourists freeze like they wax figures in that fake history museum on Bienville. They staring at the dude. The folks that start off going away from Willie turn back, coming to look at the dude. Now the tourists giving angry looks at Willie, irritated Willie's sound invading the dude's and looking like to bust Willie's guitar and turn it to ash. Willie stops playing. *The dude's not bad, goddamn it.* Willie ain't heard many like him. Pissed Willie off, white man play a beat like that and make it sound joyful-sorrow with sound of a colored parade band coming back from a funeral. The white guy stop, then pick up a slower tune, tourists throwing green into his hat like he's collecting for the church. So Willie ain't in tune with the guy's harp, but he don't like being outshined and he start slapping out a rhythm on the strings with the heel of his hand, and in seconds he lay the guitar flat on his lap so he can use both hands to pound out a shuffle with that slow Mardi Gras Caribbean sounding beat. He kick his can out a little farther .

Shit. The dude never look at him, never even give him no apperceived eye-glance. And the tourists still reaching out them arms and dropping paper into that dude's hat. In two tunes Willie's sure the guy make fifty bucks. Fifty! Some blimp of a woman drop two quarters into Willie's can. Clunk, clunk on the bottom. No one else. Nothing more than two quarters for Gatemouth Willie Brown.

The dude play maybe half an hour making money. The crowd growing. Then he put the harp in his right side pocket, reach down to take the cash out of the hat and stuff it in his left pocket, take off his shades, then put that hat on top his head and walk off. Goddamn if he don't never look back. Not one time he give a wave or call thanks to Willie for backing him on a couple tunes. And Willie wants to drown that white man in the Mississippi, push him into the wheel of a paddle steamer. Yes sir, that dude don't deserve no mercy.

Next day Saturday, after the flow of drunk guys in town for the Saints' game slow down, Willie slide around the corner onto Saint Ann where Tuba Fats playing with Henry Thibodeaux on clarinet and some sixteen-year-old kid outta the ninth ward blowing a valve trombone. Stupid. Tourists don't like no valves on a trombone. They like the slide, the growl, even when it sound like shit.

"You see that white dude on harp?" Willie ask Fats. Fats shake his head no.

"Well, he still playing on my spot."

"He fucking know how to blow that motherfucker."

"Well, he ain't s'pose to be taking my tips."

"He talk to you?"

"Maybe three words full."

The next day, the white dude's back mid afternoon. Fucker sit the same place next to Willie's spot. Willie kick his can a little farther out. Today Willie bent on turning some bread when the dude playing, to back the white dude, keep him from hogging. Then he pull out his bottleneck slide and put out a little melody on a top string where he don't need to change tuning, just slide on the string trying to make it sound good. The dude never look at him. Don't even glance to say he like or don't like it.

After a half-hour, the dude clear his hat and cram cash into his pants' pocket *Damn. Must be seventy-five dollars.* But nothing for Willie. It's racist. No count about the money. The dude is a fuckoff racist. Hating Negroes. Taking advantage.

The dude come back three days in a row. After the first day, Willie keep putting out his can. He get a little, but the tourists giving most to the dude. And that ain't the usual for the white guys crowdin' in on a black man's gig in the Quarter. Them tourists pity the blacks playing the street. They give to music men like giving money to eight-year-old pickaninnies tap dancing for coins. Guy still don't talk much. Willie's sister-in-law say the white man a murderer. But Willie don't see that in him. Maybe he steal, but Willie don't see him killing nobody.

So Willie decide to broach the guy. "Hey, mister, how about you splittin'?"

"You said you didn't split."

"I changed my thinking."

The dude shrug. But he don't share nothing with Willie whose can still only get a few coins and rare green, nothing higher than a one.

On a Friday, Willie take the wife to the doctor early in the morning. They got to ride the streetcar to City Park. "Come on, Hermonie," he say but she staring out of her wheelchair like her skull gone empty. "We going to the doctor," he say. That git her and she begin wailing and moaning. She saying something like "Nah" but only Willie knows she's real upset cause he's been listening to her crazy talk for so long. She got dimension since hurricane Camille and that be's hard to take care of cause Willie ain't got no money for the doctors she need.

But the next day Willie back on his spot. Well, the dude, he don't show. And then Willie get confused 'cause he likes the guy's playing, even though the honkie ain't generous with his take. And in truth,

Willie make more with his can when he's playing next to the dude collecting with his hat than when Willie making all the sound himself.

After the lunch crowd, Willie take a smoke break with Tuba Fats. "That guy asking 'bout you," Fats say.

"What you tell him?"

"I tell him you taking Hermonie to the doctor."

"None a his business."

"He ask. Like he want to know you do drugs, steal from the church collection plate. Stuff like that."

"What you say?"

"I tell him I don't know you real good. But I tell how sick Hermonie be."

"Don't be telling him no more. He not like a bro."

"But he blow good."

Well, the dude come back. Willie decide he going sing a song while the guy wipe out his mouth with a tissue over his finger before blowing his harp, like cleanin' shit out the stable before puttin' the horse in. Then the dude just sit back and listen to Willie, the dude's hat still on his head down over his eyes, his legs stretch out.

Willie finish his song and light up a joint he been saving.

"Sing that again," the dude say.

"I just done it."

"Just sing it again."

So Willie knock the glow off the tip of his joint and put the butt in his shirt pocket for later and start singing again. The dude's got the right Eb harp out of his pocket and he play along cross harp, not like he want to solo, but like he toting a cotton bale delicately down a wharf with some wharf rat working an hour rate. Bale be heavy and need to be tipped just right to ease the weight, and the feet need to set just right on each step testing the wood planks for imperfections to avoid losing control. It take feel; can't be learned. *The dude got it.* And the tourists come like swarm of roaches drop off banana leaf trees in the Garden District. And they looking at Willie who's trying his best to look like a lead. Willie kick his can a little farther out while Willie singing and the guy back him for maybe only the second time. Damn if the greens don't start almost flowing over the side of Willie's can. And from that song on, for many days, Willie sing and make money, the dude back him. And when the dude leave, he divvy up equal the bills from his hat and give 'em to Willie no matter how much them tourists put into Willie's coffee can that still sit separate out in front of him.

Every few days the dude come for more than a month. He might teach Willie a song, or tell Willie how to play one of his standards better than he doing. Tuba Fats bitch at Willie making money cause it cut down on Fats' take... Fats been the big draw on the square for more than a decade, and Fats don't take to be second best.

A week later it still hot, and Willie hear the word pass and creep through the Quarter—through the artist vendors hanging them pictures on the fence around Jackson square, pictures of the cathedral and the Cabildo, and them drawings of famous people that no one know who they are 'cause they all look drawed the same, and the tarot-card readers, the living statues, and tap dancing seven-year-olds with beer can scraps sewed on the soles of their sneakers and scamming tourists for tips –"Hey, Mister. I bet you a quarter I can tell you where you got them shoes." *"Okay."* "They on your feet!" *"Aw, Jesus."*

The whisper come through all them folks like a wind before one of them storms like red-hot Tobasco. The word be out. "A guy showing like I-don't-be-dressed-like-no-cop coming down Royal" go around the square in a flash, then up and down Decatur, out to the park across the streetcar track. Willie and the dude hear the word. They look around. Willie spot 'em first. Then dude see 'em too. Jeans, open-neck shirts with a collar. Not tourists. And blue sports jackets with a bulge near the heart; they carrying heat.

The dude take cash from his hat and put it in Willie's can. Then he reach into his jacket inner pocket and pull out an envelope he give to Willie. Willie hurry to hide the envelope in the lining of his guitar case so the cops don't see nothing when they walk from the tarot-card reader, who smiling like she ain't never had dope in her possession since Christ be born in Bethlehem. In seconds, before the cops see him, the dude disappear into the shadow of Pirate's Alley. The dude hold back long enough to see the cops coming. Willie looks down, shake his head when the two dickheads be asking him questions. They not locals. Feds maybe. Willie see the dude shoulder his pack and the dude's gone when the cops move on to jaw on Tuba Fats. Fats just smile and say he don't know nothing.

Willie never see the dude again. In the envelope is enough money to add to Medicare and welfare and get Hermonie into a nursing home for a while where she be watched 24-7 so she don't hurt herself. And Willie's coffee can still doing good filling up on its own now without the dude, like the dude left some good vibes in Willie's axe when he disappeared. And soon, Willie's playing bring swarms of tourists that throw money his way, like he's a healing cave at that Lord's place in France.

Chapter 60

While in New Orleans, Hiram arranged for a new identity with new papers that he was more confident would conceal him, and that he would use when he was permanently located.

He was sure the cops in the Quarter on the day he stopped playing with Gatemouth Willie Brown were out for drugs, and not him. He was happy in Louisiana and he went to Lafayette to play harmonica and washboard in a Zydeco band. He stayed in a motel run by a friend of the fiddle player, living quarters where he didn't need documents and he could work on his memoir, which was now more than 200,000 words.

It was quiet in Lafayette, and Hiram continued to dream of finally settling down when he got his last identity papers. He'd definitely decided to settle in Maine. He'd made three trips to make himself known, establishing an identity, working as a guide for climbers in Acadia National Park. He'd volunteered for neighborhood watches and attended a church. He donated to the library and attended book club readings. He liked the librarian and often joined her for coffee at the Ebb Tide, a fish chowder, home-cooked-food restaurant that served free coffee when it was snowing. It was a society foreign to his former existence, but it was out of the mainstream and people lived their own insular lives with rare curiosity about strangers who they ironically depended on to feed their economy. He knew he'd be happy there.

Maria Petulant

Maria was back on the habit. She hadn't received any money from Max Rojas and she needed cash. She called Max.

"Where's my five hundred dollars? You've had plenty of time to catch him," she said to Max's answering machine.

Max called her back from New York the next afternoon when Maria was still in bed asleep after a late night gig.

"We haven't caught him yet," Max said.

"Well, I'm right about him being here."

"You've seen him?"

"No. But I know a musician's sound. In the Quarter."

"You need to see him," Max said. "Keep looking."

"You owe me," Maria said.

"When it leads to capture."

"He's here, I tell you," Maria said.

"Call me when you see him!"

The lying bitch. She promised cash. Maria had been listening out for Hiram McDowell for months. Even spent time walking the Quarter during the French Quarter Festival. She hadn't seen him or heard him for six weeks. "I'll be back in touch," Maria said before Max hung up.

———◆———

A month later Maria had a gig at the Shrimp and Oil Festival singing with a New Orleans traditional band—"Early in the Morning," "Second Line," stuff like that—and she heard McDowell's sound buried in a zydeco band near the river. She was on stage between numbers when she heard Hiram and she left in the middle of a tune to track him down. She found him in minutes, saw him playing in an adjacent tent, couldn't recognize his face from all the hair, but he was the right height and the sound was his. She called Rojas. "He's here," Maria said.

"Stay with him."

"He'll be playing tomorrow and I think the next day. Least the festival's that long. You coming?"

"Keep in touch with me every time you see him or hear him. I'm on my way."

"You owe me a thousand dollars for this."

Rojas broke the connection.

Hiram

It was late the next day when Hiram saw Maria on stage. *Damn it.* He blocked his face with his hat. She probably couldn't recognize him at this distance in a crowd. And the stage lights were in her eyes. Still, he'd have to leave, but after his last gig tonight. He couldn't let his musician friends down without warning.

————◆————

It was past midnight on the last night of the festival. The crowds were thinning except at the music venues. The zydeco band played in a canvas tent with a stage and seating for more than two hundred on wooden folding chairs. Hiram played harp and washboard behind the front line next to the drummer and the acoustic bass. He saw Maria enter the tent. She was plainly visible in the glow from the stage lighting. And he saw the woman from Montana, the one with Paige Sterling. He'd been found.

He dropped slowly to his knees moving to his right behind the bass. The tune was almost finished. The crowd attention was on the front line and the singer. He unstrapped the washboard and left it at the edge of the stage platform. He lowered himself down three feet to the dirt. Bent over, he shuffled the ten feet to the tent edge. On his belly, he squeezed under the edge of the canvas to the dark exterior that faced the river. He paid a man for a balloon-tired bicycle and headed for Lafayette. An hour later, he had his pack and his traveling gear and was on the road west. He planned to soon head North, go through Mississippi in territory he knew well, trek through Arkansas.

He rested for only short times for more than two weeks, until he felt he had erased any chance of that woman tracing his movements. He was moving to the less populated states of Northern Nevada, Northwest California, Idaho, and Wyoming.

Chapter 61

Winona Payman meets Hiram traveling as Pete Lake

Sixty-one-year-old Winona's firm, trim glutes settled on the top step of two unpainted wooden steps that sank two inches into the desert dirt after years of being the only entrance to her trailer home through the side door. The trailer sat on a four-acre lot that had no boundary fence, or any markings for that matter, just twenty-eight trailers scattered and angled to one another in the northwest corner where the hookups were. The trailer park with no name was owned by a sixty-year-old wizened bachelor who tended his bar in Elko and showed up at the first of every month in Winnemucca to collect rents, but never in between.

Winona was thin and limber. With her forearms resting on her thighs, she cradled a glazed pottery mug with a missing handle between her knees. The aroma of black coffee in a tin pot over a butane gas two-burner stove surrounded her. The white cotton shift —thin and stretched—was crumpled high on her thighs and did not hide the outline of her panties or sagging, once-ample breasts. She contemplated with fondness a '77 faded-red Ford pickup truck with flat tires and a tailgate down with the bed loaded with cardboard boxes wrapped in plastic to protect against the weather. The motor hadn't run for more than two years but it served its purpose to store pots with succulents and cacti she brought in from the desert on her plein air painting excursions.

The sun burned a hole in the morning blue sky well above the horizon, and she squinted when she looked up to see her neighbor Kitsy, a plump short woman in shorts and a tee shirt, coming down a worn, grassless path from the second trailer to her left. Kitsy was carrying a metal mug with a handle and coffee hot enough to steam. Winona moved over on the steps to give room to Kitsy, who sat without speaking. They sipped coffee for many minutes.

"There's someone in that abandoned camping trailer in among them trashed cars on the southeast corner," Kitsy said.

"No one could live there," Winona said.

"I seen him from afar on my walk this morning."

"Maybe that government surveyor's back."

"He weren't the kind to come back to a trailer he left more un two years ago."

"Well, it's no harm," Winona said.

"What if he's a murderer? He rape people? Steal? No normal man live in a rusted out camping trailer too small to stretch out in."

"Call Harold then."

"I called Harold. He's down a deputy. Can't take the time."

"Harold scares me sometime, Kitsy," Winona said.

"We never find someone good to be sheriff."

"He's mean as a snake."

"Well, he'll ease my mind, mean or not. Can you call him? My phone's cut off now."

Winona put her hand on Kitsy's arm and nodded.

"Obliged," said Kitsy.

Sheriff Harold came by Winona's trailer the next afternoon. He wore pointed-toe white-on-black tooled leather boots, jeans, a plaid shirt and his deer-skin brown wide-brimmed Stetson with a sheriff's badge pinned on the front. "Ain't nothing there now," he said. "Someone looked to have slept there recently. But not last night. It's a piece a junk but he'd cleaned up the inside some. Cooking maybe over a sterno. Found a can there."

"You know it was a man?" Winona asked.

"No place for woman to want to go."

"Kitsy's scared."

"Got nothing to ease her worry," Sheriff said. "No doubt someone's been there. Can't tell if he's still there. Call if either of you sees him again. Maybe I'll get to talk to him." He paused. "You got a gun, Winona?"

"I don't believe in guns."

"Well, maybe you can find something to protect yourself. Wouldn't feel good something happened to you."

"Can you check in on Kitsy at night? She'd appreciate it."

"Kitsy take care of herself."

"She's scared of the people around her sometime. Make her feel better to have you look in."

"Ain't got enough help to be babysitting the likes of Kitsy."

"Maybe just look in on the park sometimes."

"It's private property. Needs its own security."

"We take care of each other, Sheriff. But we need to know the law's around."

"We crush crime in the county pretty damn good, Winona."

"Just to give us a feel that we got protection."

"Can't make folks feel different. They're protected best there is."

"Thank you, Sheriff."

"In the name of God. As long as I know you. I'm Harold. Don't be saying Sheriff. Make me feel like the enemy."

Winona smiled. "Harold," she said. Calling him Harold didn't come easily. He was one creepy specimen of male macho.

A couple of weeks later the Sheriff came by Winona's.

"You seen anymore of the guy in that trailer."

"I think he's all right. Kitsy talked to him. Said hello to him when she saw him walking toward that junk pile."

"I'll walk down there, see if there's anything about."

"I'll go with you, Sheriff."

"You think you'd make a deputy? Woman on patrol?" he laughed.

"Get me a police hat," Winona smiled. "I could use the pay."

"No pay. Just the honor," the sheriff said.

"Rather have a badge and some money than honor!" Winona said. *Sheriff doesn't see any sarcasm in that*, she thought.

"Lookee there," the sheriff said, pointing to a rabbit that knew he'd been spotted and froze in fear. The Sheriff unholstered his revolver, steadied his arm, and took aim.

"No. Don't," Winona cried.

But the trigger was pulled, the shot released. The rabbit fell over kicking and making a pitiful high pitch scream before going limp and silent.

The sheriff turned the breathless creature over with the point of his boot. "Got him in the heart," he said. "Aimin' for his head, still ain't bad for fifty feet. It's new. My Smith and Wesson Magnum.

Winona didn't speak as the sheriff walked back. "Coyote will eat him."

They walked on in silence.

They were coming up on the trailer in among maybe fifty rusted, crushed, and mangled vehicles, mostly autos except for a pickup truck and a few vans. The trailer rested on a single two-wheel carriage, both tires flat. The side door was missing the hinges. The hinges that remained were now brown with rust. The trailer back was slanted and the front curved... shaped like a comma facedown. On the back was the only window, cracked and gray-opaque.

"He been here recent," said the sheriff, pointing to a circle of ash from burnt-stick pieces that had been rubbed indistinctly and scattered with a boot.

The sheriff looked inside the trailer. "He keep it clean a trash. Give him that," he said.

"Is this dangerous? Him staying here?"

"I ain't no prevaricator for the future. But seems he'd done something by now if he was going to."

"Why would a man sleep here? That place for homeless in Elko is still open, isn't it?" Winona asked.

"Far as I know."

"I wonder why he's here."

"On the run, I'd say. Don't want to be found."

"Isn't this illegal?"

"Hard to jail a man for sleeping in a junkyard. And we got too many deadheads in town already."

"Even to identify him? Take his fingerprints or something?"

"We got a way to do that. But it ain't worth the time without some reason."

"Maybe you can drop by more often. See if he's here. Take him in."

"I'll try for you, Winona. And give us heads up the moment you see him. We'll check him out for you best we can."

"We'll keep an eye out," Winona said before they turned to walk back. She tried to remain upbeat, but the vision of the bloody rabbit carcass was fixed in her mind.

———◆———

Weeks later, Winona took the bus to Reno to buy artists' supplies. She was gone for the day and got back late at night. Next morning Kitsy came over as usual to sit with Winona on her steps. They drank two cups of coffee each in silence. Then Kitsy spoke. "That man. He back," she said.

"You saw him?"

"I talked to him."

"And?..."

"He fixed that window wouldn't open over the sink. Got the toilet to flush with the handle back in place. Don't have to reach down in the tank no more."

"I'll call the Sheriff. He said he'd check him out. Is he still here?"

"Yep. Said he'd be by today to jack up the side of the trailer so the floor don't tilt no more."

"You trust him?"

"Much as you trust any man."

"I'll call the Sheriff," Winona said again. She started to get up to go inside for her phone but Kitsy put her hand on Winona's arm with enough force that Winona sat back down and picked up her coffee cup.

"Don't think he deserve that, Winona. He doing good. He rented a double wide from Mr. Parson. Paid him cash up front. And he keeps out of sight of us and everybody. He hurtin' no one."

"But you don't know him."

"He's a good man. Down on his luck likely. Let's leave him be for a while."

Winona sat quietly thinking. There was a risk. She couldn't forget that.

"You be painting here today?" Kitsy asked.

Winona nodded.

"I'll bring him by. You can make your own mind straight out. "

"Has Sheriff Harold been by?"

"Ain't seen him in more than a month, and that was in town."

"And you don't think this man is a criminal?"

"Don't know what he done, but he don't deserve to be turned over to the law. I'm pretty right about that."

Winona thought for a moment and didn't object. Kitsy was good in judging people. She'd learned by her mistakes over the years. And she was honest to the core.

The man said his name was Pete Lake. Winona found him reserved but friendly. He was appreciative of a cup of coffee. He spoke well—certainly educated but vague on his past. She showed him her art work, those ready for a show in Ogden, Utah next month and many others in progress. He seemed interested but expressed no unchecked exuberance. He commented on the nature scenes, the mountains, the desert, the vast landscapes that made the bulk of her reputation and sales.

They sat at an unpainted, weathered picnic table near Kitsy's trailer. Kitsy made brownies for the occasion and showed Winona the repairs Pete had made.

"I was wondering if I could fix up that van," Pete said. He pointed to a weathered, rusted VW van from the 1960s that was parked on the gravel bed next to the unpaved drive that led to the highway about half mile north. "Does it run?" Pete Lake asked Kitsy.

Kitsy shook her head. "Not mine. Belong to Winona."

"The tire went flat," Winona said. "I haven't used it in couple months. Kitsy takes me in her pick up." She waved toward Kitsy's trailer where a Chevy pick up was parked.

"Who lives over there?" Pete asked, nodding at another trailer.

"Man died almost three years ago," Kitsy said. "His daughter and her kids there for a while."

"I rent it now," Winona said. "I store canvases and paint supplies there to keep my place livable."

"And those two rigs near the road?"

"A single mom and her mother. And a man works trash pickup," Kitsy said.

This is a relatively safe place to avoid identification, Winona thought. *No one here cares about a stranger's past. They're too busy hiding their own secrets to pry into the lives of others.* She was curious about this well spoken stranger.

"What did you used to do?" Winona asked Pete.

"A little of everything. Whatever came around."

"Why you here?" Kitsy asked. "Ain't the best place to find work."

"Taking some time off," Pete said.

He's on the run, Winona thought. *Someone's chasing him. But he doesn't seem dangerous. He even seems kind and thoughtful.*

Chapter 62

Winona

Winona drove. Hiram sat in the front passenger seat of the now functioning "Pete-restored" van, declining to drive. She wasn't sure why. She stopped at a familiar spot off route 400 near Star Peak. Hiram had come to hike while she painted plein air but instead Hiram sat on a rock as she set up her easel and carefully squeezed paint on her palette. She set up solvents and water and pocketed painting cloths in her apron. She sat on a three-legged folding stool. She adjusted the canvas facing west.

She sketched the scene—desert with mountains, grasslands, a farm building to the right, a few cows and wild horses. She kept the vista wide, maybe ten miles of horizon, the mountains maybe thirty miles away, some with snow peaks, the occasional cloud drifting at 20,000 feet.

Hiram didn't move watching her. She wanted to ask him if he would hike but thought better of it. He seemed to want to stay for a while and she liked that. She enjoyed being around him.

She'd made all the marks she'd need on the gessoed background. She began to lay quick drying washes for the basic shapes of sky and mountains and foreground.

"Can I do that?" Pete asked.

"I think you can probably do what ever you set your mind to."

"Make a picture?"

Winona cleaned a few brushes. "I've got a sketch pad, pencils, and an eraser. If you'll bring me that canvas tote bag from the van."

Pete found a rock to sit on a few feet away from her. "Just draw what you see," she said. She was already defining areas on the canvas with a burnt umber wash. "Define the horizon. That's the essential line to build the rest of the drawing. You're taking a vast image and contracting it to a few square inches. Proportions of objects need to relate on paper the way you see them in reality."

"Should the horizon line be curved?" Pete asked.

"Why would you want to do that?"

"The earth is round. I'm drawing the horizon at the edge of the earth. Shouldn't it be curved?"

"The horizon line will disappear as you put in the landscape. You use it for reference."

"But the proportions. If I'm trying to get the proportions right, wouldn't the horizon on my drawing show a curve?"

She saw his point. He was thinking like a scientist. "I don't know if you can appreciate the earth's curvature from this view."

"We're what? Five, six thousand feet?"

"But the horizon can't be seen."

Pete drew for a while. She glanced occasionally to see his progress. His lines were too meticulous, the shading too dense and unvaried. Pete saw her interest. "The curvature of the horizon idea didn't make any difference," he said. "I've been to the highest place on earth. The horizon is obscured by clouds and 8,000-meter mountain peaks, but I always had intense awe for how minuscule we are; the earth is this globe where distance is measured in light years and the bigness of things is incomprehensible because we don't know the boundaries of the universe. As I was watching you get started, I have some of that feeling from on high here. I love the vast topography that perpetuates a respectful insignificance. I begin to feel lost sometimes, inspired at others."

Winona put her brush in a jar, placed her palette on her knees, and surveyed the landscape hues altered by the ascending sun. After a few minutes she said: "Do you like creating art?"

"Not as much as I would like. I get the feeling that what I see as beauty in our world and want to capture will never be possible. I'd always be hampered by inadequate imitation."

Welcome to the club, Winona thought. After a pause, she said: "Some of the great artists do that for me. Give me reality expressed in different ways with skill that pleases me."

"I just know I could never develop skills to that level. It would eventually depress me."

"To try is not a failure though. And you never know what you might discover."

"I guess. I'd have to think about it."

"Try some other subjects. The van maybe."

They broke for lunch, leaning against the van on the shady side and eating sandwiches and brownies with lemonade that Winona had brought in a cooler. "Are you religious?" she asked Pete.

"I don't know." He smiled. "Are you?"

"I was. I think about it now but not with enthusiasm."

"It's tough to go on sometimes without thinking about why we're here and what's beyond."

"It's why I like painting in the West," Winona said. "It opens the mind to metaphysical possibilities."

"That only a special person can divine. It's not easy for me."

She swallowed and looked at Pete. "Oh, I think almost everyone discovers some sense of where they are or are not in the scheme of things."

"I think few."

"Everyone has their individual experiences, their own thoughts."

"Not many think philosophically about truth and existence and what we're supposed to do."

"You seem intent on the subject. What is it that humans should be thinking about?"

"Is there life after death? Is there a God that can intervene in human life?" Pete said.

"How did you come to an interest in that?"

"I'm writing a memoir. I want it to have an impact."

"I don't think anyone knows. Religion and faith help fill the unknown, don't you think?" Winona said.

"And without the faith, that's where fear can creep in," Pete said.

"Why fear?"

"Afraid of doing something or not doing something during your time on earth that will mess up your access to an afterlife. Incur the wrath of God. Prevent obtaining something others have."

"But if there is a God, He loves us."

"Or she?"

"Or She."

"Most believe God loves us only if we love him."

"So where are the rewards?" Winona asked, cleaning up the trash that had been placed on the cooler and stuffing it into a plastic bag.

"I've come to believe we find our rewards here on earth," Pete said. "I'm almost sure now."

"Heaven and hell?"

"I guess. I think we shape our heaven or hell by our actions on earth."

"And you don't mean building monuments and bridges. Even climbing mountains?"

"Right. It's society and culture where we find ourselves immersed in the conscious time we're given as humans during life. We make our heaven and hell by how we influence the humanity we live in. How we contribute. How we integrate. How we build to make it better."

"How did you ever come to that?" Winona asked.

"Writing this memoir. I've been told I had to know what made people do what they do to write anything significant."

"And you believe when life stops, our body returns to the elements. We don't exist."

"I don't know about the soul. Does an idea exist? Is there anything about a thought that is like a molecule we will eventually identify as matter and know its presence?"

"What did you do before?" Winona asked.

"I was a doctor."

"You made a good living?"

"By wealth standards, yes."

"And that didn't suffice for your heaven on earth."

"It turned out to be hell."

"What happened?"

"I was among the best. I made mistakes but not in patient care."

"Don't you miss it?"

"Sometimes. But my life is getting better now."

Winona put the cooler on the back seat of the van. "Glad things are working out for you," she said.

"And what about you?" Pete asked.

"I want to be a significant painter. I believe in the importance of art." They started back toward the easel. "That sounds pretentious, doesn't it?

"Not at all."

"Unrealistic?"

"I'm no art expert. But I agree with perfection. And I know I like what you're doing."

Winona started painting again.

"I think I'll try to draw you," Pete said. "Do you mind?"

"You could find better subjects," she said.

"I don't think so," Pete said.

Winona's painting became rote, her brush strokes placed with no thought and little purpose. She thought about her life. What was holding her back? The hurts from a broken marriage, from children who had severed any links of love, from a social setting that condemned her for a family fiasco that ended with the loss of respect and caring. She painted to fight loneliness and avoid human contact that could hurt her again if she were to get involved. And here was Pete; she couldn't suppress her interest. *It's my hell, I guess.* And being with Pete made her believe she had to get busy creating her own heaven. She had liked the suffering too much, as if it made her existence justified. She resolved to change. She'd get herself back on track.

For many weeks, Pete worked on his memoir in his trailer. He still hiked and exercised daily. He liked being with Winona and he soon ate meals with her when she was alone and invited him. He rarely went to her trailer during the day; Winona had many friends who stopped by frequently, some daily. He did not want to be a topic of conversation. He often helped her with the packing and the shipping when she sent paintings to galleries who carried her work in Mendocino, Aspen, Provo, Santa Fe, and Boulder. He came to enjoy an intellect whose ideas were deeply considered and saturated with concern for others.

Chapter 63

New York
Sophie

Months after Sophie had finally evicted June and moved back into her apartment, Paige invited her to an afternoon concert at Lincoln Center and an early dinner at Lincoln Restorante. Sophie was stunning in a knee-length fire engine red dress, black pumps and a thin black belt at her trim waist. Crystal teardrop earrings glittered in the light filtering through the glass restaurant walls that opened to the exterior. Paige thought, *I've lost Sophie's vibrant and youthful glow and brisk movements years ago. I look like a living corpse ready for display in a funeral home.* She felt a pang of jealousy. Looking at Sophie reminded her. She'd passed through the looking glass into the land of the loveless elderly.

After they were seated, Paige ordered a bottle of California Chardonnay. She stroked the crystal glass stem as she spoke. "Any word from Ann and Billie?" she asked.

"Ann's doing better. Robert is working fulltime now that Ann can take care of herself during the day. And Billie's developed new lines of drum equipment. He's doing okay financially. And Tasha just had a baby girl."

"Any word from your father?"

"Not about the manuscript."

The waiter came poised with a pen and pad. Sophie studied her menu with excessive intensity. Paige had not opened her menu and continued to look at Sophie, pleased that they were together. Finally, they made decisions. The waiter wrote down their choices and left.

"He's finished writing. He insists I find a publisher," Sophie said.

"You know I've tried. But no one is interested. He still doesn't want to talk to you."

"I need to talk to him. Tressler still doesn't like the way the biography's going. Incorporating the memoir could make the biography the best of the year. Tressler believes that. And your father would always be credited for what is used."

The waiter approached with a tray.

"What about the money?" Sophie asked.

"I'd be sure he's compensated the way he wants, even if I have to use my advance."

"I'll ask," Sophie said.

"He could call me."

"He's sure that would lead to betrayal."

The waiter held up his hand to get their attention.. "Which of you had the ragout?" he asked.

Sophie received a manuscript from her father a few weeks later. Hiram called her to see that it had arrived.

"Can I take it to Paige now?" she asked.

"Still no other way?"

"There is no better way, Dad. I'm sure. Call me soon. I think she'll want to ask questions."

Chapter 64

Paige worked on Hiram's manuscript. The last chapter ended at the time of his conviction. She called Sophie.

"There's nothing about his escape or his time on the run," Paige said.

"He doesn't see that as part of the memoir."

"It's essential for current updates."

"I know he keeps diary notes now."

"I need those."

"You won't pay without them?"

Paige paused. "No. We'll buy what he sent. But convince him to send what he has written since then. We'll pay extra for that."

"I don't think he'll do that," Sophie said. "But I'll ask."

Paige sent a revised draft to Tressler who called for a meeting the next week with Sophie, Paige, and Charles Gibson. Manuscript pages were scattered across the conference table and two screens displayed images from two laptop computers in front of Sophie.

Tressler still said he wanted better writing. He read an example of what he thought was bad.

"What's wrong with that Mr. Tressler?" Paige asked. "I have details accurately describing McDowell's activity."

"What do you think, Charles?" Tressler asked.

"It doesn't read well for me," Charles said. Sophie saw the hurt in Paige's eyes. She took criticism of her writing personally.

"It's still not objective..." Tressler began.

"It is!" Paige interrupted.

"Just listen for a minute," Tressler said. "I read this and it still reeks with your moral judgments that seem increasingly more inconsistent. We need no judgments. Just reporting."

"Give me an example."

"The foundation fundraiser."

"It's objective."

"No it's not. Almost everything said is about excess, about potential abuse of donations, of celebrities whose only desire in life seems to be fame and admiration."

"That's accurate," Paige said.

"No. It's in the writing. You chose details that outweigh charitable work that must have occurred. That's spinning the narrative to your opinions."

"I tell you, I spent a lot of time on this. The foundation *was* excessive. McDowell's fundraising was to support his lifestyle as a world-class mountain climber and was minimally concerned with healthcare for the indigent. The time he spent in saving lives was miniscule."

"That's your judgment."

"It's a right judgment."

"Make your writing allow the reader to make that judgment. How many hours did he spend? How many lives did he save? How much time did he spend on the mountain? Weigh that against the description of the excess."

"It'll kill any engagement of a reader."

"Not with good writing. Present happening as you observed it, or as others described it. Balance it as best you can. Keep your personal judgments and opinions out of the writing. And let the readers come to their own conclusions. What do you think, Charles?"

"I think you're right about making the writing as objective and neutral as possible. Present truths without prejudice. If an automobile for his collection is worth $600,000, don't say it would take the average person half a lifetime to save for that."

"That's a truth," Paige said.

"Maybe. But as presented, it's a judgment that the car costs too much. It would take the same amount of time for the average person to save that much for an operation for his sister, or his mother," Charles said. "And you would consider that just. You're not writing to insist $600,000 is too much for a car, any car. You need to state the cost. The reader will decide if it's too much or just right, based on their own experiences and opinions. You should be writing McDowell's biography with facts, not opinions."

"It's an important distinction Charles makes," Tressler agreed. "The readers have to be allowed to form their own opinions from facts presented. Otherwise it borders on propaganda, and that's not fair and will turn readers off in droves."

"What do you think, Sophie?" Paige asked. "He's your father. Do we have a just description of him and moral judgments?"

Sophie tensed. She was not pleased with how Paige was presenting her father in the biography. It didn't gel with her changing opinion of her father as a human being. He'd made mistakes. But he wasn't evil. He hadn't managed marriage well, but he'd loved her, and Ann, and Billie. She was sure of that now. And with her recent conversations, she knew prison and being on the run had changed him. She glanced apologetically at Paige. "I don't think he's as bad as the book makes him out to be," she said.

"You thought it was wrong to kill Jeremy," Paige said.

"I've come to think he assisted in Jeremy's desire for suicide. I'm sure of it now."

"That's the side of McDowell you've got to explore," Tressler said, "present without innuendo, condemnation... or undo praise for that matter."

"I agree. Let the reader decide," Charles said.

"Maybe. But there's not much to discover that's going to make him saintly," Paige said.

"Make him human," Charles said. "We can't characterize him as a monster. We have to present the truth of everything he's done, then let the reader find the monster or the saint," Charles glanced from Paige to Sophie.

"We need to know everything about his activity after he was sent to prison," Tressler said.

"And on the run," Charles said.

"I need to talk to him," Paige said. "He doesn't want to go back to prison. He speaks only to Sophie to keep the chances of exposure to a minimum. He'll be tough to find."

"Is that true?" Tressler asked Sophie.

Paige sighed. "Max thinks she might get him in New Orleans," she said. "She's had sightings."

"Go with Paige," Tressler said to Sophie. "I'll pay expenses. You need to be the first to see him."

Sophie prayed that night she'd see her father and that she could know him again. Paige needed to get the biography right too. Her father deserved justice, but she was sure now he deserved vindication too.

Chapter 65

Paige had Sophie over to her home office after Sophie finished her day at the studio to discuss slides for the biography.

"What do you think of the Charles guy?" Paige asked.

"Stuffy."

"You like him?"

"Not really," Sophie said. She was sorry she said that. She didn't know why she didn't want to admit she appreciated Charles's ideas on the biography that supported an honest presentation of her father. And, for a man, she thought of Charles as gentle and caring. And she was touched by his shyness.

"Well, we're stuck with him for an editor," Paige said. "We've got another meeting on Monday. Can you be there?"

"Sure."

Sophie reviewed photos from Nepal. Paige picked out ones she thought they ought to run by Charles.

"Want to get together this weekend?" Paige asked.

"I've got a regatta," Sophie said.

Paige looked puzzled.

"For crewing," Sophie said. "We're ranked now. And on Sunday I'm going with a friend to Connecticut to sail. She's teaching me."

"You're a social butterfly," Paige said unenthusiastically. She was disappointed Sophie wouldn't be with her.

"Are you still seeing the Rosenthal guy?" Sophie asked.

"God, no. Not for months. I'm too involved in the writing. And I've decided to start to contract as an independent investigative reporter. I think I'll take it on full time when the biography is finished."

"What about the special?"

"I told him I wouldn't do it. I don't want to expose your father again. Your father doesn't deserve it."

———◆———

On Monday Charles Gibson made Paige and Sophie wait for more than an hour. He was apologetic as he led them to the conference room, but he seemed pressured.

"You're getting a nice tan," Charles said to Sophie.

"She's learning to sail," Paige said.

"Most of it's from crewing," Sophie said.

"Where do you do that?" Charles asked.

"We practice on a lake in New Jersey and the weather's been great."

Charles displayed the slides of the foundation's fundraising night his secretary had tracked down.

"They seem sensational to me," Paige said. "Excessive. The Bugatti. The string quartet. Over the top, and really not necessary. Isn't that exactly what Tressler was against?"

"Maybe. But it was what impressed the photographer at the time," Charles said. "I think we can use it."

"What is the stack of books with the woman in the miniskirt for?" Sophie asked.

"For your father's book about the foundation and Nepal," Paige said. "They were selling books and auctioned off some others with personal comments by your father and the author."

"Is the controversy going to be in the biography?" Sophie asked. "About truth of events in the book?"

"It's a part of your father's past that should not be hidden. The errors were documented on national TV twice," Paige said.

"By you?" Charles asked.

"No. By a colleague."

"My father wasn't aware of the errors," Sophie said. "Should the fault of the author be emphasized in my father's biography?"

"Your father knew, Sophie," Paige said. "He had to know. There has never been any evidence found that a child was saved and schooled through your father's generosity. And he must have read a galley before publication."

"I don't think so. It wasn't important to him. He did it to help the foundation. He didn't do it for himself!"

"I don't believe it."

"But there's doubt about his involvement," said Sophie angrily. "He really trusted the author to report accurately."

"I'll look at it more carefully," Charles said. "And check with Mr. Tressler to get his reaction."

Sophie presented the photos from Nepal that showed the foundation staff and hospital.

"These were for my book on the plight of women in Asia. My brother and I stayed at the foundation hospital in Nepal much of the time. I thought there might be some useful shots."

"We can't use published photos," Charles said.

"They haven't been published. There's been little enthusiasm about publishing my documentary and I'm sure nothing will ever come of it."

"I'm sorry," Charles said.

"They said my photos weren't raw enough. Too much beauty. Needed more journalistic exposure. More sense of evil and violence."

"That's bullshit," Paige said. "It wasn't your photos that changed their minds. Their market disappeared."

"Publishing isn't doing well these days," Charles said.

"I've seen Sophie's photos," Paige said. "They show the desperation of women in many parts of Asia. One series shows a beautiful young girl banished to a goat shed for her menstruation. Devastating."

"Let's consider that," Charles said. "It could relate to the environment the foundation served and be an important perspective on McDowell."

Chapter 66

Charles met with Sophie and Paige two to three times a week. The three worked well together. Sophie contributed to editing and rewriting on many sections.

Charles began to use Sophie as a reader for books in production and as he depended on her more for opinions, he included her in editorial staff meetings for certain books—memoir, nonfiction, and fiction.

And often in the evenings, Charles would invite Sophie to the opera, Lincoln Center, openings of Broadway shows, and Shakespeare in the park. On weekends they wandered the mazes of the Metropolitan and the spirals of the Guggenheim. Sophie shared her love of the arts and Charles detailed his knowledge of ancient civilizations and their contributions to modern culture. They perused art galleries in Chelsea and Soho and went to readings and concerts in the Village.

"He's really creative," Sophie said to Paige.

"Do you love him?" Paige asked.

Sophie blushed. "It's not like that. We're just good friends."

"You'd be the best thing ever to put some zip into Charles' life."

Sophie blushed. "Don't be ridiculous. He's so Eastern. Sometimes I wonder if my Southern upbringing doesn't irritate him."

"Don't put yourself down, Sophie. Suck it up and go after him."

"I'm not like that," Sophie said.

"He likes you."

"Like a baby sister maybe."

"Horse poop," Paige said.

Charles invited Sophie and Paige for the Fourth of July weekend at the family house in Connecticut. Paige and Sophie drove up Friday afternoon; they would return late Sunday. A grand party for extended family and friends was planned for Saturday on the lawn with a view of the ocean. Saturday night was a ball at the yacht club with more than four hundred invited. Sunday would be a brunch at the house for family and houseguests before departure.

The house was a late 19ᵗʰ century but well preserved and a crew of attendants kept the grounds pristine. Sophie and Paige shared a room in the guesthouse where Charles's younger sisters both had their own rooms.

Sophie and Paige unpacked and dressed for dinner. The walk to the house from the guesthouse was under a covered walkway under a vaulted roof, stretching about seventy-five yards. Mrs. Gibson greeted them at the door and offered a tour of the house.

"This was my family's summer property from before this house was built near the turn of the century. Charles Eastlake was involved in the design of this house, although it is not known if he ever came here."

Along the wall of the entrance corridor were seven full length portraits of family debutantes in white gowns and gloves. "This was done by John Singer Sargent," Mrs. Gibson said, pointing to a radiant young woman with a roguish pose. The last portrait was contemporary with the debutante sitting with a mysterious side-glance. "This is Eleanor," Mrs. Gibson said, "Charles' fiancée. She's a cousin of my sister's husband twice removed. She and Charles played together on the terrace out front when they were in grade school."

Sophie's heart sank. *Fiancée?* What a fool she'd been. She was only a friend to Charles and she'd let herself believe there was more.

"It's a beautiful portrait," Paige said.

"I forgot the artist's name. He's not one of my favorites. I thought he made Eleanor look ten years older than when she came out."

In the dining room were other portraits of the family. "That is my husband's great uncle who is rumored to have dined with Edith Wharton when in Paris,"

Mrs. Gibson smiled.

The kitchen was hot and noisy with preparation for the evening's dinner. Sophie counted the pheasants lined up on trays for precooking—seventeen. The upstairs bedrooms housed tester beds from different periods. Mrs. Gibson pointed out furniture by Belter and a faux bamboo dresser made by Pottier & Stymus. "My grandfather was an avid collector of the best contemporary furniture of the time," Mrs. Gibson explained.

After the tour when Mrs. Gibson left, Sophie and Paige stood together with glasses of wine enjoying the view of the ocean on the stone paved terrace.

"That was a little humbling," Sophie said.

"As she intended. I got a little sick of her pompous self-importance," Paige said.

"Charles doesn't seem that way at all."

"I would have never guessed. He's the most down to earth male I can ever remember meeting. And all this wealth and family? A total surprise."

"I made my debut in Louisville. Compared to those dresses, I looked like Little Orphan Annie."

"New Yorkers are out of control sometimes. It's almost obscene."

"But not Charles."

Paige smiled inwardly at Sophie's defense of Charles. "He's the best. He made crucial changes in the biography without ever once making me feel bad," Paige said.

"Do you know fiancée Eleanor?" Sophie asked.

"Never met her. Heard she's in Paris, flying in tonight for tomorrow's events."

"Did Charles ever mention her to you?"

"I didn't even know her name. She looks like the socialite extraordinaire. Way out of my league."

"Maybe we'll get to meet her," Sophie said without enthusiasm as she glanced behind Paige.

Charles Gibson approached. "Mother gave you the tour, I hear," he said.

"What an amazing family," Sophie said with muted enthusiasm.

Charles smiled weakly. "Are you settled in?"

"Very comfortable," Paige said. "Will we get to meet your fiancée?"

"I hope so. She's on the red eye tonight. Should be here early in the morning."

"You've known each other since childhood?"

"Forever," Charles said.

The announcement for cocktails in the library was made by a strolling servant.

"Thank you for coming," Charles said. "I think you'll enjoy the festivities tomorrow." He turned to speak to an elderly couple that had just emerged from the covered walkway.

At the lawn party the next day, Sophie worked the crowd in ways she'd learned growing up in Louisville society. It had been years, and she was concerned about the impression she was making. She had only a brief chance to greet Charles, who was hosting the party. She was curt and evasive. He seemed puzzled by her demeanor. She was ashamed and angry that she'd let her feelings about Charles soar so high.

"Have you seen Eleanor?" Sophie asked Paige during a break.

"They've been engaged for eight years, Sophie. It's an arranged marriage that neither seems to want to consummate."

"How do you know?"

"I asked his brother."

Sophie was a fluster of emotions. Maybe he could care for her.

"He loves you, Sophie," Paige said, "I can see it."

Sophie wanted it to be true but she wouldn't admit it. "Why is he still engaged?"

"I think it allowed them to do their own things. She's interested in politics. She doesn't have time for romance."

Sophie couldn't speak. She worried that her earlier treatment of Charles had offended him. She wanted to believe Paige so badly. She wanted Charles to care. But good things in her life always disappeared. And she suddenly couldn't believe that it wasn't happening to her again.

"It's getting late. We'll need to get ready for the ball," Paige said.

The ball was in the grand ballroom of the country club. Christmas tree-sized crystal chandeliers glittered from the ceiling. Food service with sterling silver hinged-top serving dishes and iced displays of shellfish and salmon were at one end of the room. A full orchestra played continuously.

Paige sat at a circular side table at the edge of the dance floor as Sophie danced with a man she'd just met, a college classmate of Charles. A diamond clip that gathered her long dark hair glittered in the light from the chandeliers. She was stunning in a strapless, formal red dress with a tight waist. As she twirled, the silk fabric undulated around her ankles revealing dress pumps sparkling with red stones.

She's beautiful, Paige thought. Paige had helped Sophie with her dress. Sophie had been so down about her misjudgment of Charles.

"It's too tacky," Sophie had said of the dress, looking in the mirror.

"It's elegant. You'll knock 'em dead," Paige said.

"I wish it were true," Sophie said with no self-confidence.

Sophie danced with rare breaks for three hours. Young men returned for a second and third dance and cut in at will to be paired with such a graceful partner. Sophie pulled it off without a wrinkle.

At the end, before going to the car to return to the house, Sophie and Paige sat near the club portico on a bench waiting for their car to be brought from valet. They heard two men's voices, standing near the drive and hidden by a line of eight-foot tall boxwoods.

"Who's the broad in the red dress?" one said.

"Works at Charles' publishing company."

"Wasn't Eleanor upset? I mean, an employee. She's a photographer. Hardly a respectable invite."

"Eleanor's pissed, no doubt."

"Eleanor probably doesn't even know she's here."

"She's the best looking here. You're interested, aren't you?"

"Not for an employee."

"Well, I'd like to know her a lot better."

"She's from the South."

"I don't mean to marry her."

"Don't waste your time. Her father's convicted of murder."

"Jesus, does anyone know?"

"Charles. I'm not sure about the family. They'll know by tomorrow morning."

"Is that the euthanasia trial guy the FBI is hunting? Secretary of something?"

"That's the one. That wither your hard on?"

The men got into their cars. Sophie held back tears.

"Assholes," Paige said.

"I wish I were someone else."

"You can't escape who you are," Paige said. "And you're great. Always believe that."

But Sophie didn't feel any better.

On the drive back from the yacht club to the house, Sophie convinced Paige to take her back to the City early. They made their excuses before retiring and expressed their gratitude by writing notes on the Crane stationary found in the desk drawer of their room. They left their notes on the entrance hall side-table. They left in the morning before other guests were up.

In New York, Sophie continued to work with Charles on the biography and as an assistant on his editorial duties with other works to be published. But she declined social gatherings.

Paige met Sophie after she finished work at the studio on a Wednesday to go to Bloomingdale's to shop and eat in a restaurant on Madison Avenue.

"Charles talked to me yesterday," Paige began after they were seated and had ordered. "He came to my apartment."

Sophie tried to maintain disinterest.

"He wanted to know why you changed."

"I told him," Sophie said. "He's already asked me."

"He wanted the old Sophie back, he said, 'What did I do wrong?' he said."

"I told him I'm too busy with work," Sophie said.

"He doesn't believe that. Why don't you be honest with him?"

"I can't lead him on. I'll never be anything more than a murderer's daughter and his employee."

"It's not true," Paige said.

"It's the myth that lives on. And how could I ever dump that burden on Charles. It would ruin what he has."

"He loves you, Sophie. I told him about those guys at the ball. He hurt for you. For the injustice of it all. He said it would never matter to him. And I believe him."

"I can't do it. He doesn't see how it would ruin us."

"I told him how I felt about Eleanor," Paige said. "Told him I thought he'd been insensitive about leading you on when he was engaged to his childhood sweetheart. 'Eleanor and I have never been in love. We'll never marry. We've never even been friends,' he said."

" 'You were wrong to deceive Sophie,' I said. He teared up. A grown man sitting in front of me fighting not to cry. I felt sorry for him."

Sophie said nothing. Her heart ached. But she knew that her past would always be a barrier to a truly open relationship.

"Would you see him again?" Paige asked. "He broke the engagement and insisted Eleanor make it public knowledge. He wanted me to tell you that."

"It doesn't change reality," Sophie said.

"Don't make a mistake here, Sophie. Look forward. He loves you. You love him. That doesn't happen to many people very often. Don't let it slip away because of public opinion about your father. Charles doesn't care. And he accepts the truth of your father's innocence."

Sophie changed the subject. But that night she couldn't sleep. She lived with deep sadness that she would always see a future ruined by her past.

Chapter 67

Winona

Winona drove the van on the first long distance trip in a long time. With Pete's restoration, it cruised easily on highways at sixty-five for the first time she could remember. Pete wrote in his notebook. He looked good. He'd trimmed his beard and hair for the trip. He decided not to wear a hat. And he'd bought slacks, an out-of-date but well-made sports jacket and a white dress shirt with a button down collar at Goodwill in Salt Lake City.

"It's running smoothly," she said. "I'm surprised."

"That I could do it?"

"Don't be difficult." She smiled.

They were going east on I80.

"You always liked VW vans?" Winona asked.

"They captured a generation, but it's not my favorite," Pete said.

They rode in silence. "What's your favorite?" Winona said.

"I bought a '34 Bugatti a few years ago."

"Sounds expensive."

"Paid $190,000, sold it a year later after restoration work for just over $600,000. I loved that car."

"Because you made money?"

"No. Not all about money. It had beautiful lines. And it functioned like a cheetah in full stride."

"A car that old?"

"Handmade, it had the feel of a real car. A physical experience. It hugged the road with a few inches clearance. The firmness of the steering made you feel in charge. I tested it on the Bonneville flats before I had it restored. It was an unforgettable experience."

They rode in silence, Pete lost in thought. It was the first glimpse he'd allowed her of his former life.

"That sounded pretentious, didn't it?" he finally said.

Winona smiled. "More than a little," she said. "But I thought you were sincere about your love for the car."

"It was all the profit stuff?"

"You really paid that price for an automobile?"

Occasionally, like now, she had a rare glimpse into his past, but not really much about Pete himself. *How could anyone spend that much money on a car?*

And she decided to break their unspoken vows of probing the past... his bringing up the car allowed that. "What did you do back then?" she said.

She regretted the question instantly. She feared it would change their friendship. Had she opened wounds he'd suffer?

She liked his interest in her. He asked her about painting, but he never asked about her husband, who was remarried now living with a stalwart of exclusive society. *I miss my children. As they used to be anyway.*

Pete had avoided talk about previous family. And he never asked why she was living alone in a trailer in the mountain desert. She'd probably tell him some day, to explain that her husband had destroyed her, falsely accusing her of infidelity, severing her from friends by lying about her innocence of wrongdoing and spreading evil stories of her past... all to marry a wealthy, connected divorcée who could assure him a lifestyle he wanted in his retiring years.

"You wouldn't believe what I did," he said. He paused as he seemed to think about whether he wanted to tell her or not. "I told you I was a doctor. Well, I was a surgeon."

Winona's former and only husband was a doctor.

"And you made that kind of money?" she asked.

Pete laughed. "I inherited a lot."

Winona was curious but did not ask. It was more than Pete had ever revealed about himself or his past. She wanted to know more.

A lot more. But she feared the danger on silencing him forever if he thought she was prying.

They rode on past two exits more than sixty miles apart. Pete was back to making notes.

The VW passed an eighteen-wheeler. Winona smiled at Pete, proud to be passing anything with the van. She could see a smile of pride in his return glance.

"What makes you really want to paint pictures?" he said. "You've never said when I've asked you before."

'Why do you ask?" she asked.

"I'm working more things out for my book. It's ready to be edited. And I was wondering."

"You're writing about me?"

"Not exactly. I'm writing about me, mostly." He smiled. "Sort of arrogant sounding. But I'm interested in why people do things. I want to write something that will please and I've been told I need to find myself and learn more about others to have any chance of writing something significant." He paused. "And you spend a lot of waking hours creating pictures to please people. What drives you?"

She thought for a moment. "It keeps me busy. I enjoy it."

"No. Not that. What does making pictures of sand and rock and sky do for you? What do you accomplish?"

"You mean like relieve tension? Forget haunting memories? Make me sleep better?"

"It's got to be more than that. Don't you want to change people in some way?"

From the back window of a sedan that cut in front of the VW, a child waved frantically with a right hand, fingers spread, mouthing something unintelligible.

"What do you mean?" Winona asked.

"You know. Produce an emotional response in them. Something that changes them for the better?"

"I never thought about it. I think painting has been an escape."

"A release of tension?

"Maybe."

The sun was midmorning high. She adjusted the visor.

"I don't think I expect the same reaction from viewers who see my paintings. Even the ones who claim to like them."

"What happens to make you like the paintings you like?" Pete asked.

"I have favorites. I saw Vermeer's 'Girl with the Pearl Earring' on a trip to the Netherlands. He's made her beautiful for me. Beautiful in ways I wouldn't have discovered looking at her in real life or a photo."

"Are there others?"

"I love Sargent's 'Lanterns.' Do you know it?"

"No."

"Children with paper lanterns in a garden. Sharing innocence without guile. It's not just the technical aspects, or the subject matter. He was able to show me something about innocence that I'd lost as an adult. *Especially after my divorce.* Some of his portraits have given me insight into human nature too."

"So as a viewer you get pleasure from some intellectual or visual discovery about people."

She thought for a moment. Checking her speed with a quick glance. "I don't think that's all."

He was taking notes again.

"There is an Andrew Wyeth painting of rocks in water of a stream," she said. "I didn't even like the painting when I first saw it. It was too photorealistic. Almost surrealistic. But as I stared at it, it changed me in ways that I didn't realize until much later. He'd created a memorable image, and from that memory I think I realized that there can be beauty in the image of pebbles and rocks at the bottom of a clear stream. I found beauty in what had been ordinary, even for-gettable, for me. He didn't create emotion. He taught me new ways to think and remember. And that was pleasurable. And probably what I would like to do with my landscapes and seascapes. To awaken new ways to see things. Appreciate through things that are not possible by photographs or just staring."

Pete wrote intensely now. Then he clipped his pencil on the cover and closed his notebook.

"Do you feel the same about sculpture?" he asked.

"There is a head study of a woman grieving over the loss of her son by Jean-Batiste Carpeaux. 19th century art. Some think it's too sentimental. But the grief he captured tears my heart."

"So great art evokes empathy?"

"What's your point with all this?" Winona asked.

"Trying to judge what makes people do what they do. And what makes them successful at what they do." He made a quick note. "Is it giving pleasure to them in some way? Or just making them see and think about things in new ways?"

"Couldn't it be either?" Winona said. "And maybe more. I saw an exhibit a few years back in Atlanta. When I was married and before I started painting seriously. I didn't go on my own. It featured an artist's paintings and sculpture. She'd been a EMS technician, riding an ambulance in her pre-artistic life. Her work was internal organs, blood, broken limbs and bones, crushed skulls, excrement."

"What motivated her?" he said.

"I was appalled. Angry really. It was grotesque. What was she trying to do to the viewer? It didn't give me pleasure."

"You remembered. Maybe that was her purpose."

"But I hated her for etching in my brain something unwanted and that I couldn't forget. It was space she didn't deserve."

"She had a political message?"

"I'm sure. But I don't know what. She seemed anti-establishment and in a rage about humanity so that it gave her satisfaction to destroy the human form."

"Bizarre."

"And I resent her success."

"But it can't be lasting success," Pete said.

Winona downshifted to brake, then returned to cruising gear.

"For me, that she is accepted by the art world, makes millions, and counts herself among the greats without shame, says we've lost our cultural compass to beauty."

"It has to be related to experiences of her past, too," Hiram said.

"I wouldn't think when creating art, very many artists start out to make a viewer think or feel a certain way."

"I like what you do," Hiram said. "It pleases me." He looked to Winona to make sure she knew he was sincere.

Winona put on a blinker to exit at a rest stop. "I got to pee," she said.

She eased off the highway onto the access to the facilities.

"The more I think about it," she said, "I think human culture deserves the artists' attempts at beauty. It's defining."

"Can a culture gorging on capitalism resist creating for wealth?" Pete still took notes now leaning forward with his note pad on the dash.

She pulled into the lined parking space at the rest stop.

"It must have an effect. But probably most great art is created with altruism still. Only time will tell. The future will seek beauty in the past, " she said.

"The futurists may not find a lot to please them from our generations," Pete said, opening the side door and stepping down before heading to the men's room.

The exhibit was in the town hall in Ogden, Utah. Hiram helped transport and hang canvases. Winona asked him to stay for the reception. "Food may be a little iffy in quality but these receptions always seem to have a few unique items that are fun to try." He circulated as Winona made contacts.

Highlighted alone on a wall with special track lighting was Winona's painting of Nevada's horizon. A best of show ribbon and a wood and brass plaque sat on an easel in front praising her career. Pete stared and returned many times to gaze. Winona deserved recognition.

They drove back the same night. When they said goodnight, Winona leaned forward and kissed Pete on the cheek. He reached out and took her in his arms and held her for more than a minute.

Chapter 68

The sun was down and the stars were out. Hiram sat on a folding chair outside his trailer, editing his diary notes on his knees. Winona ran up, winded from the effort.

"Thank God you're here," she said.

Hiram looked up at her. "What's the matter?"

"Kitsy's at the emergency room. A truck totaled the pickup. From the sound of it, I don't think she'll live."

"Where is she? Is the VW gassed?"

"Yes."

"I'll drive," Hiram said.

At the ER in the strip mall, only a technician and a nurse were standing next to Kitsy, who was lying on a gurney.

"Has she been conscious?" Hiram asked.

"No," the nurse said, adjusting a pack of fluid on an IV pole.

"Do you have oxygen?"

"I can't find the mask."

"You must have a nasal catheter."

"I looked."

"Where's the doctor?"

"We can't locate him. We called the x-ray tech. He's not answering."

Hiram quickly checked Kitsy. He took a stethoscope. "What's her pressure?"

"90/60."

Hiram listened to the chest, then the distended abdomen.

The tech took a call on his cell. "Air Mercy is tied up, at least two hours. Maybe more."

"Ready the ambulance," Hiram said. "We'll leave for Reno in five minutes. You the driver?" Hiram said to the tech. "Yes," the tech said.

"Call the state patrol. See if we can get an escort."

Hiram found a syringe. He released the trapped air in a pneumothorax with a stab between the ribs that went to the hilt before air bubbled into the syringe followed by a mixture of blood and yellow fluid. Kitsy's respirations slowed. Her blood pressure rose. She was still unconscious.

"Start another line. We need expanders. Balanced salt. Electrolytes."

"What about the x-ray?" the nurse said.

Hiram ignored her. When he finished securing a temporary drain, he said, "Draw blood for a type and crossmatch. See if there's a way for the police to get it to the lab before we arrive. We'll need at least four units of blood. Let's go!"

Winona stepped forward. "What can I do?"

"Follow in the Van. We'll be at St. Mary's in Reno in less than three hours with an escort. Be careful. Follow the speed limit and don't try to keep up with us."

In minutes, they were on the way west. Twenty miles outside Winnemucca, State police entered from an on-ramp to lead the way.

"Get the surgeon on call on the speaker," Hiram said to the nurse who transferred the request to the driver.

Hiram introduced himself over the radio. "Vehicular accident. Female about sixty. Unconscious. I relieved pressure from a pneumothorax. She's ventilated now. Abdomen distended, no bowel sounds. A ruptured spleen tamponaded now by a blood filled abdomen," he said. "Multiple fractures. I've stabilized the spine. We'll need blood."

The surgeon asked many questions. Hiram answered. "What's your name?" the doc asked.

"Peter Lake."

"Trained?"

"Surgery." *He wondered where I went to medical school,* Hiram thought.

"Do I know you?"

"I don't think so," Hiram said.

They arrived in just under two hours. Kitsy was taken immediately to the operating room. Winona arrived half an hour after surgery began.

"I've got to go," Hiram said, shouldering his backpack.

"Take the van."

"No. You'll need it."

"Can I reach you?"

"I wish. But no. I'll keep in touch."

"What about Kitsy?" Winona asked.

"If she makes it through surgery, she's got a good chance of survival. Never the same. But she'll live."

"She needs you."

"These are competent folk. And Kitsy needs you most of all. I can't stay. But, I'll be sure to be somewhere close until she's discharged. Not leave until I know she'll get better."

Chapter 69

After Kitsy regained consciousness, it took her a few days to orient and think cohesively. When Winona arrived, as she had every day since the accident, Kitsy reached out to grab Winona's arm to guide her to sit on the bed.

"It's him," Kitsy said. "I saw a wanted poster on a bulletin board when I was on a stretcher waiting for surgery, just before they gave me that anesthetic."

"Who?"

"Pete. His name is Mc... something. Wanted for murder."

"Are you sure?"

"It's him. I told hospital security."

"What did they do?"

"They said they'd spread the word."

"Did you tell them about Winnemucca? Where Pete stayed?"

"Yes. Of course."

"My God, he saved your life, Kitsy. You would be dead if it wasn't for his kindness."

Winona closed her eyes.

"It wasn't wrong," Kitsy said. "He's a murderer."

"He's not. He's falsely accused."

"But convicted. Escaped from jail. It said so on the poster."

"He'll go back to jail because of you. I've got to go."

"I had to tell. I prayed about it."

"He was your friend, Kitsy."

"I didn't do no wrong."

Winona gathered her belongings from the closet and under the bed. She put them in a shopping bag.

"You going to warn him?" Kitsy asked.

But Winona was out the door.

Winona drove the van as fast as it would go. Four and half hours later, she turned onto the dirt road at the trailer park. It was past midnight, the sky clear but moonless. Among the dark shapes of the trailers, three sheriffs' vehicles flashed beams of red and white into the night. A fire department ambulance was positioned with the front end toward the trailer Hiram had rented, the headlights reflected from the aluminum siding. Winona parked as close as she could and started toward her trailer. A deputy stopped her, gripping her arm. She twisted away. Two men were sliding a body bag into the back of the ambulance.

"What did you do?" she screamed at the deputy.

"He put up a fight," the deputy said.

The Sheriff got out of one of the cars and approached Winona. "Best you don't stay here tonight," he said.

"I live here."

"I know that. But that man dead, Miss Winona."

"You the one that killed him?"

"He got his due."

"He didn't have a weapon."

"He was shooting at us. Ask the deputy. He'll tell you."

"You lie. He didn't believe in guns."

"Best you don't worry yourself. I can take you down to the motel. Spend the night there."

"I'll do fine here," Winona said.

"It's a crime scene."

"Because you killed an innocent man?"

"Best you rest, Miss Winona," the Sheriff said.

Max heard of the capture on the news and called Paige in New York. "He's dead."

"Oh no. Where?" Paige asked.

"Somewhere in Nevada."

"Are you going out there?"

"Yes. I want to tie up loose ends."

"I'll go with you."

"It'll take at least eight hours. And get the daughter. Let the family claim the body."

"Won't he be considered escaped from custody? Return the corpse to prison?"

"I don't know. But I'll sort it out. And the girl will be helpful."

Chapter 70

Paige arrived with Sophie at the trailer park in Winnemucca in a rental car from Salt Lake Airport. Max had already started her investigation. They sat cramped knee-to-knee in Winona's trailer.

"Can you tell us what happened?" Paige asked Winona.

"They shot him," Winona said.

"He put up a fight?" Paige asked.

"He wouldn't have resisted," Winona said.

"McDowell had five bullet wounds," Max said. "I got to the coroner. A senile retired general practitioner."

"Did he suffer?" Sophie asked.

"No. Impossible. Three wounds in the back, one through the chest, one to the head."

"He didn't have a gun," Winona said. "I know that."

"Did you hear the shots?" Max asked.

"He was dead when I got here."

"But you think the Sheriff killed an unarmed suspect?"

"The sheriff doesn't take prisoners, Miss Rojas." Winona was crying. "He's not a gentle person."

"Can you tell us how they found him?" Paige asked.

Max spoke up. "Sheriff won't say. Or the deputy. I asked them."

"My friend was in the hospital in Reno," Winona said. "She saw a poster with McDowell's picture and told the authorities."

"And you came right back here?" Paige asked.

"As fast as I could."

"You wanted to warn him? He was an escaped criminal."

"He was a human being," Winona said.

"And you were afraid of him?"

Winona bristled at the interrogation.

"Did you know him a long time?"

"A few months."

"And you never suspected he was a murderer? Never asked?"

Winona refused a response.

Paige touched Sophie's hand. "We need to get his belongings."

"I'll take you," Max said.

Winona followed Sophie out of the trailer. "I'm so sorry about your father. He was a good man."

"Could I talk to you about it? I haven't seen him in years now," Sophie said.

Lingering around the crime scene, Max asked if police were around. A man said Sheriff had called police in Elko to investigate. They were on their way. Max whispered to Paige, "Get his things before anyone shows up. Put what you can find in the trunk of my car. Then get Sophie to take photos of everything near and far. I'll start interviewing."

The sun was up. Paige and Sophie found Hiram's backpack and his travel equipment. Then Sophie photographed the inside and outside of the trailer and the surrounding ground. Then took more distant views of the trailer park and surroundings. She joined Max and Paige to leave before the Elko detective showed up.

"Did we violate a crime scene?" Sophie asked Max.

"They haven't established anything close to a crime scene yet. They aren't eager to preserve evidence," Max said.

Sophie and Paige rented motel rooms. Max joined Paige and Sophie in Sophie's room to look through Hiram's possessions. There was no gun or evidence that Hiram had carried any weapons.

"I expected we might find notes, or a diary," Paige said. "We know he was writing more for his memoir."

"Ask the Winona woman. I want to be sure I find any witnesses to the shooting," Max said.

It was after midnight but Paige and Sophie returned to Winona's trailer.

Winona listened to Paige and Sophie describe what they were looking for. "Notes. Or a notebook."

"There was nothing in the trailer?" Winona asked.

"No."

"He did write sometimes down in the junk yard, a place he stayed for a while."

Winona took Paige and Sophie across the four acres to the camping trailer.

"He stayed here?" Sophie asked.

"When he first came here," Winona replied. "And then on and off he might sleep down here on a beautiful night or when there were strangers in the park."

Sophie teared up. "His life was not easy," she whispered.

"There were times when he seemed down," Winona said. "But on most days, he liked who he was and what he was doing."

"What did he do with his time?" Paige asked.

"Traveled and wrote his memoir. Sometimes he helped me with shipping my paintings, or setting up my supplies." Her voice was tinged with sorrow.

They looked in the camper. There was a hinged door below a small sink. Inside, behind a collector tank, Paige saw written notes rolled up and fastened with a rubber band in a coffee can. They went outside into the light.

"This is it," she said to Sophie. "His diary notes."

Sophie held the notes and slumped down to the desert earth to sit cross-legged, tears blurring her father's hand written description of his time since his escape from prison.

Chapter 71

New York

Paige carefully consolidated Hiram's notes into a narrative draft. Max was hired to track down as many witnesses to Hiram's fugitive years as possible. Max easily found the key influences in Hiram's life and Paige interviewed each one. Some of the interviews were conducted over days as Paige got to know the individuals. Tressler then called a meeting with Paige, Sophie, Charles, and he included the CEO of the outsourced publicity agency he used, the firm's chief legal consultant, two assistant editors and Mildred Cox, present owner of the firm.

"You know why we're here," Tressler began.

"I don't, Harmon," Mildred Cox, the owner, said.

"You know, Mildred, it's the McDowell biography," Tressler said, irritated with Mildred Cox's dismissive tone and her feigned innocence of the meeting's purpose just to be contrary.

"I'm not a writer," Mildred said. *You're not much of anything except excessive inherited wealth,* Tressler thought.

"I need your input," Tressler said to Mildred Cox, "we'll be arousing criticism, calling attention to sensitive issues like right to life with this biography. I want you aware. No surprises when we release." He turned to the others. "We've got to get this one right. You've all read this draft. What are the changes needed?"

Paige stood to address the group. "We retrieved McDowell's diary notes that gave great insight about his activities and thinking from prison until his death. I was able to interview many of the people he stayed with and knew during this period. With intellectual intensity, he searched for reasons for his decline and he looked to building a new life under a new identity completely separated from the past. He became a compassionate person in ways that were antithetical to his past. I've restructured the biography to emphasize his enlightenment to a new way of existing. I wanted the biography to reveal his revelations, not to simply detail his foibles and wrongdoings."

"He was guilty of murder. Society judged that. Stick more to the facts of the trial," legal said.

"I didn't get the draft," Mildred Cox said.

"We delivered it by courier," a junior editor said.

Charles spoke. "The problem is that no matter how detached we try to be from conclusions about McDowell's guilt or innocence of murder or euthanasia, with the new diary notes found at the trailer park where he was killed, he seemed to have changed from the life-devoted-to-me he lived before the trial. He'd been intelligent, but self absorbed with personal achievements and fame. He was so involved with his admirable image that his life became a selfish pursuit of wealth and recognition."

Sophie did not feel confident about contributing to this meeting but Charles' words gave her courage to speak. "My father was a dedicated surgeon and caregiver who saved lives and provided better quality of health and living for hundreds of thousands of less fortunates. He was not selfish," she said.

"Some would think he had an arrogant disdain for human kind," an editor said. "He didn't have many friends."

"That's your opinion," Sophie said. "It's not the truth we now know."

"He is convicted of killing his grandson. That's pretty damn arrogant in the views of many," legal said.

"What's the point here?" Sophie asked Tressler. "I think Paige has created the fairest possible presentation of my father in the biography. Is this meeting for her to change it again?"

Tressler stood to look down at those around the table. "Paige's material from McDowell's notes after he escaped from prison is her best writing. He did change. He was smart enough to have hidden enough cash away for existing on a poverty level indefinitely without getting caught, and he began to think about his past," Tressler said.

"He made friends. He helped others. Paige describes him as a man redeemed by genuinely caring about the people he engaged with. And he took some responsibility at least for being the cause of his troubles. And many may feel that is a troubling representation, that the evil is minimized. But that's wrong. It *is* a biography based on truth and not myth."

"This is not about whether murder or euthanasia was committed," Paige said. "It's about a human life, a life judged harshly by the public and the press."

"The motives and means of McDowell's death will always be front page interest," an editor said.

"Paige has done well with that presentation," Charles said.

"You wrote most of that," the editor said with rancor.

Charles continued. "People will have preformed opinions about euthanasia or assisted suicide before they read the book. We can't change that. I've always felt we should be treating the writing of this biography as a coming of age. McDowell grew after his time in prison..." Charles said.

"We didn't try to change a reader's opinion," Paige said. "We've presented the life of McDowell, and euthanasia really was a minor part of that."

"You did," Tressler said. "I believe the balance is right. Very little needs to be done with the manuscript. We will treat this as a coming of age. Not the evolution of a murderer."

"I don't see what all the fuss is about," Mildred Cox said.

"In some ways, we should honor McDowell," Charles said. "This is not about living life on the edges, on the top and bottom, it's about discovering who you are."

"Biography has to deal with the truth," legal said.

"Everything is true. Facts have been vetted," Paige said.

"And the writing about McDowell's motives and actions is accurate," Charles said. "It's how we chose the emphasis in what we write. It's not just describing events with statistics, narrative descriptions, societal judgments of what is moral and what is not."

"That's just gobbledygook," Mildred Cox said.

"Of course we have to have the happenings," Paige said, "I've got that. But Charles is right. Especially with the new material from McDowell's new friends, we can make this story about a failed surgeon who finds himself to make a new beginning with new perspectives and potential."

"A nemesis of hubris with a rise from the ashes," Tressler said.

"Who wants to read that?" Mildred Cox asked.

"It's what's right," Tressler said. "It's what we should do."

"Reveal the inner soul," Paige said. "We can do that with what we've got." She was looking at Charles.

"Redo it. Vet it. Keep everyone in this room involved." Tressler glanced around the room. "Will it work from the publicity view?" Tressler asked publicity.

"We can make it work. We'll have to revise all the copies, but I like the thrust of where you're going."

"We need to go for final approval with the board in three weeks," Tressler said. "Be sure we are not vulnerable on any legal issues."

"Can I meet the author?" Mildred Cox asked.

"Jesus, Mildred. You're looking at her," Tressler said pointing to Paige.

"Charles Gibson has provided invaluable support, Mrs. Cox," Paige said.

Mildred Cox didn't respond for a few seconds. *A senior moment,* Paige thought.

"Well, at least someone is valuable," Mildred Cox said, staring vaguely out a window.

Chapter 72

The Mc Dowell biography was released and Tressler hosted the traditional launching party for authors, agents, reviewers, and friends of the firm. Paige signed copies for an hour before her thirty-minute reading. Charles sat in the front row of folding chairs lined in a square; Sophie stood behind the seated guests, admiring Paige's reading voice. She had not seen Charles since Paige had talked to her about his confessions to her, Sophie refused to accept his calls. She couldn't bear to maneuver through a paper-thin conversation avoiding all the feelings for him that haunted her and that hadn't decreased in intensity. She couldn't bear bleating platitudes about ideas of claimed mutual disinterest while she really wanted to tell him of the pain of her longing to be with him, to share with him all that she felt and was.

Paige returned to her table for signing books again after the reading. Sophie whispered in her ear her congratulations and thanks. She slipped out the front door. She shivered at the blast of cold air that engulfed her. She moved quickly to walk back toward her apartment.

She crossed a street at the light. Charles startled her when he came up to her side.

"You can't avoid me forever," he said.

"I'm not avoiding you," she said.

"Really, Sophie. You can't tell me you haven't been avoiding me."

He was a kind man. He was unlucky to care for her. She wished he'd never had to deal with her and her unrequited love.

"Let me buy you a cup of coffee," he said, pointing to a Starbucks across the street.

"Thanks, but I..."

"I won't let you refuse," he said.

They sat at a small round table for two amidst a jangle of coffee machinery and the din of a coffeehouse filled with customers.

"I've got news," he said. "I'm leaving New York."

Her mind went blank with the shock of it and she held back her tears and turned her head away.

"I'm going to build a literary journal of fiction for Pagelli, the movie director, in San Francisco."

The surprise of his leaving was quickly replaced by the devastation of his no longer being near her.

"I want you to be managing editor," he said.

She was overwhelmed. She clasped her hands and squeezed her eyes shut. Could she ignore the change in her life and profession? Could they ever recapture the camaraderie they had once shared in New York in a new city?

"Say you'll take it," he asked desperately.

Her resistance collapsed. She pressed her fingers to her eyes to hold back her tears of happiness.

"I'll pay moving expenses and rent for the first six months," he said.

She led him out to the street to walk side by side, hand in hand.

"You'll go?" he asked.

Sophie squeezed his arm. "I love you, Charles Gibson. How soon do we leave?"